FLESH

Insatiable Series

Book 3

Patrick Logan

This book is a work of fiction. Names, characters, places, and incidents in this book are either entirely imaginary or are used fictitiously. Any resemblance to actual people, living or dead, or of places, events, or locales is entirely coincidental.

ISBN-13: 978-1519136473
ISBN-10: 1519136471
Third Edition: February 2017

Books by Patrick Logan

Insatiable Series

Book 1: Skin

Book 2: Crackers

Book 3: Flesh

Book 4: Parasite

Book 5: Stitches

The Haunted Series

Book 1: Shallow Graves

Book 2: The Seventh Ward

Book 3: Seaforth Prison

Book 4: Scarsdale Crematorium

Book 5: Sacred Heard Orphanage

Family Values Trilogy

Witch (Prequel)

Mother

Father

Daughter

Short Stories

System Update

Prologue

SWEAT BEADED ON THE BRICKS, tiny droplets of perspiration in the form of condensed humidity. It was unbearably hot in the basement, and the air was thick, housing equal parts dust and water.

A hand suddenly reached out of the hole in the floor, the long, thin fingers stretching skyward. Bright sunlight from the open doorway splayed between the digits. As the arm continued to stretch upward, a thin forearm cleared the opening, followed by the inner side of a knobby elbow. Without warning, the arm came down on the hardwood, the fingers splaying out, desperately seeking purchase on the dusty floor.

There was a grunt, and then another hand appeared, only this one was heavy, almost *bulbous*, the fingers not clearly discernable from each other, each blending together like a mitten. When it landed on the floor above, it did so with an ungainly thud.

The hands and arms tensed, and a figure rose clumsily out of the basement, collapsing onto the floor and rolling onto its back with another series of grunts.

Grey shafts of light continued to penetrate the abandoned Estate, slipping through tiny cracks and holes in the boards that covered the windows. A large flood of light spilled through the open front door, reflecting off the dust motes that fluttered in the newly disturbed air.

Hot. Too hot.

The naked figure flipped onto its front and then labored to its feet, remaining hunched at the waist, hiding its upper half from the offensive sunlight. The thing's mottled flesh was covered in sweat, but unlike the bricks in the basement below, the beads were not individual entities, but had coalesced into a sheen that covered the entire surface of its entire body. With several desperate, lurching strides, it made its way to the back of the house, creeping its way along the cabinets that lined the kitchen, then strafed the wall as it tried to stay out of the direct sunlight.

The back of the house had been boarded up, but it managed to pry these rotten planks off without much effort, despite having to resort to using its only good hand.

A sigh escaped the thing as it exited the house and entered the still cool and dewy morning air, the shadow provided by the peaked roof of the Estate protecting the area from the sun's onslaught for the time being.

It wouldn't last long.

The shambling mass avoided the large swimming pool, its meandering gait taking it wide to avoid an unfortunate misstep. When its feet left the cobblestones and touched the cool grass, another wave of relief washed over it, culminating in a veritable shudder that made its progress look robotic, as if filmed at a low framerate.

At the back of the property was a culvert, an ancient cement tunnel that led beneath a small two-lane road.

The figure collapsed in the shady interior of the tunnel, not bothering to push aside the network of spider webs or detritus that lined the interior of the forgotten passage.

Cool; the cement was cool, and was a welcome relief to his overheating face and stomach.

As it shut its eyes, the skin on its naked back just above the left shoulder blade suddenly began to stretch, pushing the already extended membrane to its maximum. An outline became apparent beneath the blistering white skin, a protruding oval about six inches across; an oval with six knobby, articulated limbs.

The skin on the figure's back puckered, then tore. A groan escaped its chapped lips, but it wasn't a manifestation of pain; rather, sweet relief washed over it as the tension from its stretched skin was momentarily relieved. A warm wetness spread from the spot on its back from where the cracker had budded, a wetness that could only be one thing: blood.

It didn't matter.

What mattered was the cool cement on its stomach; what mattered was the relief from its stretched skin.

The individual points of the cracker's appendages, all six of them, slowly pressed into its skin, making small indentations just outside of the wound. A moment later, the hole that it had erupted from slowly began to become obscured, a layer of milky white skin pushing up to the surface. Another few seconds and the ragged, bloody hole was completely replaced by this new layer of thin white flesh.

A cracking sound echoed off of the undulating walls of the culvert; six cracks, all the same cadence.

Crack. Crack. Crack. Crack. Crack. Crack.

Then the cracker was gone, leaving what was once a boy lying face down on his stomach, alone, his skin beginning to stretch again, the outline of another cracker slowly becoming visible beneath the surface.

PART I – BUDDING

1.

THE MAN WITH THE bushy red beard raised his head from his lap and looked around.

The bathroom was filthy, the walls — which might have once been white, or in the very least eggshell — were now so streaked with dirty grey smudges that they seemed to meld into an obscene background color. There was the usual graffiti, phone numbers etched with red pens and promises of sexual acts of the kind that might have once made him blush. There were the ubiquitous swastikas, drops of blood, promises of castration, and various curses, each less intelligible than the last. But none of these were of interest to him.

The slurping sound from between his legs stopped for a moment, and he turned his gaze downward.

A pair of bright green eyes stared up at him, expectant.

"Don't stop," he instructed the woman.

The woman nodded and then buried her head in his lap once more.

No, none of the graffiti bothered him, except for one.

He leaned forward, and the woman kneeling on the floor between his legs shifted to accommodate his movements. Her pace quickened, clearly misinterpreting his gesture. On the left wall of the bathroom stall was a picture of a large shape, something akin to a morbidly obese man, crudely drawn with a green crayon. It was a generally featureless mass, except for two vertical lines in yellow at the center of its head. Beneath the shape were two words: *Oot'-keban.*

The man's breath caught in his throat and he blinked hard, not believing what he was seeing. He leaned forward farther, reaching out with his hand to wipe some of the grime away.

The woman protested, again pulling her head up, but this time, instead of indicating for her to continue, he used his other hand to push her head to one side.

She grumbled something but he ignored her, moving closer still to the crudely drawn shape. When his eyes focused in the dim light, a sigh escaped him. It wasn't a person after all, just a green circle. And what he had first thought were yellow eyes were just a row of lights that went all the way around the shape. The words beneath the space ship weren't *Oot'-keban*, either, but *Art Cabin.*

Spaceship. Just a fucking alien spaceship.

He slumped back onto the top of the toilet seat, his heart rate finally returning to normal. The woman between his legs set about returning to her business, but any semblance of *mood* in the grimy stall was gone.

"Naw," he grumbled, using the palm of his hand to push her forehead away again.

She looked up at him, her mouth open, incredulous. She had a shock of white-blonde hair pulled back in a tight ponytail, which was obviously meant to serve two purposes: the color was supposed to make her look younger, and the tight ponytail was meant to stretch out her skin, smooth some of the wrinkles.

Both attempts failed; this was a woman who had been around the block, a fact that was reflected in her tired face.

"What you mean, 'No'?"

She smacked a piece of bubble gum loudly and pushed a stray strand of white hair from her face.

The man began to stand.

"I mean, 'no' — not in the mood anymore." His words were languid, apathetic.

She smacked the gum several more times before slowly pulling herself to her feet.

"Well, you're still paying me," she informed him, her mouth tight. Her hands smoothed and lowered the short jean skirt that had ridden up when she had squatted.

He looked away, pushing the stall door open behind her. The woman stepped backward.

"Fine," he said absently, hiking up his own jeans.

He tucked himself back in and then zipped up his jeans. Then he reached into his wallet and pulled out a fifty. He hadn't even put his wallet back into his back pocket before her manicured hand reached out and snatched the bill from him.

Then she blew a large pink bubble and turned away, stepping out of the stall and going over to the large, cracked mirror above a porcelain sink.

"Thanks," she said between chews.

"Whatever," he grumbled.

The man stretched his back, then watched as the prostitute leaned close to the mirror and opened her mouth wide, using one of her fingers to wipe away smeared lipstick from the corner of her lips.

As the man left the stall and made his way toward the door leading back to the bar, the woman turned to him again.

"There are pills for that, you know," she said, her expression tight.

"Pills? For what?"

The woman's large green eyes drifted down his body and her gaze lingered on his crotch.

The man laughed.

"It's not me, baby, it's you," he said, and then laughed again at the confused look that fell on her pale face.

The palm of his hand struck the back of the door and pushed it open an inch. Music and loud voices articulated their way through the opening. Now it was his turn to stop and face her.

"Anyways," he continued, the smile still plastered on his bearded face, "that was my last fifty. Care to buy a fella a drink?"

2.

AN ARM SLOWLY SNAKED its way around her neck, the fingers dissecting her chin that had been driven protectively into her chest. The girl grunted, trying to shake the man's body from her back, but he was too heavy, his center of gravity too high up on her shoulders. On her elbows and knees, she crouched herself into a tight ball, trying to build up as much potential energy as possible, conserving her strength for one final explosive move.

Just as her assailant's fingers reached his bicep on the other side of her neck, but before he could lock in the chokehold, the girl exploded, turning her head quickly into the choke while at the same time sliding one of her legs flat. The spontaneity and precision of the movement caught the man off guard, and in one smooth motion, she turned her body over, flipping her assailant onto his back.

Breathing heavily, she found herself on top of the man, sitting on his chest, staring down at his tense face, his eyes staring up at her in surprise.

But this man was a brown belt, and his surprise was only temporary.

The man bucked her unexpectedly, and she, being at least thirty pounds lighter, became airborne, her body launched up toward his head. Her first instinct was to come down on his head with her elbows, driving his head into the mat beneath them, but she fought this urge and attempted instead to land gracefully.

In the end, her intentions were irrelevant, as immediately after he bucked her, the man slid down her body, grabbing ahold of her right ankle as he passed. In one smooth transition, he hooked her heel under his arm and gave her leg a yank, pulling her onto her back for the second time in the last forty seconds.

"Fuck," she swore, momentarily dazed when the back of her head made contact with the ground.

This time, the man didn't make the mistake of slowly locking in his hold; this time, his grip was fast and furious, and before she knew it, her ankle was wrenched completely sideways, and with one of the man's legs laced across her chest, she found herself unable to roll out of the heel-hook.

She grunted and tried to reach for the man's leg, to defend against the ankle lock by putting him into one of her own, but he twisted his legs away from her. Her fingers reached across the mat, desperate now, the pressure building in her quad, trying to seek out any part of the man's body that she might be able to attack.

Nothing—her desperate fingers found no purchase.

The man grunted and increased the pressure on her ankle.

"Tap," he demanded. He yanked her foot again, turning it so far that it was almost perpendicular. "Tap."

The girl shifted her hips, trying to buck him as he had done to her in an attempt to get him to loosen his grip so that she might pull her leg out from beneath his armpit and yank herself to her feet.

It was no use. His grip was solid, unbreakable.

"Tap," he repeated a third time. He twisted her ankle beyond ninety degrees as he spoke, emphasizing his words.

Now it was her turn to do something unexpected. Instead of trying to turn into the hold and protect her ankle, she turned against it. This only helped tighten the man's grip, as her foot became even more anchored in his armpit. This move, a seemingly basic mistake, actually surprised the man, and she felt his grip loosen for a moment. Yet she did not alter course and try to get out of the hold; she had tried that already and knew it wouldn't work. Besides, as before, the man's surprise was short-lived, and he quickly clamped his arms down, doubling the pressure on her ankle.

With a grunt of her own, she twisted her hips as hard as she could, and an audible pop filled the gym. This time, the man's surprise was so great that he completely let go of her ankle, his eyes bulging from his sockets in horror. At this point, however, it didn't matter—she was already out.

"What the fuck?" The man's face twisted as the girl's leg suddenly came free just above the knee and he was stuck holding nothing but a prosthetic limb.

The girl used this prolonged surprise to her advantage, and quickly scrambled on top of the man's chest. Then, staring into his wide eyes, she brought her right elbow down in a high arc. She heard the man's nose crunch, and then felt the unmistakable warm sensation of blood on her forearm.

"Corina!" someone shouted from off to her right.

She ignored the cry, and raised her arm to deliver another crushing blow when a meaty hand grabbed her forearm from behind.

"Corina!" The man's breath reeked of stale coffee, a scent that strangely brought her around.

Her entire body went limp, and she allowed herself to be pulled off. The man's hands immediately went to his broken nose, his eyes watering.

"What the fuck, Corina?" he said, his voice coming out nasally and high-pitched.

Corina turned her large hazel eyes to the floor, immediately ashamed of what she had done. The man that she had brutally elbowed quickly scampered to his feet, grabbing the heel of her prosthetic leg and tossing it like a loose helicopter blade into the corner of the room.

"Fucking bitch," he muttered, staring at the blood that filled his palm.

"Take a walk, Teddy. Go get cleaned up," said the man who'd grabbed Corina's arm.

The man with the broken nose waved the old man away, but he said nothing further and turned his back to both of them.

Corina, eyes still downcast, pulled away from the now loose grip on her forearm, turning her foot sideways to balance herself on one leg. Then she turned and looked at the man who had prevented her from delivering what would have probably been at least another half dozen blows.

There was no humor in the man's heavily lined face. His eyes were a rich blue, and they focused on her intently, trying to figure out if she had calmed down. Above his eyes was a thick thatch of eyebrows that were knitted tightly, the inner corners nearly touching in a Scorsese sort of way. The man—who Corina assumed was in his late sixties or early seventies, although she had never asked him directly—had short grey hair cropped close to his skull. Despite his age, the man's grip had been tight, and so was the rest of him. Sure, like everyone his age his skin had lost some of its elasticity, and in a few key places it sagged a bit—beneath his chin, on the underside of his wrists, around his knees—but he would never be mistaken as one of the out-of-shape bingo players from down the hall. No, years of jiu jitsu and boxing training had turned his physique into a rock—a rock with a light layer of moss covering the surface.

"I'm sorry," Corina whispered, looking away from her mentor's face. For nearly five years she had been coming here, turning his dojo into her own personal shrink to work out her problems.

Her attention was drawn to the bloody smear on the underside of her forearm. Obviously, it would take more than physical activities, irrespective of how violent, to exorcise her demons.

The man's voice matched his physique; hard and gravelly.

"Sorry's not going to cut it this time, Corina," Mr. Gillespie said.

Her eyes snapped up.

Not gonna cut it?

This wasn't the first time that someone she had been rolling with had ended up bloody—all the other times Mr. Gillespie had just told her to shower up.

But none of those partners had been Teddy Manfred, the son of the man that owned the building that Mr. Gillespie leased to run the dojo.

Corina shook her head slowly, the sweaty strips of short brown hair clinging uncomfortably to her cheeks and scalp.

"I need this," she pleaded. "Please, Mr—"

He cut her off.

"Corina, you broke Teddy's nose." His voice softened. "You know what he could do to this place."

Corina felt tears welling in her eyes. This was all she had—he couldn't take this away from her.

"Please," she begged.

Something in the old man's face broke, and his hard expression became flaccid. He brought a hand to the heavy lines around his mouth and rubbed them.

"Look, Corina, just take some time off and I'll talk to Teddy. But you need some real help, and I—this place—can't give it to you anymore."

"How much time is 'some'?" she asked, ignoring the last comment.

Mr. Gillespie's blue eyes focused on hers.

"A month," he said. "Two would be better, but a month will do. Will give me some time to smooth things over with Teddy and his dad. You know Teddy—he's a fucking prima donna, thinks he's UFC champion or something." He paused, then repeated, "A month."

Corina nodded. She would go mad without the gym for a month, but knew that she was getting off easy—besides, she knew that no matter how much Mr. Gillespie cared for her, he was not a man to go back on a decision once it had been made.

The man returned her nod and walked to the corner of the room and collected her prosthetic leg. He handed it to her, and Corina locked it into place. She opened her mouth to say something, but then closed it again. There was no more to be said.

Instead, she headed to the change room in silence.

A month. An entire month without the gym.

"Fuck."

3.

IT WASN'T THE MAN'S dark skin, or the fact that he was six-foot-four and two hundred and sixty pounds of mostly muscle in a place that was populated by fat white men with burgeoning bellies, long grey beards, and tattoos marking most of their exposed pale flesh that made him stand out. No, it was something as simple as his shirt; not the *shirt* itself, as this was nothing more than a beige button-down with short sleeves. Rather, it was what was on his shirt: the patch on his triceps just before the bottom of the sleeve, the one that read 'Askergan County PD'. And, more specifically, it was the gold star on his chest that read: SHERIFF. Sticking out like a sore thumb in this place was an understatement.

But there was one man in the bar that didn't lean back and take notice, and that was the man with the red bushy beard and the crooked teeth that had emerged from the bathroom. Following only a few seconds after a pale woman with a blonde ponytail and jean skirt that was barely long enough to cover her ass cheeks, the man walked across the room, aware of but not acknowledging the sheriff who sat alone at the bar. He took the seat right next to the muscular police officer.

"Whiskey," the sheriff demanded, and the barkeep, a young man with jet black hair that was shaved on the sides but with a healthy crop on top, just stared at him.

The sheriff cleared his throat.

"Whiskey," he asked again.

The bartender sneered but obliged, turning his back to the sheriff and reaching for the lowest bottle on the glass shelf. "And get one for my friend here, too."

A moment later, the bartender turned back around with two rock glasses, one in each hand, the bottoms coated with a golden brown liquid. It was barely enough whiskey to cover the bottom, let alone a full ounce.

This didn't seem to bother the sheriff, and he downed it in one go. He twisted the glass back and forth in his meaty black hand.

"Another," he demanded, and the skinny bartender reluctantly took the glass from him.

"Do you like trivia?" the sheriff asked, turning to the man beside him.

The man with the red beard didn't respond.

"Well I do," the sheriff continued. "I have a few favorites, too. Wanna hear them?"

Again, the man to his left said nothing.

The sheriff continued, unfazed.

"Who is the only man in NHL history to score two overtime goals in one game?" the sheriff asked.

The man with the red beard cleared his throat.

"Chris Campoli," he said. Then he brought his own thimble of drink to his mouth and swallowed.

The sheriff smiled. This time, when the bartender turned with another glass of whiskey, the sheriff took a small sip and put the glass down on the bar instead of drinking it all at once.

The barkeep turned back to the shelf and began drying some pint glasses, doing a terrible job of pretending he wasn't eaves-dropping.

"How about this?" the sheriff continued, this time keeping his eyes straight ahead, focusing on the mirror on the wall be-hind the bartender. "Who has the most three-on-five short-handed goals?"

The man with the red beard smirked; he couldn't help it. This was too easy.

"Mike Richards."

Again, the sheriff laughed.

"Good, good. But now—"

The sheriff hesitated. A flicker of movement in the mirror caught his eye. Two men were approaching them from behind, two large men wearing jeans and leather vests—straight out of the eighties. Following close behind was the blonde with the ponytail and red lipstick that had come out of the bathroom right before the man with the red beard.

The sheriff swiveled in his chair to face the men that ap-proached.

The larger of the two men, an oaf who was nearly as big as the sheriff himself, stepped in front of him and pointed his pudgy finger aggressively.

"You're not welcome here."

The sheriff, unfazed, smiled, revealing a row of perfectly white teeth.

"You must have me mistaken for someone else," he said. Then he puffed his considerable chest and brought his own fin-ger to the star on his vest, tapping it several times. "The name is Sheriff; Sheriff Paul White."

The biker sneered.

"This ain't Askergan. You're out of your jurisdiction."

Again, the other biker snorted.

"DICK-tion."

Sheriff White rolled his eyes.

The biker took offense to this and took another aggressive step forward, closing the distance between himself and the sheriff to under three feet. When he extended his finger again, the sheriff's face suddenly changed—his smile disappeared, hiding those brilliant white teeth behind his thick lips, and his hazel eyes went cold.

The movements were quick for such a big man; not lightning quick, but much faster than either of the bikers could have anticipated.

The sheriff's hand shot out and he grabbed the man's outstretched finger, yanking it hard to one side, snapping the bone just beyond the first knuckle. The biker cried out, and as he instinctively turned to look at his hand, the sheriff reared back and drove his massive fist directly into the man's face.

The biker never saw the blow coming and stumbled backward, taking the girl down with him as he collapsed on top of a round table. The table broke under his immense weight, smashing several pint glasses and spraying the stunned occupants with frothing liquid and glass fragments.

"What the *fuck*?!" the other biker shouted, his eyes darting from his fallen friend and the girl and then back at the sheriff. "You *fuck*!" He took a step forward.

During the altercation, the man with the bushy red beard had slipped off the stool and now, as the sheriff readied himself, his right leg going forward, his fists raised up in front of his face, the man casually took one step to his right. The biker took another step forward, and that was when the man with the red beard delivered a vicious kick squarely to the side of the biker's knee. The blow had been timed perfectly, and the biker's forward progress was immediately halted, a cry escaping his lips.

Both of his hands immediately went to his knee as he careened sideways, hopping on his other foot, trying not to fall.

He lost the battle.

Another table was broken and more beer was spilled.

"Yeah, I think we better go," the man with the red beard said. The shock was beginning to wear off, and the men that had been sitting around the first smashed table now helped the biker with the broken finger to his feet.

The sheriff nodded.

"Like, right now!" the man said.

The other half dozen men in the bar were standing now, inspecting their beer-soaked clothes. The man with the torn knee was still wailing on the ground, but they stepped around him, not taking heed.

"Go!" the man with the red beard suddenly shouted, and the sheriff, on cue, quickly turned and ran to the door.

The other man followed.

The sheriff scrambled to get the car door to his cruiser unlocked as the door to the bar banged open behind them.

The man with the red beard turned back to the bar, just as the sheriff opened his door and jumped into the driver seat.

"You *motherfucker*!"

It was the man that Sheriff White had punched, his head tilted to one side, his uninjured hand probing his already swelling jaw. He turned his head to one side and spat a glob of blood onto the tarmac. The man with the red beard thought he saw a flash of white in the red splotch—a tooth, perhaps.

"Get in!" the sheriff yelled, and the man quickly obliged.

The sheriff peeled out of the parking lot, his squealing tires leaving the bikers in a cloud of dust and a trail of burnt rubber.

Thankfully, they were only about a dozen miles outside of Askergan, and despite the bikers' obvious fury, the sheriff knew that they wouldn't dare follow. And if they did, well, things would be very different on his turf.

Still, part of him knew that Sabra and his drug dealing bikers would come; after all, they had to get the drugs that were pervading the County into it somehow. When they came, he hoped that they would be ready.

After a minute or so, the sheriff's adrenaline drained and his heart rate returned to normal. He turned to his passenger.

"Classy joint you got there."

The man smirked, keeping his eyes straight ahead.

"Yeah, you fit right in," he replied.

The sheriff grunted. It had been almost five years since he had seen his friend, and despite his appearance—the red beard, the shoulder-length brown hair—and his choice of drinking establishment, he could tell that not much had changed.

"Let's get you cleaned up, Coggins. Askergan needs you; Askergan needs the good boys again."

Andrew Coggins's smile faded, and he kept his eyes trained on the road ahead.

The good boys—Askergan needs the good boys.

Coggins, still silent, eyes focused ahead, reached up and flicked on the cherries.

4.

THE INTOXICATING SMELL OF fresh lawn clippings filled the warm summer air. The clusters of potted dianthuses that marked the steps of the pale blue porch were in full bloom, and a smattering of bumblebees hovered above them, gorging themselves on the newly exposed nectar.

"Oh, shoo," Mrs. Mullheney grumbled, swinging her hand-carved wooden cane over the tops of the flowers. "Get out of here, you little buggers."

The bumblebees scattered, but the minute the woman with the thickly lined face turned and continued down the porch and then made her way to the barn at the back of her property, they returned in earnest.

It had been her husband's idea to turn the rarely used wooden shed into a small gift shop, and Mrs. Mullheney had initially scoffed at the idea when it had first been proposed. It seemed only fitting that she went ahead with the conversion a year after he passed. Status quo, anyone from the town that knew of them might say, as it was no secret that the hard woman had spent the better part of a century impressing her iron will on the man, turning what few good ideas he had had into her own. But, as usual, Mrs. Mullheney could give two shits about what the nosey townsfolk had to say.

What was unexpected, however, was the fact that she actually enjoyed running the store.

Mrs. Mullheney pulled an old set of keys out of the pocket of her ankle-length white dress and opened the gleaming chrome padlock.

She wasn't really sure why she liked the store that much. After all, she never really sold more than a few hundred dollars' worth of merchandise a month. A practical woman, she supposed that running the small store, which was open but for a few hours every day—eleven to two, no exceptions—gave her some purpose, aside from finishing the crossword puzzle in the otherwise unread daily newspaper. The crossword puzzle was still more important, of course, but running the small gift shop added more *purpose* to her otherwise meandering existence.

Mrs. Mullheney pulled the door wide and inhaled deeply. It smelled better in the shop that morning; better than usual.

Probably because it didn't rain last night.

Anytime it rained with enough vigor to soak the roof, some of the cascading water inevitably leaked through the old shingles and wet the oak wood ceiling. This, in turn, tinged the air in the small shed turned *shoppe* with a hint of mildew that drove Mrs. Mullheney nuts. And, in addition to her disgust at the smell, she found that on days following a night rain she would have to walk around the side of the shed and open the door and window a half hour early to make sure that the rows of teddy bears and handmade throws didn't start to take on the scent of mildew. And all of this meant that she had less time to finish her crossword.

Mrs. Mullheney pulled her glasses from her nose and let them rest on her narrow chest, held there by a long, beaded chain. Then she turned her nose to the ceiling, closed her eyes, and drew a deep breath.

Wood. Wood and earth and cotton.

Mrs. Mullheney smiled and put her glasses back on before setting about getting things prepared before her first visitors might—or might not, it mattered little to her—arrive. So long as the store was open at eleven.

Mrs. Mullheney bent to retrieve the 'OPEN' sign from the floor beside the open door, and then rose with all of the equally predictable snaps and pops from her spine and knees. She reached back outside the shed and hung the sign on the nail below the window, only she kept it turned so that it read 'CLOSED'. At eleven, she would turn the sign over.

Next, she picked up a clipboard from the small table inside the door and flipped it to the first empty page. Using the pen clipped to the cover, she wrote today's date on the upper right-hand corner and then turned her attention to the first row of shelves and began to take inventory.

Twelve teddies all in a row.

Mrs. Mullheney systematically went from shelf to shelf, counting off each of the two dozen or so types of trinkets and teddies first in her head, then out loud, and then writing them in the ledger.

Fourteen hand-knit throws.

The store never sold more than a few items a day on average, and even that number was heavily biased by the weekend days and just three or four specific weeks in the summer. But it didn't matter; the *shoppe* was open every single day, rain or shine, snow or sun, from eleven to two.

Eighteen tiny American flags in eighteen identical miniature ceramic cups all bearing the Askergan County name.

A smile unexpectedly broke across the elderly woman's thin lips.

Bert would be happy, she thought. *He would be so happy.*

A strange thought indeed, as emotional exchanges between Mrs. Mullheney and her husband when he had been alive had been, well, *infrequent.*

Thoughts of her husband caused the woman's smile to quickly transition into an expression of sadness. But there was no time for that. Never was. There was only time for inventory before the shop opened. She shook the emotion away and checked her watch: it was a quarter to eleven. Mrs. Mullheney picked up the pace.

It was while taking inventory of the second-to-last shelf, the one on the back wall across the door, that she first noticed something out of the ordinary.

Mrs. Mullheney's face twisted at the sight of the orange ornamental buoys with the white rope in the traditional looped pattern and the same, nearly ubiquitous 'Askergan County' name emblazoned in white on the front. She remembered stacking the toy buoys neatly after closing yesterday, stacking all seven of the Frisbee-sized trinkets on top of one another like a child's stacking game, minus the protuberance in the center. Now all seven were loose on the ground

The wind, maybe?

It had been windy last night, but truthfully, wind was a common feature of her home being so close to the water. And yet today was the first day that the buoys had fallen.

Mrs. Mullheney moved closer to the scattered stack of orange buoys and then reluctantly bent to pick them up. When she eventually managed to straighten her back out again and went to put the buoys on the shelf, her hand froze in midair.

There was something hidden behind the fallen stack of buoys at the back of the shelf, tucked away nearly out of sight.

Mrs. Mullheney squinted through the thick lenses of her glasses. It was white, about the size of a small dessert plate, and flat on the top. Her lip curled into a snarl, and she slowly backed away from the shelf and toward the door, reaching blindly behind her with her left hand until her knobby fingers reached the oak cane. Feeling the hard, knotted wood in her thin hand imbued her with courage, and she stepped toward the shelf again, slowly bringing the cane out in front of her body.

She spied the thing once more: it was exactly as it had been moments before. Tilting her head, she managed to make out more of the creature from behind the orange trinkets, and thought that perhaps, based on the wide, flat, and apparently hard-looking shell, that it might be some sort of crab.

A crab? Askergan has no crabs. Crayfish, catfish, and the occasional mussel, but no crabs.

Raising one thin white eyebrow, Mrs. Mullheney reached out with the rubber foot of her cane and used it to push the closest orange buoy off to one side. She kept her eyes firmly locked on the crab as she did this.

It didn't move.

Mrs. Mullheney swept the cane the other way, pushing two more buoys out of the way, one of which crashed to the floor and rolled a few feet to her left. She ignored it and squinted until her eyes became but slits.

The shell, which she had previously thought to be a completely smooth surface, appeared upon closer inspection to be riddled with hundreds of tiny holes. And its legs, at least the three legs on the one side that she could see, were unlike any she had seen given her limited crustacean exposure; there were knots and thick cartilaginous bulbs all the way down the length, something that reminded her of an extremely arthritic digit.

Malted? Could it be a shell from a malted crab?

Surely a living, breathing—she listened closely and convinced herself that the barely audible rhythmic puffs of air were indeed coming from it—crab would have moved by now, right? Especially after the buoy had fallen to the floor?

There was only one way to find out.

Biting the inside of her lip, Mrs. Mullheney reached out with the cane with the intent of probing the crab-thing at the back of the shelf.

The rubber foot never made contact with the shell.

A fraction of an inch before the cane reached it, Mrs Mullheney heard a series of rhythmic cracks, and the creature seemed to lower on its haunches. She pulled the cane back, tilting her head to one side in a mixture of curiosity and confusion. She heard another crack, a resounding noise that echoed off the inside of the *shoppe*, and then the thing flew through the air with such speed and grace that the elderly woman didn't even manage to stagger backwards before it landed directly on her face.

She tried to scream, but the legs quickly splayed and then flattened, two of them crossing over her lips, preventing them from opening. Eyes wide, her arthritic hands reached up and tore desperately at the shell, trying to pull it from her face, trying to *breathe*. When she finally managed to hook her fingers beneath one edge of the shell, she felt a horrible suction on the side of her cheek where the bulk of the oval mass had landed, followed by the intense pain as the dozens of tiny teeth dug into her flesh. Mrs. Mullheney's eyes rolled back in her head and she collapsed to the floor, her wooden cane falling from her arthritic fingers and banging loudly off the oak planks.

For the first time in over a year and a half, the 'OPEN' sign at *Mulhenney Gifts and Snacks* was not hung below the window at exactly eleven o'clock.

5.

"GOOD MORNING, MRS. DREW."

The lady at the desk, a woman in her late fifties with iron-colored hair pulled back into a tight bun and vibrant green eyes, looked up from her computer screen.

"Morning, sheriff," she said curtly with a nod. "There's a fresh pot of coffee on the stove."

Sheriff Paul White grinned; Mrs. Drew always made a pot of coffee in the morning, but didn't always make it *on the stove.* On the stove meant that she had brought in her own beans, the ones that she roasted and ground in her house, and used a French press to produce the most ridiculously amazing coffee he had ever tried. He had once heard of a feline or rodent or some sort of creature high in the mountains of Belize or Chile or some equally exotic locale that ate only the freshest coffee beans. Farmers would follow these creatures around and root through their dung to find the beans that had undergone a fermenting process in their guts. Supposedly, these beans made for the best coffee in the world — or so it was said.

Well, the sheriff thought as he made his way to the stove and breathed in deeply through his wide nostrils, *short of sifting through shit,* this *is the best coffee in the world.*

He grabbed his mug off the counter and poured himself a cup of the thick, dark liquid. The intoxicating aroma of the fresh coffee brought a smile to his lips.

Today is going to be a good day.

His smile faded as he remembered who he had requested to come down the station for the second time in three days.

Please be a good day today. Please, today let us find him — find the boy tired and bruised, but safe and alive.

The sheriff took a sip of the coffee, but he barely tasted it. His thoughts had drifted elsewhere, and the seductive hold that the brewed beverage had had on him was lost.

Please.

Mrs. Drew's voice drew him back.

"Gregory Griddle and his boy, Kent, are waiting for you in room one," she informed him. "Just like you asked."

Sheriff White nodded and took another sip of his coffee. It tasted bitter.

"Williams is in there with them keeping them company," she added.

"We are going to have some help come in today, I—"

But before the sheriff could finish his sentence, the door to the police station swung open, the tiny bell above the door announcing his arrival.

"Speak of the devil."

Andrew Coggins strode through the doorway, head held high. There was a world of difference in his current appearance compared to the previous night when the sheriff had collected him from the biker bar. His long red beard had been trimmed, now cropped closely to his face, which actually looked good on him, serving to fill out his otherwise narrow face. His hair had been brushed and was now slicked back away from his face, revealing his small brown eyes. He had changed his clothes, too, and was now sporting a pair of jeans and a plain white t-shirt.

He still looked tired, and there was a hint of pink in the corners of his eyes, a lasting reminder of too many nights filled with whiskey and bathroom encounters, but he looked *much* better. But when he spoke he sounded different; his voice was deeper, more serious than the Sheriff remembered. It was Coggins, but it wasn't *the* Coggins of old. This was someone a little different, like an identical twin.

"Well, well, well," Paul said, peering over the rim of his cup of coffee. "Look what the cougar dragged in."

Coggins offered him a quick glance, but ignored the comment. Instead, he turned to Mrs. Drew at the front desk.

Mrs. Drew had first joined on with Paul after her husband, the late Sheriff Dana Drew, had gone missing during the blizzard of six years ago. Paul had to give her credit; even after he had been found—dead, murdered by a deranged psychopath, or so the story went—and her adopted daughter still pining away in a coma, she had stayed on. Mrs. Drew had been critical to getting the town back to normal after the snow had been cleared. She had been important to Paul as well, as without her, there was no way that he would have been able to simply pick up the responsibility of the sheriff's badge after his mentor, his *friend*, one of the good guys, had been so ruthlessly murdered.

Sheriff White took another gulp of the hot liquid before putting the cup down on the counter. It tasted sour.

"Mrs. Drew," Coggins began, but then stopped himself. His eyes turned downward and he cleared his throat. "Mrs. Drew, I can't—"

The woman raised a slender hand, stopping him cold. Coggins looked up again, the expression on his face as legible as the headline on a tabloid newspaper: shame.

After the young Lawrence girl had been found—alive, thank God—Coggins had disappeared, fading into the snowstorm just like one of the many flakes that left after that horrible week. He had missed the sheriff's funeral, and hadn't stopped by the station since. Every once in a while, maybe once every two weeks—more frequently during the holidays—Sheriff White made his way up to the long-term care facility in Darborough and checked in on Alice Dehaust. The facility required that he sign in at each visit, and he always made a note to check the log to see who had been in to visit.

Of course, there was Mrs. Drew—or was it *Ms.* Drew now?—and his own scrawlings on that mostly empty sheet of paper, and once in a while there was another name or two, childhood friends, perhaps, but never in the six years since the incident at Mrs. Wharfburn's had he noted Coggins's name.

Yep, Sheriff White could recognize that expression from a mile away. Shame.

"Deputy Coggins," she said, her voice calm, even. Her bright green eyes stared at the man for a long while, until Coggins was forced to break the stare.

Deputy Coggins.

"It's good to have you back," she finished simply, her thin lips revealing no expression. Mrs. Drew, unlike her late husband, who'd liked to joke around with his deputies, was impossible to read.

There was an awkward pause as the two remained in their position in the police station reception area but a few feet from each other, her seated, him standing.

Paul thought he could read Coggins's thoughts as they careened through his skull.

Should I apologize? Should I tell her how sorry am I for her loss? What should I say?

In the end, saying nothing was probably the best course of action, and Sheriff White stepped forward quickly to break the unease.

"Good to have you back, Coggins."

Coggins turned to him, his face reddening.

"Like I said last night, we need you."

Coggins looked confused, as if he was unsure of why he was actually back here, in the station where it had all started — why he had agreed to come back to join the police force, even if only on a temporary basis. For a brief moment, Paul thought that the man might become overwhelmed and just bolt to the door, never to be seen again for another six years.

He wondered if he would blame Coggins if he tried.

Good ones — we're the good boys.

"Come," the sheriff said, taking a step toward the man and gently grabbing ahold of his arm. "There is someone you need to meet."

6.

THE SMALL APARTMENT SMELLED of cumin and sweet peppers, a delightful concoction that hit Corina's small, upturned nose even before she opened the door.

Inside, the smell was nearly overwhelming.

She tossed her keys in the small crystal bowl on the table by the entrance, and then leaned over and removed her running shoes, adding them to the pile on the other side of the door.

The apartment wasn't much more than a glorified rectangle, with the kitchen off to the right of the front entrance and opposite the apartment's only bathroom.

Corina headed to the kitchen first, coming up behind her mother and gently resting her hand on the woman's shoulder as she shook the wrought-iron skillet, sautéing the vegetable stir fry as only mothers knew how.

Marley Lawrence nearly jumped out of her skin.

"Jesus, Corina, you can't sneak up on me like that," she said, turning to face her eldest daughter.

The woman was tall and athletic, with long brown hair that was pulled back in a ponytail, revealing small ears adorned with a simple set of silver stud earrings. Despite her trim physique, she looked older than her forty-odd years, a fact that was reflected in the dark circles that hung beneath her hazel eyes and the deep grooves that lined the corners of her mouth.

"Sorry, Mom," Corina grumbled, reaching around her mother and grabbing a sizzling square piece of yellow pepper from the skillet. She shook it in the air for a few seconds in a poor attempt to cool it before popping it into her mouth.

"You're going to burn yourself," her mother scolded, turning back to the stove.

So long as I don't freeze.

Still chomping on the yellow pepper, mouth wide, breathing heavily in a further attempt to make it palatable, she brought a hand up and pushed a wayward strand of short brown hair out of her face. When her calloused fingers brushed against the top of her ear, her mood grew increasingly sour. The ear ended much sooner than it ought to, coming to an abrupt halt just above the second ridge. The blizzard of six years ago had taken more than just her leg, her father, and part of her ear; it had —

Corina shook the thoughts from her head, wondering why now, why today of all days, these thoughts had come flooding back.

"Where's Henrietta?" she asked, trying to change the subject of her own thoughts.

"In your bedroom, watching TV. Why don't you go get her and set the table? Dinner is almost ready," her mother replied.
.

Corina swallowed the pepper and nodded.

The rest of the apartment was pretty much the same as the entrance and kitchen: plain and ordinary. There was a small dinner table across from the kitchen, and an even smaller family room adjacent to the dining room, which housed a leather couch, a chair, and a small TV. The apartment only had two bedrooms, one for Marley and one that Henrietta and Corina shared. It was a bit strange sharing the room with her sister, who was a decade younger, but Corina didn't mind. In fact, she didn't sleep well when she was alone, and it helped to have the girl in there with her. It was strange that an eighteen-year-old would need comfort from an eight—*'Almost nine, don't call me eight'*—year-old, but *strange* was an appropriate way to describe their family.

It had taken nearly three years for the insurance to pay out after Cody had been killed, what with the still uncertain circumstances surrounding his death.

Need to rule out suicide, they had said, which was ridiculous and insulting. *Just procedure.*

Procedure, as if what was left of the Lawrence family were undergoing some sort of simple surgery, setting a broken finger or cauterizing a nose prone to bleeding, perhaps.

The debt that Marley had racked up during those three hard years—necessarily so, as she had trouble walking anywhere with the toes missing on her left foot, which like most of Corina's ear had also been lost to frostbite—had been substantial, and when the insurance money finally came in, thanks in no small part to Sheriff Paul White, the money had barely covered it.

Moving out of the city had helped curb some of the bills, as did selling their house and now leasing the apartment. But money was—and always would be ever since the paltry advances on Cody's last book dried up—a stressor in the Lawrence household, something that Corina despised more than anything.

Corina bit her lip and tried to put on a happy face when she pulled open the door to her room. Henrietta, her long, curly, and most unruly mop of blonde hair spilling down over her shoulders, lay on her stomach on Corina's bed, the lower bunk, her face propped on her hands.

The girl's brilliant green eyes went wide when she saw her sister.

"Corina!"

Henrietta scrambled to her feet and rushed to her sister, wrapping her in a tight embrace. Despite their age difference, Henrietta was very tall for her age, and was only a few inches shorter than Corina, who was not short by any stretch. The girl's enthusiasm immediately brought Corina out of her funk, and she found herself smiling despite herself.

Corina tried to run her hand through the girl's hair, but her fingers almost immediately caught in the unruly ringlets and she pulled it out.

"Not so hard, kiddo," she said, easing her sister away from her. "You're gonna knock Captain Hook over."

Henrietta looked up at her and smiled. Corina mimed a peg-legged walk, tapping the shin of her prosthetic leg for effect.

"Argh," she grunted, squinting one eye and balling one hand into a fist and the other into a makeshift hook.

Henrietta laughed.

"Go on, little one, go wash your hands. Mom says dinner is almost ready."

Henrietta snapped her own sock-covered feet together and raised a hand in mock salute.

"Aye, aye, Captain."

*   *   *

"Delicious as always, Mom," Corina complimented between mouthfuls.

She looked over at her mother, who was staring off into the distance, her plate mostly untouched.

"Yeah, Mom, it's really good," Henrietta followed up.

Marley shook her head slightly.

"What's that, dear?"

Corina frowned.

"We just said that the dinner is good; yummy. You should try some."

Reminded of her meal, Marley looked down at her plate, but instead of bringing her fork to her mouth, she laid it back down on her placemat and turned her eyes to the counter. Corina followed her gaze and noted the stack of torn envelopes and sheets of tri-folded paper, which could only be—*were* always only—one thing: bills.

"What's the matter, Mom?" Corina asked hesitantly, even though she already knew the answer.

"I think—I think—" Marley couldn't hold her daughter's gaze, and she looked away. "I think you need to get a job," she finished simply.

Corina slowly put her own fork down on her plate and folded her hands calmly in front of her.

"How many times do you want to go over this, Ma?"

Marley's eye flicked up and she glared at her daughter.

"You're eighteen now, almost nineteen—"

"Thanks, Mom. I know how old I am," Corina said, glaring back just as hard.

Marley shook her head, her tired face beginning to sag. It was times like these that she looked *much* older than her age. Even though Mama Lawrence had been Cody's mother and not Marley's, Corina was reminded of the woman now.

"Corina, please, we—*I* need some help." She gestured to the pile of bills on the counter behind her. "The bills keep piling up, and I can't take any more shifts over at the home."

Corina stared at her mother for a moment. There was a time when she had been pretty, very pretty, with soft features, a delicate, almost upturned nose, and big hazel eyes that could draw the attention of any man in the room.

But not now.

Now she was just old; old, tired, and desperate.

It was not a good look on anyone, much less Corina's own mother.

Anger slowly displaced the embarrassment and ignominy she felt for her mother then, and this anger soon bled to her deceased father; she was furious that he was gone, that he had left them. Fueling this feeling was the fact that Cody had opted to take Henrietta with him when he had entered the blizzard. These feelings were mostly irrational, especially given her delicate condition at the time when Cody had left Mama Lawrence's home, but still...her father had picked her—a fact that could not be denied.

Corina's gaze slipped downward, and she found herself staring at the pink plastic of her artificial leg that peeked out from just below the hem of her jeans.

Without warning, she brought a fist down on the hard plastic and her eyes shot up again. Everything suddenly came rushing back, as it was apt to do at times like this: her dead father, her amputated leg, the missing piece of her ear, being kicked out of the dojo for nearly a month, and even the patches of white skin on Henrietta's neck and hands that had never regained their normal flush after being frostbitten.

"I told you already! I'm not working, Ma, not in this shit—"

"Hey!" Marley said, her eyes darting to Henrietta, who had buried herself in her meal in an attempt to drown out their bickering.

But it was a weak look, one from a defeated mother, a look akin to caving and letting her daughter stay out past curfew.

"I hate this shit town," Corina continued, her teeth clenched, "and I won't work here. I need to train, Ma, you know this. I'm not ready to work."

Her thoughts quickly drifted to what had happened that afternoon, how she had gone spastic again and was now suspended from the training facility for a month.

Corina pushed these thoughts away.

"I need help, Corina."

The woman's fragility and weakness angered Corina more than anything; she couldn't even stand to stare at her mother's downcast face, her eyes welling up and in danger of spilling over at any moment.

When did you become so fucking weak? What kind of role model is that for Henri?

Corina stood with a start, her chair toppling noisily onto the parquet tiles behind her.

Marley's tired eyes looked up at her.

"It's not my fault that Dad is gone, Mom." Corina jabbed at her chest with a stubby nail. "It's not *my* fault."

7.

"COGGINS, I WANT YOU to meet Deputy Andrew Williams," Sheriff Paul White said, holding his thick arm out in front of him as introduction.

Coggins stared at the man across from him and couldn't help the thoughts that entered his head.

This is—was—my replacement?

The man was a little shorter than Coggins, maybe five-foot-ten on a good day, and had a shock of slicked black hair that looked as hard as frozen ice cream. The man had narrow, pointy features, a beak-like nose, and was thin bordering on skinny. His beige ACPD shirt was perhaps one size too big, and it had been tucked in tight and then pulled out of the front of his pants so that it billowed just a little, making him seem a little larger, a little thicker.

Coggins knew this, because he used to do the same.

His eyes drifted to Sheriff White's heavily muscled frame and dark, almost ebony skin, and then back at the pale, thin man with the slicked hair.

Bonnie and Clyde.

"Nice to meet you," Deputy Williams finally said, extending his hand.

The man had eyes that turned downward slightly at the outer corners, something that gave him this perpetual sleepy appearance.

Coggins took the man's hand and shook it briefly.

"Same," he grumbled.

The sheriff gave him a strange look, and when he spoke, although his words were clearly directed at Deputy Williams, his eyes remained firmly locked on Coggins's.

"Coggins here is going to be deputized... again. At least until this case is solved."

Sheriff White reached over and cuffed the side of each of Coggins's arms with enough force to jolt him. It was meant as a friendly gesture to break some of the tension, but it also conveyed another meaning: *Buck up, boy. Look alive.*

Coggins feigned a smile, revealing a row of crooked lower teeth that peeked through his thick red beard.

"Deputy Coggins, at your service."

The stern look on the sheriff's face stopped him from going into a full salute.

A silence fell over the three of them, their thoughts clearly pasted on their faces. Deputy Williams's expression was one of uncertainty, what with their shared knowledge of the fact that Askergan now only had the financial resources to support one deputy. Sheriff White looked confused, unsure if bringing this bearded, harder version of Coggins onboard was a good idea. And Coggins—now *Deputy* Coggins again—wondered what in God's name he was doing back here after swearing that he would never step back into the town again, let alone back here—back here in the police station where it had all begun.

Sheriff Paul White shook his head.

"Let's get this started," he finally instructed, breaking the silence. "Coggins, there is something that you need to hear."

*   *   *

The boy, who couldn't be much older than fifteen, had a hard time making eye contact. Sure, this was partially due to his guilt, which was especially apparent when he started talking about how he and his friends had been drinking, but there was more to it than that; Coggins didn't need his decade plus experience as a police officer to figure that out.

The boy was terrified.

"Go on, champ, tell the officers the story again," the boy's father encouraged.

The man's father, who Sheriff White had introduced as Gregory Griddle, was a good-looking man, tall and athletic, with light brown hair that was parted neatly atop his head. He had boyish, symmetrical features and a smattering of crow's feet at the corners of his eyes that were a lasting reminder that this was a man who liked to laugh—who loved life.

But he wasn't laughing now.

When the boy didn't immediately respond and bowed his head, leaving the two deputies and Sheriff White to stare at the mess of reddish-blonde hair, the boy's father cleared his throat and interjected.

"We were camping," he began, but the sheriff raised a large hand and cut him off.

"Let him tell the story, please, Mr. Griddle."

The man nodded and turned back to his boy, resting a hand gently on his back.

"C'mon, Kent, tell them the story again."

The boy's back hitched as he took a deep breath, and then he turned his face upward to meet them.

Like his father, the boy was handsome, but he still had to grow into his features, which were all just a little too big for him: his lips, nose, and even his ears were just a tad oversized for his small, round face. His eyes, on the other hand, were a dark, deep hazel — they were the eyes of a much older man, one who had seen *things*.

Coggins knew those eyes; they were the eyes that his father used to have before he passed, the same eyes shared by the rest of his father's whiskey and cigar *troupe* that had come over once a month, every month, since the first time that Coggins could remember until his very last day. They were the eyes of men who had seen things, who had seen horrible things, the eyes of men who had been to *war*.

The boy — this young Kent Griddle — began to speak, and with his words he weaved an elaborate and fantastical tale that even Deputy Coggins, for all he had seen in his time, his own eyes the same dark, dull pits as his father's, had a hard time believing.

When Kent was done, he bowed his head again, tears streaming silently down his freckled face.

"Thank you," the sheriff said softly, and he indicated to the boy's father that they could rise. "You can go now, just please stay local until I let you know different."

Gregory Griddle nodded.

"C'mon, Kent, let's get going."

The boy curled into his father's chest as he stood, and with his arms wrapped around his son, the two Griddle men left the small interrogation room. Left alone now, the two deputies and the sheriff remained silent for some time. Sheriff White leaned heavily onto the table that had just been vacated, while Deputies Williams and Coggins sat leaning against opposite walls, their thin arms crossed over their narrow chests.

Eventually the sheriff cleared his throat to speak, but before he could get the words out, the door to the interrogation room burst open and Gregory Griddle poked his head in.

"Listen," he said, almost breathlessly. It was clear that he had left his son in the car running out front—they could all hear the roar of the car's engine—and that he didn't want Kent to be alone for very long. "I—I mean, we—me and the other boys' fathers—can help. We *want* to help find Tyler…"

His eyes dropped.

"I mean, we should have kept better watch…"

"They are boys, Mr. Griddle," the sheriff interrupted, grinding his knuckles even deeper into the table.

Gregory nodded.

"But we want to help, Sheriff. We—I *need* to help. Please, call us if there is anything we can do," the man pleaded.

The big sheriff nodded, a gesture that was quickly returned before Mr. Griddle once again fled the room.

This time, there was no silence when the three officers were alone again.

"Well? What do you think?" Deputy Williams asked. "You think the boys took something else instead of just the vodka?"

No one answered.

"Acid, maybe? PCP?"

Coggins shook his head.

"This is not nineteen eighty-four," he sighed, bringing his fingers up to his temples and rubbing them. He was well past the point of getting hangovers—six years of solid drinking would make you pretty good at it—but for some reason, today his mind felt foggy. It might have been the boy's outlandish story, or the fight last night at the bar with Sheriff White, or maybe it was just being back here, seeing them all. It was fucking up his mojo.

He swallowed hard.

Or maybe it was talking to Mrs. Drew; Mrs. Drew who was sitting at the desk that Alice had manned for so many years before...

"Fuck," he swore, closing his eyes tightly.

"You alright, Coggins?" White asked.

Coggins blinked hard a third time and looked at the man who had been his partner for the better part of a decade.

"Yeah," he said, but the words came out strained and he could tell by the look on the man's face that his response hadn't been convincing.

"What, then?" Williams asked, trying to butt into Coggins and White's silent, private exchange. "Ecstasy?"

The sheriff shook his head.

"I doubt it."

With a sigh, Sheriff White straightened his back and removed his fists from the desk. His knuckles were red from having been driven into the cheap fiberboard.

"Look"—he indicated the chairs on which Gregory Griddle and his boy had sat moments ago—"these are good people. They aren't hiding anything—you saw the way the boy was even ashamed to admit that he had been drinking. And who doesn't drink when they are fifteen?"

Coggins found himself nodding. He lacked the 'spidey sense' of recognizing *good boys* that the sheriff and his predecessor had, but he had become fairly adept at figuring out if someone was lying. And, in this case, he didn't think so.

It was the eyes; that hardened look that could not be faked. And the boy had it when the father had not. This was telling enough.

"So, what, then?" Williams asked again with a shrug.

The sheriff shook his head slowly before turning to Coggins for an answer.

"It's a missing person," Coggins said, trying his best to be pragmatic about the entire situation. "A missing person—nothing more, nothing less… at this point. We can forget about parasite crabs burrowing beneath flesh for the time being. We should focus our efforts on finding the boy first."

Both the sheriff and Deputy Williams nodded in agreement.

"Alright, so what's the first thing we do when looking for a missing person?" Coggins continued.

When no one answered right away, Coggins extended his neck and made a face.

"Paul! I'm gone for a few weeks and this whole place has fallen to shit! What kind of operation are you running here?"

The comment was meant to be humorous, to break the ice, the tension, whatever membrane of anxiety had slipped over the Askergan County Police Department, but it fell flat.

"Well?"

The sheriff looked up at him, his heavy brow pushing down over his eyes. There was no humor in his face.

"We go to the last place the person was seen," he replied dryly.

Coggins kept the charade going, raising his arms out in front of him, palms up.

"That's right, children, we go to the last place the person was seen. This is what you called me back in for? You need me to regurgitate Police Procedure 101?"

Deputy Williams rolled his eyes, but Coggins ignored him.

Why hire a skinny white dude to replace me if he has no sense of humor?

Coggins remembered the hours of playing poker he had spent with the then Deputy White, riding him about anything and everything. The man used to get so worked up that several times Coggins had been seriously worried that one of the thick veins in the man's neck or forehead might burst.

When his eyes fell back on the sheriff now, however, the man's expression was blank.

"And where was the last place that little Tyler Wandry was seen?"

The sheriff swallowed hard and averted his eyes.

Coggins's arms immediately fell to his sides, and the smile on his face vanished so rapidly that it was as if it had been slapped off. Even before the sheriff answered, Coggins knew what he was going to say; the answer had been in his eyes the whole time.

"The Wharfburns' Estate," Sheriff White said dryly.

Deputy Bradley Coggins felt his entire body go numb.

8.

CORINA LAWRENCE WENT IMMEDIATELY to her room after finishing dinner, not even bothering to clean up her or her sister's dishes as she usually did.

Marley was fuming.

And then she had been irate, irrational, and violent. Corina didn't blame her; after all, what she had said was horrible.

No wonder Dad left you.

Even now, just the thought of the words she had spoken made her shake her head in disgust.

Left you—as if Cody had been fed up with her and had demanded that they separated or divorced, or that he had found himself a young trophy mistress and had fled town with her.

Left you—implying that Corina and Henri might be able to go and visit him, to hold him, to hug him.

Corina started to cry.

Cody Lawrence had left because he wanted to save Henrietta, of course, and she knew that... but still, her mother had a way of getting under her skin like no one else.

Corina wiped the tears from her eyes and crawled onto her stomach. She propped herself on her elbows and switched on the small TV at the edge of her bed, quickly flipping through the channels to try and find something stupid on to distract her before she tucked her pride between her prosthetic leg and went to apologize. Tonight, however, the task was proving more difficult.

She wants me to get a job, to help pay some of the bills.

This is what Marley wanted, but Corina wanted to get a job and make money and *move out*. It wasn't that she didn't love her sister and get along amicably with her mother *most* of the time, but she was turning nineteen soon, and she needed to spread her wings—figure out what the hell she wanted to do with her life. And to keep training; she loved training.

Corina had been completely lost after what had happened at her grandmother's house more than six years ago, and had accidently stumbled on the MMA gym one evening while wandering the snowy streets in Downtown Pekinish just after they had moved. Usually she just wandered the streets aimlessly, practicing walking with a normal gait, lost in her own thoughts, but on that particularly frigid November afternoon, a man had been standing outside the gym, a man in his mid-sixties, dressed in only a pair of gym shorts. His muscled chest and arms, which looked like they belonged to a man at least two decades younger, were covered in sweat. At first, Corina had tried to hurry by, to slide by without being noticed, which was something she had become rather adept at over the past few months. But then someone had hollered from inside the open door of the building, and her attention had been drawn back.

"Mr. Gillespe! Get back inside and *roll*, you old fart!"

Her eyes met the old man's then—this *Mr. Gillespe*—and for a brief moment, she saw her father in those eyes, even though Cody hadn't been particularly athletic or even interested in sports; there was something in those eyes, a kindness that was difficult to describe.

"What's up, kiddo? Got a bummed knee?"

It probably would — *should* — have been considered creepy, a mid-sixty-year-old shirtless man calling out to a fourteen-year-old girl passing by, and it probably looked that way; only it wasn't, not at all.

Corina had looked down at her jeans then, wondering what the man was talking about.

Bummed knee?

A second later, she realized that she must have been walking with a limp; the actuators in the knee probably had gotten cold and weren't working as fluidly as they should have been.

Corina blushed and pulled up the ankle of her jeans, revealing the metal rods that connected the plastic leg to the artificial foot buried in a running shoe.

"Bummed leg," she informed the man.

Corina wasn't sure why she had even bothered to answer the man, let alone why she had chosen *that* answer. She supposed that she'd been looking to evoke a reaction, something on either end of the spectrum — pity or fear, or maybe something else.

Her confidence wasn't at an all-time high, what with finishing her grade nine exams while in the hospital bed recovering from the amputation, while her mind was busy trying to piece itself back together, to form walls and barriers that were necessary for her to continue on. And then shortly after she had been fitted for the leg and released from the hospital, they had been forced to move to Pekinish County to a small apartment in order to conserve money. Couple that with being homeschooled from grade ten onward, and you had the ideal recipe for a loner.

But now there was this man, this *old* man, who reacted to 'Bummed leg' not with surprise, fear, or disgust, but with something else. Something she hadn't experienced before.

"So what?" Mr. Gillespe replied.

Indifference.

For the first time in countless months since the blizzard and the death of her father, uncle, and grandmother, someone hadn't handled her like a precious vase—like something so fragile that it would break simply by breathing on it.

Apathetic.

"You ever trained before?" Mr. Gillespe asked, his breath coming out in thick clouds in the cold air.

The man was blocking the open doorway to the building behind him, and despite her efforts, Corina couldn't see around him to figure out what the hell he was talking about.

Trained?

"Rolled? Jiu jitsu? Muai Thay?"

Corina must have made a face then, as the old man laughed.

Someone hollered from the open door behind him again, but he just waved them away.

"MMA," he clarified.

When Corina still failed to react, the man threw up his hands.

"You know? Mixed Martial Arts?"

Still no response.

What is this crazy old man talking about?

The man rolled his eyes.

"Where have you been living?"

"Now? Pekinish."

Mr. Gillespe shook his head.

"Not what I meant. Anyways, why don't you step inside the gym and take a look."

And against all logic and 'stranger danger' doctrines impressed on her since even before she could form rational memories, she had gone inside.

And that was six years ago.

Memories of smashing Teddy's nose with her elbow flashed in her mind.

Fuck.

No, she wasn't fragile anymore—although she wasn't sure she had ever been *fragile*. *Fragile* was typically reserved for something that was easily broken, and once broken was thereafter unusable. Corina had been broken, but she had rebuilt herself into something stronger, something better.

Corina rubbed the sore spot on the underside of her right forearm where it had made contact with her sparring partner's face.

She wasn't fragile; she was strong—solid as a rock.

The TV suddenly stopped airing whatever sitcom she wasn't paying attention to, and a news reporter with cropped blonde hair and a serious face filled the screen.

"Breaking news," she started in a dry tone. "We have gotten word that a fifteen-year-old boy by the name of Tyler Wandry has been missing since Saturday—more than two days ago. He was last seen at Askergan KOA Campsite."

Corina's blood ran cold at the name of the place.

Askergan.

A photograph appeared in the upper right-hand corner of the screen of a boy with a shaved head, small dark eyes, and a prominent scar that ran from the outside of his right eye down to just below where his lips met.

"Tyler Wandry," the woman continued, her hand instinctively dropping to the bottom of her short yellow dress as it billowed from a gust of wind that struck her from behind. This seemed strange to Corina, as she had thought that the dirt road and the embankment leading down to the lake in the background were computer generated; she simply assumed that all newscasts were done in front of a green screen—even news from rural Askergan County.

"If you have any information, please contact the number on the screen now."

Even though the segment was over, the cameraman kept the feed rolling for just a second too long and the image on the TV suddenly turned sideways, presumably as the camera was removed from the tripod. The image twisted and then froze, and Corina, who had been holding her breath ever since the blonde reporter had uttered the word 'Askergan', experienced a sudden intake of air that was so violent that she immediately started to cough.

"You okay, Cor?" Henrietta asked from the family room.

Corina didn't hear her sister.

She had never been to the house that had been onscreen, which had been mostly out of focus and tilted at an odd angle, but that didn't matter; *she* had never been, but her father and uncles had. Even though the sitcom had come back on now, the image of that house remained in her mind, as if it had been permanently etched onto her retinas.

It was the place that she had spent six years trying to destroy with MMA training. It was the place responsible for why she and her nine-year-old sister shared a bedroom, and why her mom was always at her throat for not helping out with the bills. It was the place that had robbed her of part of her ear, her left leg, and all of her teenage years. The image onscreen had been the Wharfburn Estate.

*   *   *

The bus took a long time to show up outside the Lawrence apartment, too long for Corina's liking. It was as if the universe were slowing things down for her, giving her a chance to reconsider her actions, doing anything and everything to keep her from going back to Askergan.

No. No I'm not turning around.

Immediately after seeing the house on the news report about the missing boy, she had made up her mind. And when Corina's mind was made up, it was *made up*. After a night of fitful sleep, she had kissed her mother and her sister and had headed straight for the bus stop.

It was barely seven, and the sun was taking its time rising into the sky, a subtle indication that the oppressing heat of summer would come to an end before long. But it was already warm out and Corina was sweltering in her *Gillespe MMA* sweatshirt and faded blue jeans. Slung over her shoulder was a dark green canvas backpack in which she had stuffed a change of clothes.

As she waited for the bus to arrive, she reached into the bag and rooted around in the inside pocket until her fingers found the small, folded piece of paper. She pulled it out and unfolded it, slowly, carefully, trying not to make the small tears along where it had been folded any larger. When it was flat, Corina stared at her uncle's handwriting for a moment, reading those three words over and over again in her head.

Corina wasn't sure why her uncle had given this piece of paper to her at the hospital six years ago, as it hadn't made much sense to her then. In fact, several times since, she had debated throwing it in the garbage, if nothing else but to signify a complete letting go of the past. But for some reason, she had never been able to let go. And now she was glad.

Deputy Bradley Coggins, the three handwritten words read.

'Deputy Bradley Coggins is a man that you can trust; is someone that you can talk to,' her uncle had said when he had handed it

over. And that was it; no further, drawn-out explanation, and Corina had been too doped up to think to ask any questions.

Deputy Bradley Coggins is someone I can talk to? What, is he a shrink?

But after seeing the Wharfburn Estate on the news, she had made up her mind that that was exactly what she was going to do.

Corina folded the yellowed piece of notepaper and put it in her pocket.

She was going to find Deputy Bradley Coggins and ask him the questions that she should have inquired about years ago.

She just had to make one stop first.

9.

THE POLICE CRUISER PLUGGED along Highway 2 at a moderate clip, the interior silent. Sheriff White was behind the wheel, his thick hands clutching the black leather steering wheel at ten and two with such precision that Coggins wondered not once but twice if there was a driving instructor in the backseat taking notes.

Coggins himself was in the passenger seat, shifting uncomfortably in his new —*old*— police uniform, trying to get used to the way it restricted his movements. And the heat…

Why do they make the damn things out of thick cotton? he wondered, repeatedly pulling the beige short-sleeved button-down shirt away from his chest in an attempt to fan himself.

Coggins had been staring out the window of the cruiser for almost a half hour, the deluge of thoughts rushing through his head all at once making it feel like a dam—one he had taken years to carefully erect, brick by brick, whiskey by whiskey, toothless prostitute by toothless prostitute—had suddenly given way. In a way, the heat and his completely suffocating ACPD shirt were a blessed distraction.

Sheriff White cleared his throat.

"So, you ever gonna tell me what happened up there?"

Coggins rested his forehead on the passenger window. Then he scratched at his beard. His fingers came back wet with sweat.

"I told you already," he replied flatly.

The sheriff shook his head.

"I mean what *really* happened."

Coggins shrugged. Truth was, what had *really* happened six years ago at the Wharfburn Estate was buried away, tucked not only behind the dam that was suddenly springing multiple leaks, but in a safe that was embedded in the bottom of the concrete basin. A safe with one of those old-fashioned dials. A safe to which he had forgotten the combination. But when he had heard the words that had come out of young Kent Griddle's mouth, the fantastical story about a crab-like parasite clinging to his friend's *skin*, clawing its way beneath, he thought he remembered the first number to the safe's combination: it was a six.

I need a drink.

"Coggins? You alright?"

Coggins turned to look at his old friend, and was surprised that the man was no longer staring straight ahead, but had turned to face him, concern plastered on his features.

Fail — you fail your driving test, Mr. Paul White.

"Fine."

The words came out dry and hoarse and he cleared his throat.

"Fine," he repeated, attempting and failing to inject life into the singular word.

"Don't look fine, Coggins."

The sheriff took a deep breath, his eyes flicking back to the road for a brief moment before returning to Coggins.

"Look, Coggins, am I going to be able to count on you? Are you gonna be able to keep it together?"

Coggins thought of the sour expression that Deputy Williams had made when Paul had informed them that Coggins was to come with him to the Estate, while Williams was to stay back with Mrs. Drew and hold the fort. At the time, Coggins had felt proud—an almost completely foreign feeling over the past six years—but now he almost wished that Whitey had told *him* to stay back at the station.

They hit a bump, and Paul's head brushed the ceiling of the cabin.

Come to think of it, he wished that Sheriff White had never shown up at the bar on Monday.

The good boys—Askergan needs the good boys.

Coggins took a brief look down at his trembling palms, their movements a reflection of his need to imbibe, and the idea of him being one of the *good boys* seemed almost comical. He balled his hands into fists and tried to force the shakes away.

Dana Drew had picked him as a deputy, and Dana Drew knew the good boys.

"I'll be fine," he said at long last, bringing his gaze to meet the sheriff's eyes and holding the stare.

"Good," Paul replied, a hint of a smile crossing his thick lips.

Then his hands went back to ten and two, and his eyes returned to focusing on the road ahead.

"So," he continued after a few more minutes of silence, "you gonna tell me what happened up here?"

Coggins ignored him and stared out the window, desperately trying to find enough gum in his mind to keep the memory dam from exploding.

*   *   *

"God damn it," the sheriff grumbled when he first spied the small AC News van blocking more than half of the small dirt road roughly a quarter mile from the Wharfburn Estate.

"How do they get here so fast?"

Coggins shrugged.

"Dunno. But you know what they say: the only things that can survive a nuclear explosion are cockroaches and news reporters. It has something to do with their DNA."

The sheriff chuckled and slammed the cruiser into park.

Coggins laughed as well, despite himself.

"Did you miss me, big fella?" he asked as they exited the vehicle.

"No," White replied bluntly, but the smile that remained etched on his face said differently.

"Really?" Coggins teased. "Then how come you hired my twin to replace me?"

The sheriff turned to face him as they walked the short distance from their cruiser to the news van. As they approached, the chubby cameraman looked over at them, jammed the final corner of a sandwich into his fat face, and nudged a woman with blonde hair and a yellow dress that sat beside him on the van's bumper. Together they stood, and after the woman shifted her hips and pulled down her dress, they hurried over to them.

"Twin?" the sheriff asked.

"Deputy Williams."

When the sheriff's brow furrowed in confusion, Coggins started to tick off items on one hand.

"Tall, thin…"

Coggins paused as the attractive blond reporter approached. Her cameraman, still a few paces behind her, desperately trying to keep up, fumbled to switch on the old-fashioned over-the-shoulder camera mid-stride.

"Sheriff! Sheriff!" the woman squealed, smoothing her short blond hair with the hand not holding the mic.

The sheriff and deputy ignored her and kept striding forward.

"...dark hair? Slicked, *dark* hair? And *white*, my God, Paul, can't get any more clichéd than that; Tonto and the Lone Ranger."

The sheriff raised an eyebrow. "Tonto was a native and the Lone Ranger was white," he offered.

Coggins shrugged.

"Close enough."

"Sheriff? Just a few words for me and the people of Askergan... for AC News," the woman interjected.

The sheriff pushed by her, and now she was following them instead of running toward them, which Coggins preferred. The cameraman huffed and did an about-face, now struggling to run back the other way. The red light on the oversized camera resting on the man's broad shoulder was on, and Coggins made a note to watch what he said. It was, after all, his first day on the job.

"But you forgot one thing," Coggins informed the big man beside him, holding out one final finger.

Paul turned to him, stopping for a brief moment, his eyes still squinted, his expression dubious.

"And what's that?" he asked.

"Funny—that man is dry as a nun's cunt, my friend; no humor in that skinny face."

Well, it wasn't *really* Coggins's first day on the job, and he thought he could get away with that one.

A small smile passed over the sheriff's face, and Coggins was reassured that the big man hadn't lost all of his sense of humor.

The sheriff stopped abruptly and did a slow turn, his smile fading. The blond woman managed to stop in time, but the cameraman, trying to pull up his mom jeans without dropping the camera, bumped into the reporter and she, in turn, bumped into Sheriff White's broad chest. The reported turned and glared daggers at her cameraman.

Sheriff White placed his hands on his hips, a subconscious peacock ritual, making him seem nearly twice his already impressive size. Coggins made a face; even though he had been gone for a number of years, this seemed out of place for the big man—for most people, aside from a professional wrestler. It was just weird.

"Nancy, why did you bother coming up here? You know every single question you're gonna ask will be met with the same answer."

Nancy? They were on first-name basis?

The reporter turned to face the cameraman, indicating that he should point the camera at the sheriff. She swiveled her hips and then smoothed the front of her short dress that barely made it to mid-thigh. After a deep breath, she cleared her throat and held the mic out in front of her.

"Sheriff Paul White," she began, her voice suddenly changing, becoming more *professional*, "are there any leads on the missing boy? On Tyler Winicky?"

The sheriff rolled his eyes.

"No comment. At this time, the investigation is ongoing, and we are not in a position to discuss any details."

The reporter's face went sour, her bright red lips turning downward. She looked back at her fat cameraman and rested her hand on the top of the lens, indicating that he should lower the camera. The man, looking as if he might pass out from all the running, obliged, and then proceeded to head back to the truck, where he nearly collapsed on the rear bumper.

"Paul?" Nancy asked, once again turning back to the sheriff.

Coggins watched as the woman reached up and laid a gentle hand on the sheriff's shoulder, her bright green eyes sparkling. She was pretty, Coggins realized: full lips, big green eyes, and a smoking body.

One of the sheriff's eyebrows raised, and his eyes quickly darted to Coggins and back again.

Coggins smirked. It all made sense now.

Tsk, tsk, Paul. Relations with the media, a definite no-no.

The reporter's hand fell away, and she cleared her throat.

"Anything you can give me, Sheriff. Anything at all."

The sheriff seemed to mull this over for a minute before slowly shaking his head.

"I'm sorry, Nancy, I really have nothing right now. Just a crazy story from a bunch of scared kids whose friend went missing." The sheriff shrugged. "That's all I've got, really."

The reporter lowered her gaze, and Coggins sized her up a little more. She was younger than he and the sheriff, maybe by a good five years or so, but she was undeniably pretty, even if her features were a little small. She had smallish breasts, but ample hips and ass, which was made more evident by the fact that she had to continually tug at the bottom of her yellow dress to keep it from riding up and showing her underwear. Coggins glanced from the sheriff and then back to the reporter.

Lucky dog, he thought, his thoughts turning briefly to the woman that he had solicited in the bathroom of the grungy biker bar. *Lucky dog.*

When Nancy raised her eyes again, her expression had softened, a look that Coggins knew well: the pleading of a present or past lover.

Lucky, lucky dog.

"Tell me this, then, Sheriff: do you think that this is related to the string of kidnappings over in Pekinish a couple of years back?"

Sheriff White looked skyward for a moment, then bit the inside of his lip.

"Don't think so, no," he said, slowly shaking his head. "Doesn't seem to fit the bill. Besides, this is a missing *boy*, while, as far as I know, all the missing kids in Pekinish are female."

Nancy nodded slowly.

"And have you talked to anyone over there? The police over in Pekinish?"

The sheriff frowned and turned away from the woman, taking large steps in the direction of the Wharfburn Estate.

"You said one more question."

Coggins watched as the reporter hurried to keep up with the big man.

"But no," the sheriff continued, "I haven't spoken to anyone over there—yet."

The woman stopped following then, knowing as all the good reporters do when there was no information to be gleaned from a source, no matter how personal their relationship.

The woman nodded at Coggins, then hurried back to her colleague, who was still resting on the back of the truck, his thick torso still heaving with deep breaths.

When she was out of earshot, Coggins placed a hand on the sheriff's shoulder. The big man kept walking.

"Really?" Coggins asked, his voice dripping with humor. "Really, Paul? Nancy Whitaker of AC News?"

When the sheriff pulled his arm away from Coggins's grip, the deputy laughed. But another few paces and the Wharfburn Estate came into view, and the chuckle caught in his throat.

For a few minutes, Coggins had returned to his old self, teasing the big sheriff. But now, with the Wharfburn Estate looming before them, all the humor left him. Instead, all he felt was dread, pain, and despair. This was a horrible place—a place of nightmares.

10.

THE MORNING WAS ALREADY hot and humid when Corina Lawrence arrived at *Gillespe MMA*. At half past nine in the morning, the doors were still closed, but Corina knew that Frank Gillespe would be inside, cleaning wrestler sweat from the mats or taping up new rips on the ancient punching bags.

Corina waited for the bus doors to hiss closed and drive off before swinging the small canvas duffel onto her shoulder and hurrying across the street. Concentrating hard, she tried to make her gait look as natural as possible as she jogged across the road, pulling her prosthetic leg beneath her and pushing it back behind like her good leg. When she got to the other side, she resumed walking again, slipping the bag from one shoulder to the other. Corina hadn't packed much in the duffel bag, just a handful of light clothing, but now she was beginning to regret not packing more; she had no idea how long she might be back in Askergan.

Back in Askergan.

The thought drove a shudder through her, but she willed this sensation away. She had been waiting her whole life for this, for a chance to figure out what had happened to her and her family, and getting cold feet on a hot morning like this was out of the question.

Corina banged on the steel door with a flat hand, listening closely as the echo of her knocking faded and was followed by stirring. There was a momentary silence, and then she heard some shuffling steps coming toward the door. A second later, the latch was removed and the door pulled open.

"Frank," Corina said quickly, "I need a favor."

The man in his mid-sixties standing in the doorway eyed her suspiciously, his wiry black-and-grey eyebrows knitting together.

Without waiting for an answer, Corina pressed forward, swinging first her good leg then the prosthetic one across the threshold.

Frank Gillespe stepped aside and allowed her to pass. When she was fully inside, he closed the large metal door and latched it again.

"I'm going back to Askergan," Corina said bluntly when Frank turned to face her again. "I'm going back to Askergan to finish up some business."

Her eyes were trained on him, trying to read his reactions. For once, the man looked tired: thick, dark circles clinging to the underside of his eyes, the lines around his mouth pulled downward a little farther than usual. She often forgot that Frank would turn seventy in just a few short years, probably based on how good a shape he was in and his seemingly ineffable energy storage. But as soon as she had said those words— *Askergan*—his strength seemed to have been sapped.

Corina had purposely pushed thoughts of how this conversation would go during the bus ride over, worried that the more thought she put into her actions, the less likely she would be to carry through with them. But now, staring at his tired, incredulous expression, she was riddled with guilt and embarrassment.

You're not a kid anymore, Corina. Grow up; move on.

She shook her head.

"I need to borrow some cash," Corina continued quickly.

Frank Gillespe surprised her by immediately nodding. Without a word, he turned and made his way slowly to the small office at the back of the gym, just beyond the boxing ring.

"Come with me," he said, his voice, as always, mixed with gravel.

Now it was Corina's turn to nod.

She stared at the back of his grey cut-off t-shirt and thin cotton track pants as she followed the man that had guided her through so many tough times over the years, and she slowly became lost in thought. And, as her mind was wired to do, it soon drifted to what might have been—what might have been if her father hadn't insisted on heading to Grandma's house that Christmas, what might have happened if she hadn't broken her leg playing outside. Her thoughts darkened.

What would have happened if I hadn't found Frank back when I was struggling along on one leg?

"Corina? Are you listening?"

Corina shook the thoughts from her head.

Focus, she scolded herself.

When she raised her eyes, she realized that Frank had stopped walking and had turned to face her again, only this time his eyebrows were high on his forehead. A multitude of creases splayed outward on his forehead, congregating around the outer corners of his eyes like a nest of snakes.

"I said, *'I knew this day would come'*."

Even though Corina had heard the comment this time, she still didn't respond; she didn't know what to say.

The thing was, she'd known this day would come, too. In a strange way, Corina thought it was the reason why she had accepted Frank's challenge all those years ago, why she trained so vigorously for an opponent that hadn't reared its ugly head—an opponent that manifested as her past.

Until now.

"I am only going to ask you one thing, and that's it," Frank continued, his expression, while still tired, shifting from surprised and suspicious to paternal.

Corina nodded as Frank turned again and reached into his office. She heard him fiddle with a metal box on his desk, pulling out a stack of worn bills. When he turned toward her again, he held the stack out to her. She hesitated, waiting for his question.

Now it was her turn to be suspicious.

"Are you sure?" he asked, his lips pressing together tightly.

Corina bit the inside of her lip as she mulled the question over.

Truth was, she wasn't sure—not at all. The thought of going back to *that* place—to the exact location that had taken so much from her and from the ones that she loved—was terrifying. But both she and Frank had known that this day would eventually come. She just hadn't known it would be so soon.

Corina offered a slow nod in the form of response, which Frank returned.

It was time—it was time to vanquish this final demon.

Frank offered the stack of money, which Corina now saw was made up of a mixture of about ten or fifteen fives and tens.

"Then take this," the man said.

Corina thought about refusing the cash, about feigning disinterest, playing the *'oh, gee, I couldn't possibly'* card, but that wasn't her. No more faking it. In fact, if she was being true to herself and the gentle old man standing across from her, it was one of the reasons she had come to this place. Not the only reason, surely, but she needed money, if only to make it to Askergan by train.

She took the money, then reached for the man and hugged him fiercely.

Frank hugged her back.

"You never knew my dad," she said slowly as they separated. There were tears in her eyes. "You never knew my dad, but I know he would be grateful for all that you've done for me."

Frank Gillespe nodded.

Corina sniffed, wiped the tears from her face with the back of her sleeve, and then jammed the small wad of cash into the pocket of her jeans.

Over the past four or five years, Corina had spoken to Frank about what had happened in Askergan more than to anyone else, her mother included—it was her catharsis. Her uncle had tried repeatedly to reach out to her in the time since the storm, but each and every time she had politely declined—he was just too *close* to what had happened, too *familiar*. When she had spoken to Frank, the story had been abstract, with her spitting out the words like a tale that she had observed instead of one lived. That wouldn't have been possible with Jared. And now the only thing that she had from her uncle was the worn and folded piece of paper in her pocket.

Deputy Bradley Coggins—he's one of us, one of the good guys.

It had been too much for her then fragile mind to deal with, and it was better for her to shut things out—talking to Jared would have only brought back memories. Only in this place, in this holy sanctuary of the MMA world where she could pound her frustrations out on the arms and legs and faces of other equally troubled individuals, could she speak the truth—and who else would be there to listen but the holy minister of this sacred parish?

"Corina?" the elderly man before her asked, his eyebrows pulling downward. "Remember that you are still suspended for a month."

Corina smiled and leaned forward to place a gentle kiss on his wrinkled cheek.

"I'll be back long before that," she replied, then left *Gillespe MMA* for the last time.

11.

NEWLY RE-DEPUTIZED BRADLEY COGGINS found every step more difficult than the last, his body struggling to cut through the air like a fly trying to navigate through a block of softened butter.

There was evil here—*still* here—and it took all of his willpower to stop the images of what had happened in Mrs. Wharfburn's now charred front foyer from tumbling back to the forefront of his mind. He had spent the better part of the past decade trying to drown out those visions with cheap whiskey and cheaper women.

Evidently, he had failed.

"Coggins? Let's head to the kitchen, okay?"

Coggins nodded, trying hard to swallow the fist-sized lump in his throat.

His eyes lingered on the thick black char mark in the center of the room.

Dana, don't get down!

He closed his eyes and shook his head hard, bringing a hand to his left temple.

Fuck.

"Coggins?"

Somewhere far away, Coggins realized that the man had stopped, and he used the hand not affixed to the side of his head to usher the man forward.

"Keep going," he grumbled through gritted teeth. "Just a headache."

He wanted—*needed*—to be out of this front foyer immediately.

The kitchen was in desperate need of an update, the pale brown wooden cabinets with their thick metal handles indicative of a style long past its due date. The fridge and stove were equally dated, huge white plastic-looking beasts that crowded the space. For such a massive house, the kitchen was small, dated, and *stale*. But compared to the entrance and foyer, the kitchen was pretty much untouched.

The sheriff used the pad of his finger to trace a line in the dust-covered quartz countertop. In doing so, he stirred a thick dust cloud into the air, which immediately made him cough.

Coggins brought his hand away from the side of his head. Now that they were in another part of the house, a part where he had never been before, his mind started working overtime trying to compartmentalize, to render his memories once again abstract.

It worked—for now.

The trapdoor in front of the fridge was still open, the rusty metal hinge folding the four-foot square piece of tiled floor completely backward, revealing a dark passage into the basement below. The thin layer of dust on the floor around the trapdoor and throughout the kitchen was disturbed, which jived with the Griddle boy's story. Someone had been here recently.

Coggins had also found remnants of glass on the floor in the foyer before he had hurried through—the vodka—which was also consistent with Kent's story.

The sheriff nodded toward the opening in the floor.

"Might be too tight for me to fit," he offered.

Coggins frowned and shook his head.

"If you think I'm—"

The sheriff cut him off by raising a large hand.

"We'll both go."

Not what I was thinking, but okay.

The idea of staying alone in the kitchen while the sheriff went below was almost as bad as the prospect of heading into the stinking darkness alone—not *as* bad, but close.

Coggins went down first, mainly a result of physics, at the sheriff's request, who noted that if something went wrong, Paul could quickly pull him back up again.

The first thing that struck Coggins when his feet landed on the ground below was the dust: it was everywhere, suspended in the air like a miniature galaxy. He waved a hand in front of his face, but this only served to send the galaxy into rotation.

"Toss the flashlight down," he hollered to the sheriff above, his voice cracking.

He coughed and then swallowed a few times, trying desperately to moisten his incredibly dry throat. It was dry and dusty in the basement, there was no doubt of that, but there was something else about it that bothered Coggins; it smelled bad down there, *really* bad, a funk that reminded him of six years ago...

Stop it, he chided himself.

He reached up and grabbed the flashlight from the sheriff's outstretched hand and flicked it on. His breath caught in his throat.

"Sheriff?" Coggins's voice wavered. "Get your big ass down here."

There was a stirring sound from the kitchen above, but Coggins kept his eyes trained on the scene before him. Even as he took two steps to his left to allow room for the big man to fall into the basement, careful to avoid the smashed staircase, he kept his eyes aimed straight ahead.

A moment later, a heavy thud sounded from his right as the sheriff lowered himself into the room. At just over six feet of headroom, the sheriff had to crane his neck uncomfortably to avoid bumping his head on the lowered floor beams.

"God, it stinks in here," the sheriff muttered, slapping his big hands together, sending more dust swirling into the humid air. "What—?"

But the sheriff left the sentence unfinished as his gaze followed the flashlight beam for the first time.

For a few seconds, the sheriff and Deputy Coggins just stood silently in the dusty basement, staring at the wet mess before them.

There were about a half dozen, maybe more, animal pelts scattered on the floor by the back wall of the basement, some folded over themselves, others appearing as if they had been laid flat.

Skin.

Coggins shuddered and suddenly felt cold despite the heat.

Laying on the floor in front of the skins were an equal number of beach ball-sized spheres, the tops of which were ragged and broken. Coggins let his gaze fall to the crescent-shaped bottoms and noted some residual pink fluid still clinging to the translucent surface.

Given the humidity in the basement, the residual fluid meant that these too were fresh—had a considerable amount of time passed since the orbs had been smashed open, the fluid would have long since risen to mingle with the dust in the air.

From somewhere far away, Coggins heard the sheriff exhale loudly before turning to face him.

"Coggins? You okay? You're shaking."

It was true, Coggins realized, staring at the beam of light from the flashlight that jumped up and down as if held by someone suffering from Parkinson's.

He *was* shaking, but he couldn't help it.

"Air," he gulped. "I need air."

The sheriff took two quick steps toward his partner before first grabbing the flashlight from him and then wrapping his thick arm around Coggins's narrow waist.

A second later, Coggins felt his knees buckle, and if it weren't for the sheriff holding him, he would have fallen down in a heap.

"C'mon," the sheriff grunted as he carried Coggins directly beneath the trapdoor, "let's get you out of here."

Like a man migrating through Vaseline, Coggins slowly reached up and grabbed the floor above.

"Ready?" the sheriff asked.

He didn't wait for an answer. The big man boosted him out of the basement with such force that Coggins skidded a few feet across the kitchen floor.

He blinked hard, trying to clear the dust from his eyes.

Skins. Those were skins down there...

Coggins coughed and spat a thick wad of phlegm on the floor beside him.

"Coggins? You all right up there?" the sheriff hollered.

Coggins scrambled to a seated position, and after a deep breath of considerably less funky air, grumbled an affirmative.

His head was starting to clear, but he still couldn't stop his whole body from quivering.

"You okay to hang out up there for a minute?"

This time, Coggins didn't answer.

Skins—like the one that Oxford had worn, like the skin of Mrs. Wharfburn that had been peeled and discarded by—

Coggins bit the inside of his cheek so hard that he tasted blood.

Stop it.

"It looks like eggs," the sheriff grumbled from below, his voice echoing off the moist bricks and funneling up through the opening in the floor.

Eggs…

"Fucking dinosaur eggs. Coggins?"

"Yeah?" he manage to croak.

"This is fucked up… sounds just like the way the Griddle boy described it."

Coggins felt his heart skip a beat. This was his worst nightmare, coming back here to this godforsaken place that he wished he had completely burnt to the ground. And now this, finding—*good fucking Lord*—eggs?

Coggins barely stifled a moan.

"Coggins?" the sheriff's voice was more serious now.

This time, Coggins couldn't even squeak out a *'yes'*. It didn't matter; the big man continued anyway.

"What happened here? I mean, before? You ever going to tell me?"

Again Coggins remained silent, trying his best to catch his bearings and stop the world from spinning.

A drink. I need a drink.

Besides, it wasn't even clear if Paul was talking to him or to himself.

"What the fuck is this?" the sheriff grumbled from below.

Coggins heard Paul grunt. The next time he spoke, his voice was louder and it was clear that the comment was directed at him.

"Heads-up!"

Something flew out of the trapdoor a second later, landing just a foot from where Coggins sat. The deputy's eyes went wide, and sweat immediately beaded on his forehead. Using his hands to push his body, he desperately scampered away from the object that clattered loudly off the tiles. Coggins hesitated before coming completely to his feet, staring at the shape, a small, oblong object roughly the size of a miniature football, with a network of spindle-like legs folded awkwardly beneath it. The only saving grace was that it wasn't moving: the hard white surface that looked like bleached bone was inert, silent, *dead*.

His heart rate having come down a little, Coggins managed to pull himself to his feet in a somewhat organized fashion, then stretched his back and brushed some of the dust from his dark blue police pants.

Eyes fixated on the *thing*, he cleared his throat again and hollered back at the sheriff, who was struggling to lift himself out of the basement.

"What's this? Did Nancy Whitaker give you crabs, Paul? You know you can just fucking scrub them… kerosene and a wire brush should do the trick."

Dirt ticked his throat, and he turned to spit again.

The joke wasn't funny.

The sheriff finally managed to pull his large body out of the basement via a modified pull-up, and rolled over to look at Coggins. Like Coggins, the man's forehead glistened with sweat. It wasn't noon yet, but the temperature was already reaching into the high nineties.

"Very funny," the sheriff grumbled as he too brushed dirt from his pants.

Paul White pulled a pen from the front pocket of his shirt and used it to flip the crab-thing over. The six legs clattered to the floor, splaying out from around its body. It wasn't a crab, that much was clear; a crab had eight legs, and *those* legs definitely didn't have so many thick, knotted joints.

It was hideous, and Coggins shuddered. The sheriff caught the movement and looked over at him, his eyebrows once again raising up on his forehead.

"I know one day you'll tell me what happened here, Coggins."

The man's eyes softened, and when he continued his voice had dropped an octave.

"But even if you don't, I know what you must have done was the right thing. We are, after all, some of the *good* boys — even if one of us likes to frequent hookers and drink cheap whiskey in a bar with fat, drug-dealing bikers."

Coggins cracked a smile despite himself.

"Remember that, okay? Remember what Dana Drew told us."

12.

CORINA BRUSHED A LOCK of short, dark hair from the side of her face and placed her hands on her hips. As she leaned back and stretched her spine, the bus pulled away, revealing a small, inauspicious brick building with an illuminated white-and-blue placard on the lawn that read: *Askergan County Police Department.*

It had been a long ride to Askergan, and during her time on the bus anxiety had built and manifested as a pressure behind Corina's eyes. It had been six years since she had been to this place, but it appeared that all of her efforts in the gym to repress the memories had been for naught: seeing those words — *Askergan County* — brought everything flooding back like a deluge.

Six years. Six years ago she had been here with her family, when it had still been *whole*; when Dad had still been alive. She had been but a child then, an obstinate pre-teen, but memories of horrible events seemed to stick with you, to defy memory convention — the scene around the kitchen table, eating Grandma's turkey, the atmosphere festive and jovial; that scene was permanent.

Dad; I miss you, dad.

A single tear rolled down her round cheeks, and she quickly wiped it away with the sleeve of her sweatshirt.

You saved Henri by leaving—sacrificed yourself in the process, but you saved us.

And this is how it was with her, flip-flopping between being angry at her dad for leaving to revering him for saving them all. It was all just so confusing, culminating with her arrival back in Askergan.

Corina shook her head, trying to clear her mind.

She failed.

A memory of lying in the hospital bed just after her surgery came to her, but unlike her vision of Christmas dinner, this one was far from lucid, clearly the byproduct of being hopped up on painkillers. Jared was with her, she remembered that. And she remembered uttering several words to him—words that didn't make sense to her now, but words that she felt she would understand soon.

Palil. It's growing its palil *and it's still coming.*

Corina shuddered and self-consciously reached down to adjust her prosthetic leg. Her jeans had been specifically tailored—one of the Lawrence family's very few extravagant expenditures—so that a passerby would not be able to tell that her leg beneath wasn't real. There was a little extra room in the knee to disguise the bulky attachment and a tight taper on both legs to disguise the fact that the prosthetic leg was slightly narrower than her real leg.

Corina shifted the knapsack to her other shoulder and took a step onto the street, eyes focused on the glass front of the police station. Her stride was smooth and natural, one that had taken several years to perfect. She kept her eyes trained on the small brown brick building as she crossed the road and then the parking lot, trying desperately to avoid looking at the sign emblazoned with the words that incited such painful, vivid memories.

Askergan County.

Corina shuddered.

I can't believe I'm back in this fucking place.

*   *   *

Corina wasn't sure what to expect when she pulled open the glass door to the police station, but it certainly wasn't a woman in her mid to late fifties with short grey hair pulled back in a tight bun, wearing a snug-fitting office uniform: a white-and-purple-striped blouse tucked into a knee-length black skirt.

The woman looked up when the bell above the door chimed signifying Corina's entrance, and Corina was immediately struck by how pretty she was, irrespective of her age: her skin was a vibrant hue of pink, her makeup subtle yet accentuating. But mostly it was her eyes; the woman's eyes were a vibrant green that almost seemed to shimmer under the fluorescent lights. Yet despite her pleasing appearance, there was something about the way her pale red lips were slightly pressed together and the way her left hand didn't quite lay on the plain brown desk in front of her, but pressed into it ever so slightly. These subtle gestures sent a clear message: this woman was not to be messed with.

Corina glanced down at her own body and felt a pang of guilt. Wearing her jeans—tailored, yes, stylish, not so much—and an old VERMONT U sweatshirt, she looked more like a vagabond than a respectable member of society. And the dampness in her pits and between her thighs from sweating on the long bus ride didn't help her cause, either.

"May I help you?" the woman asked in a voice that was firm yet nonaggressive.

Corina cleared her throat and stepped completely into the station, allowing the door to close behind her.

"Yes, I—" She cleared her throat again and reached into her jean pocket. She pulled out the worn piece of paper and unfolded it, careful not to rip the seams. "Yes," she continued, "I am looking for Deputy Bradley Coggins."

When Corina looked up again, the woman was staring at her with a queer expression on her face. When she didn't answer right away, Corina looked down at the paper again, making sure that she had said the name correctly.

Had Jared been wrong? Was there a Deputy Coggins here?

But then the woman's face returned to its previous demeanor.

"He is not here right now," she informed Corina, her eyes now suspiciously looking her up and down. "But if you need an officer, young lady, Deputy Williams is here. You can talk to him if you want."

Corina's face contorted. She didn't want—didn't need—Deputy Williams; she needed Deputy Coggins.

"Or," the woman continued, more slowly this time, "or you can talk to me if you want—if you would be more comfortable talking to a woman."

She continued to stare at Corina, sizing her up.

Corina shook her head slowly.

"No, I just need to talk to Deputy Coggins."

"Well, I'm not sure when he'll be back. You can come back tomorrow, if you'd like."

Corina shook her head again.

"I came a long way to see Deputy Coggins. Is it all right if I just wait here?"

The woman nodded.

"Of course. There are some chairs over there that you can use. I can also get you a coffee and some snacks if you would like."

The woman indicated a row of black chairs that were bound together by their armrests in the small waiting room in which she stood.

"Just a water would be nice, Mrs...?"

"Mrs. Drew," the woman answered sharply, and then added in a softer tone, "I'll get you some water. You just go ahead and take a seat."

Corina did as she was asked, tossing her backpack on the seat beside her. While she waited, she looked around.

It wasn't much of a police station, at least not in the tradi-tional sense. There were no lanes with glass-covered window booths at the ends manned by obstinate ladies begrudgingly taking police reports, and there were no American flags hang-ing every few feet along the wall. Instead, there was just the one simple desk occupied by Mrs. Drew, and a small adjacent kitchen, where the woman now went to get the glass of water that Corina had requested. Behind the desk was a small passage that led to what she assumed were other offices and the jail cells. All in all, it was more an office than a police station.

"Here you go," Mrs. Drew said, returning from the kitchen and handing Corina a glass of water.

She thanked the woman and took a sip. The cool liquid felt good going down on this hot morning.

A man suddenly made his way to the front of the station from the passageway behind Mrs. Drew's desk. He was thin, with slicked black hair and a narrow face punctuated by two small, dark eyes. Deputy Williams, no doubt; the way he walked, with a slight swagger, was enough for Corina to con-clude that he was a deputy, irrespective of her conversation with Mrs. Drew earlier. And when he spoke in a voice that didn't quite fit his profile, as if he were putting it on, making it deeper in an attempt to seem authoritative, Corina could have closed her eyes and known that an officer of the law was speaking—she didn't need to see the gold star on the breast of his beige shirt.

"Heard the door open," he said, stopping just at the side of Mrs. Drew's desk. One hand went to his side, and Corina followed his movements to the grey butt of his gun.

Corina rolled her eyes. She knew men like this; she had submitted dozens of them over the years in the gym.

"Everything all right here, Mrs. Drew?"

Mrs. Drew turned from Corina to face the man.

"Yes, Andrew, everything is fine."

The deputy pushed his lips together and nodded curtly.

Good, just checking up on you, ye hear. Making sure everything is A-OK, m'lady.

"And you, Miss, you okay, too?" he asked, peering around Mrs. Drew.

Corina nodded.

"Just came—"

Mrs. Drew interrupted her.

"She is here to see Deputy Coggins," she said curtly.

The deputy's dark eyebrows knitted on his high forehead.

"Brad?"

He turned to Corina.

"You need to talk to a deputy, sweetie?"

Corina cringed.

Sweetie. That's what Dad used to call me.

She shook her head and was about to reply, but again Mrs. Drew answered for her.

"No, not to see a deputy. To see Coggins."

Deputy Williams seemed confused by this, and his beady eyes darted to Corina and then Mrs. Drew and back again. Eventually they fixed on Corina.

"I can take you to see him," he said bluntly.

Mrs. Drew's posture changed.

"I think it's better if she waits here."

The deputy's gaze went back to the woman.

"It's okay, he's only out there at the Wharfburn Estate—I'll take her to see him."

Corina's entire body immediately broke out in a cold sweat and her heart began to race. Mrs. Drew said something in response, but Corina didn't hear the words.

Wharfburn Estate.

Like *Askergan County*, these words carried so much weight that they seemed to crush her.

Corina was suddenly flushed into a memory, of a time when she was young, maybe only five or six years old, lying on her bed in her striped pajamas, listening to her father read.

"You sure you want to hear this one?" he asked, looking over at her with his pale blue eyes.

Corina nodded vigorously.

"But it's not that exciting…"

"That's okay, Daddy."

He wasn't lying, his essays were never that exciting—but it was the way he read them. And it wasn't just the funny voices that he used—which sometimes became a distraction when he messed up all the accents—but it was the way he read his own work. His voice exuded pride as his tongue pronounced those words, and the effect was intoxicating.

"Read on, Daddy," she said with a smile.

Although Cody Lawrence attempted a neutral expression, he failed; pride tiptoed over his features.

It took Corina a moment to realize that both Mrs. Drew and the deputy were staring at her.

Had they asked a question?

Heart still racing, her gaze jumped from face to face.

The door suddenly chimed and Corina turned to face the sound just as the door slammed into the wall behind it. A man with thick black hair aggressively parted on one side and a gnarled white beard burst through the entrance, his eyes red and wild.

"Where the fuck is my boy?" he shouted, revealing two rows of thick brown teeth clenched in a sneer. "Where the fuck is my boy?"

13.

COGGINS FOLLOWED THE SHERIFF through the kitchen, his eyes locked on the streaks of disturbed dust on the kitchen floor. He was looking at anything but the strange crab-like creature in the clear plastic bag clutched in his hand.

In fact, he was so distracted that he only noticed that Sheriff White stopped a split second before he rammed into him from behind.

Raising his gaze, he realized that Paul had pulled up in front of the French doors at the rear of the house, the meaty palm of his right hand firmly planted on the butt of his gun. He allowed his eyes to drift upward, but when he saw judgement in Paul's face, he looked down again.

That was a mistake; he fixated on the corpse of the strange white creature in the bag.

"Coggins," Sheriff White hissed, and Coggin's tired eyes snapped up again. "Stay behind me."

Coggins shrugged and did as he was told. But unlike the sheriff, both of his hands remained at his sides.

The sheriff pressed his back against the wall adjacent the exit, then used his hand to open the door nearest him all the way. Coggins crept beside him and also leaned up against the wall, but his focus was locked on the plastic bag.

The sheriff first peeked around the corner and, apparently seeing nothing but the empty swimming pool, he took two steps to his left and exited the house, glancing first left and then swinging his gun in a wide arc all the way across the lawn.

Clearly satisfied that there was no danger, aside from the risk of being forever entangled in the waist-high weeds, he leaned back into the house to indicate to Coggins to join him.

"All clear," he said.

Coggins found the whole scene a little dramatic, despite himself and the crab, and he rolled his eyes. Deep down, he knew that his reaction was just a defense mechanism, but he didn't give a shit. He casually joined the sheriff outside, and when Paul gave him a stern look, Coggins shrugged.

"Lead the way, Miami Vice," he said. "It's just my first day on the job, after all."

Yet despite his humorous commentary, he too decided to draw his gun, although he held it by his hip instead of fanning it out in front of him as the sheriff continued to do.

They followed the path through the overgrown lawn, which was mainly composed of a thicket of broken grass stalks and disturbed dandelion tops. A gnat buzzed by Coggins' ear, and he brought his hand up to sweep it away. In doing so, he caught a glimpse of the crab-thing in the plastic bag again.

It was hideous—its crispy, bleached limbs were so taut now that the pointed ends stretched the makeshift evidence bag to its maximum.

"What do you think about the boy's story now?" Coggins asked quietly, eyes still moving up and down the multi-jointed limbs.

The sheriff continued to plow ahead slowly.

"Dunno," he said after a moment of silent contemplation. "You?"

Even though he had posed the initial question, he hadn't expected the man to immediately throw it back to him. But when he tried to recall what the Griddle boy had said, he found his mind drifting elsewhere, back to what had happened here in this very house.

Bile rose in his throat and he swallowed hard.

Memories that had long since been suppressed with the help of his best friend Johnny Walker suddenly came thudding back. It was hard, really hard, to put things in perspective, to think that what flooded his mind at this very moment was anything but his imagination. After all, on that fateful time a few days before Christmas, he had gone at least a day without eating, and on top of that it had been freezing cold. The snow didn't help, either, its collective mass a disorienting blanket of non-sense that numbed his senses.

Back then, the Wharfburn Estate had been covered in a thick blanket of snow. Back then, he had been thin, in shape. Back then, he hadn't been able to feel his extremities. Now he was a little pudgy from years of drinking. And it was hot, the sun beating down on them relentlessly. So very different the two times he had been here, but they were somehow the same—the same evil had drawn him here then, and it was another evil—his hand tightened on the plastic bag, wrenching it in his moist palm—that had pulled him back.

Coggins took a deep breath and wiped the sweat from his brow, making sure to use the hand that held the pistol and not the one with his bag.

His last memory of the place was watching the skins burn in the foyer, along with the abomination that Sheriff Dana Drew had become. It was there, staring at the boiling and bubbling skin of his friend, mentor, *father figure*, that something inside of him had broken.

Deputy Bradley Coggins started to shake, and he felt a strong urge to drink.

This is fucked—what am I doing back here?

They had thought that they had gotten it all—burned all the skins and the *evil* that had descended on this place, after which then they had all gone their separate ways. Burying those secrets deep, severing all connection with those who had been involved in the horrors, as familiarity would only serve to bring back memories of a time and a place that would eventually blur into oblivion.

That was their hope, anyway.

"Coggins?"

Coggins raised his head from the ground and stared at the sheriff's face. The man's thick black eyebrows had turned upward in the middle, his expression one of deep concern.

Coggins swallowed hard.

It was a foolish hope.

"I'm fine," he lied, wiping away more sweat from his forehead.

The sheriff continued to stare at him.

"Look, I'm the cool guy from Miami Vice, you're the black guy—I'm cool," Coggins continued.

After a time, Coggins could no longer stand the sheriff's accusatory glance, and he let his eyes drift to one side, to behind the big man.

With their stare broken, the sheriff finally spoke up.

"What happened here?" the sheriff asked, his voice low.

Coggins shrugged.

"You heard the boy." He raised the plastic bag with the six-legged crab in front of him, but purposely avoided looking at it. "Fucking crabs, man."

The sheriff shook his head and indicated that Coggins should lower the hideous thing.

"No, I mean before."

The big man's face twisted, and for a moment Coggins thought that the sheriff might shed a tear. He didn't blame him;

being back here had him tearing up too. "I mean with the sheriff."

Coggins's eyes went dark.

"Nothing," he said definitively, making it clear that he
meant to change the subject. The sheriff nodded slowly.

"Anything I need to know, anything that will help me with
this?" He indicated the plastic bag with his chin.

Coggins thought about that for a moment. Of course they
were related—somehow that *fucking* thing that had possessed
Dana Drew had planted these eggs in the basement.

Evil.

Oot'-keban.

Of course they were related.

Coggins bit the inside of his lip so hard that he tasted blood.

Should have just burned the whole fucking place to the ground.

"Coggins?"

He hadn't realized that he had drifted into thought again.

"Can you handle this?"

Coggins shook his head.

"Fuck no. But if I screw up, you can always revert to my twin
that you hired."

The sheriff looked confused.

"Twin?"

Coggins waited, and eventually understanding crossed the
sheriff's broad features.

"Deputy Williams?"

Coggins nodded, and a small smile broke on the sheriff's
face.

"Not your twin," he said. "The man is a highly—"

"Face it, Paul, you missed me so much that you tried to hire
someone that looks exactly like me. You cheated on me."

The sheriff smirked and turned back to the path leading away from the house.

"Fucking hell," the man muttered just loud enough for Coggins to hear. "Maybe Sheriff Drew's judgement on you was way off. Maybe *he* was the one drinking at Sabra's biker bar when he decided to hire your sorry ass."

Coggins smiled and fell in behind the big man.

They walked in silence for the next minute, and after about fifty paces, the path led them first into a thin forest, then to a small clearing at the mouth of a culvert. The culvert, which was about fifteen feet long, cut an opening in a hill that ran up to the road above.

The sheriff turned to Coggins and pointed to the left side of the culvert. Coggins nodded and dropped to a crouch before squirreling his way to the side of the hill. The sheriff did the same on the opposite side of the opening, both of them leaning with their backs against the hill, both guns drawn now.

Their eyes met and the sheriff nodded.

Coggins watched as the man took a deep breath, then stepped in front of the culvert, his pistol aimed into the tunnel.

A moment later, he lowered his gun down and turned to Coggins.

"All clear," he said again.

Coggins made a face.

"You been watching Matlock or something? What is this 'all clear' bullshit?" Coggins asked, once again moving in behind the sheriff.

"Protocol," the sheriff answered simply.

Coggins looked skyward.

"Ah, yes, ye the keeper of the rules."

The sheriff ignored him and stepped into the culvert. Coggins followed.

The shade of the tunnel offered much relief from the hot sun beating down from above, and Coggins didn't hesitate in leaning against the back of the corrugated metal, enjoying the cooling sensation that it offered even through his police shirt. He watched as the sheriff squatted and moved a few steps into the tunnel, examining a disturbed area on the floor.

"Someone was here recently," he said, more to himself than to Coggins.

Coggins nodded and examined the interior of the massive culvert, which was large enough that the six-foot-four sheriff could stand inside without ducking, and once again let his mind wander.

He had tried to return to the deputy lifestyle—or at least *wanted* to try to continue his life much the way it had been before the blizzard. But he just couldn't do it; no matter how hard he tried, he couldn't pick up the phone and call his partner, the now Sheriff Paul White, and tell him, *'Yeah, listen, Whitey, I'm good now—good to come back to work.'*

He never made that call because he cared about the man too much to lie to him. And he couldn't face Alice, either, even though he called often to check up on her. Her condition was always the same, and for some reason, he felt that only contributed to his complacency: *No change, Mr. Coggins. Alice is still sleeping soundly.*

Maybe, just maybe, if she had awoken, if she had—

Coggins shook the nonsense from his head.

It didn't matter. He was here now, in a culvert, trying to keep cool on what must have been one of the hottest days of the year. Here, in *this* place, with Sheriff White.

But why?

Coggins had no idea.

"You think—?" the sheriff began, but the crackle of the radio on his hip interrupted him. The sound was loud in the culvert, and Coggins, still jumpy, forever on edge, felt his breath catch in his throat.

"Sheriff?" the static-ridden voice demanded. "Sheriff?"

In the background, Coggins thought he heard someone shout.

The sheriff, still on his haunches, turned to Coggins, his expression grim. There was a sheen on his dark face, and sweat had nearly soaked all the way through his police shirt. He unhooked the radio and barked, keeping his eyes trained on Coggins.

"Come in, Deputy Williams."

"Yeah, Sheriff, we have a bit of a—" The deputy suddenly shouted to someone in the background, "Get behind me! And you stay away from her!"

There was a pause, followed by the sound of more commotion.

The sheriff brought the radio to his lips again.

"Andy? What the hell is going on over there?"

"Sorry, Sheriff—listen, you need to get back here quick. Mr. ugh, Mr., ugh—" There was another pause, but this time the radio clicked off for a brief moment before the deputy spoke again. "Mr. Wandry is here—the father of the missing boy Tyler—and—"

There was another pause, but this time the radio stayed on. Coggins leaned closer to the sheriff, trying to make out what was going on back at the station. He heard two female voices, one young and the other old.

The young girl's voice: "Don't come near me."

The old woman's voice: "Stay away from her."

He recognized the older woman's voice: it was Mrs. Drew, and she didn't sound scared. Instead, her words sounded like a veiled threat, which didn't surprise the sheriff. The confidence in the younger girl's voice, on the other hand, was startling.

Stay away from us, if you know what's good for you.

"Back up! Back up, now!"

It was the deputy this time, and the next time he spoke his voice was louder; clearly, the man had brought the radio back to his face.

"Sheriff, you need to get down here—Walter Wandry has lost his mind."

"Ten-four," the sheriff replied, pulling himself to his feet. "I'll be there in thirty. Throw him in the cell until I get there."

The sheriff clicked off the radio and headed toward Coggins, intending to leave the culvert.

"Let's go," he said, reaching out for Coggins's arm.

Coggins moved a little to his left, letting Paul's hand fall short.

"You go," Coggins said. "You go, I have something to take care of around here."

The sheriff's thick eyebrows furrowed, a mask of confusion crossing his features.

"Something to take care of?" he repeated, his voice hesitant.

Coggins knew what the man was thinking—he was thinking that the *something* that Coggins was referring to was a drink.

And he wanted a drink, but that wasn't the *something*—not this time.

"I need to—"

Coggins didn't finish his sentence. A resounding crack erupted in the culvert from behind the two men, and it echoed off the irregular surface, making it difficult to determine where exactly it was coming from.

The sheriff acted first. Gun still drawn, he whipped his crouched body around. Coggins pushed off of the interior of the culvert with his foot and pulled his gun out of the holster, dropping the bag with the crab to the ground.

The object gliding toward them was moving too quickly to fire at it, and even if it were farther away, it would have been a difficult target.

Sheriff White sidestepped just in time and swiveled his hips as the flying disc came at him. At the same time, he swung his gun around, releasing the butt and grabbing the barrel mid swing.

There was another crack, but this one was deeper, more crumpling in texture, and it lacked the popping quality of the previous sound.

The butt of the sheriff's gun smashed the flying thing's shell and sent it careening back the way it came with far less grace. As it tumbled through the air, Coggins noted that it had six knobby appendages and was nearly identical to the thing that the sheriff had tossed out of the basement, the thing in the plastic bag that he had dropped to the ground.

The creature smacked against the wall with a moist smack and slowly slid down the side, leaving a trail of an opaque white substance in its wake. Then it landed in a lifeless heap at the bottom of the culvert about six feet from the sheriff. Paul immediately flipped his gun around and kept it trained on the thing, and the two men waited in silence for a moment, their heavy breathing the only sound in the now hot culvert.

When the cracker didn't move for several seconds, the sheriff finally lowered his gun.

"Jesus, Whitey, you should have been a baseball player, not a football player," Coggins said breathlessly.

Despite his words, his mind was churning, thinking about the story that the Griddle kid had told them about how the crab-thing had affixed to his friend's scalp.

That was fucking close.

Coggins kept his gun drawn as the sheriff turned to face him. There was no humor on his face.

"I need to get to the station," he said curtly. "You coming back, Coggins?"

Despite the authority of his words, the man was obviously torn; they clearly had business to take care of here, but his ties to Deputy Williams and Mrs. Drew ran deep. Coggins was reminded of when Sheriff Drew had said that he was going to check out the Wharfburn Estate and had never returned, leaving those back at the station to clean up the mess. Evidently, Paul was reluctant to leave them in the same predicament.

The sheriff nodded slowly, more to himself than to Coggins.

"Find out what's going on here, Coggins. Then meet me back at the station."

Now it was Coggins's turn to nod, and he did so enthusiastically, trying to prove to the sheriff that he was making the right decision. It was obvious that his longtime friend was still suspicious of him, and that was okay — the man had every right to be worried; Coggins's still trembling hands were proof enough of that.

"Hey," Coggins replied, slipping his finger off of the trigger and flipping the gun flat, pointing it at the culvert ceiling, "we're the good boys, remember? I'll be back... after all, you never know when I'll need that baseball swing again."

Coggins tried to smile, tried to convince the sheriff of some truth behind his words, but his lips failed to obey.

The truth was, he didn't know if he would be back.

14.

SHERIFF PAUL WHITE HAMMERED the cruiser into park and jumped out of the car, drawing his gun at the same time. He yanked open the glass door to the police station and stepped inside, his eyes immediately searching the space for danger.

No one—the reception area was completely empty. He spotted a cup of coffee—still hot, judging by the steam that exited the porcelain mug—on Mrs. Drew's desk, but she was not sitting in the chair behind it. There was a pile of papers splashed on the corner of her desk, and several more sheets on the ground.

"Hey! Williams! Mrs. Drew!"

He took two hesitant steps forward, trying to piece together an idea of what had happened here—trying to comprehend what this Mr. Wandry might have done.

There was a backpack on the row of chairs off to the left, one that he had never seen before. Other than that, the place looked pretty much the same as it had when he had left about an hour ago with Deputy Coggins.

"Deputy Williams," he shouted, raising his considerable voice so that the baritone speech bounced off the walls of the small station.

"Back here, Sheriff!" Deputy Williams's voice drifted up to him from down the long hallway, and the sheriff felt his heart rate slow. "Back here, boss," the man repeated.

"Coming," he replied.

Although he didn't holster his gun, he did lower it to his side as he hopped over the swinging half door that separated the reception area and the back of the station where his and the other deputies' desks were, as well as Askergan County's only cell.

The sheriff hurried down the short hallway flanked by filing cabinets, passing the closed door of the interrogation room where he had spoken to Kent Griddle and his father, before coming upon Mrs. Drew, Deputy Williams, and two other people he had never seen before in his life. The first was a pretty young woman who looked to be in her early twenties, with short brown hair cropped and tucked behind small ears, and a round face with large green eyes and a small, upturned nose. His eyes quickly flicked to the cell, and he was accosted by a much less pleasant sight: an extremely thin man sporting only a stained white undershirt and a pair of black sweat shorts. His jet black hair was parted aggressively on one side, in stark contrast to his long, scraggly white beard. The man was holding a pockmarked hand to his nose, blood leaking slowly from between his thin fingers. Even from where he stood, at least a dozen feet from the man, the sheriff could see the track marks on the inside of the man's elbows.

He took two steps forward, and Deputy Williams, who, like the young girl and Mrs. Drew, had been staring at the man in the cell, turned slowly to face the sheriff.

The man had a strange smirk on his face. He ran a hand through his slick black hair and then scratched behind one of his ears that stood out on the side of his head.

While the sheriff did see some similarities between his two deputies, as Coggins had been keen to point out, the men were hardly twins. Williams had large white teeth jammed into a wide mouth, which were pretty much the antithesis of the over-crowded chicklets that Coggins had. And where Coggins had a red beard, Williams was always clean shaven, showing off the dimples—two in the left, one in the right—in his round cheeks.

"What happened here?" the sheriff asked, his eyes darting from Williams to the man in the cell behind him.

"Mr. Wandry—" Deputy Williams began.

The man in the cell suddenly took a step forward and pulled his hand away from his face, using both bloodied hands to grab the bars.

"It's Walter Wandry, you fucking cunt," he sneered, revealing a set of brown and yellow teeth.

"Hey!" the sheriff shouted, stepping forward. He holstered his gun and raised a thick finger and pointed it at the man. "You watch your mouth."

Walter smiled at the sheriff, then turned his head to one side and spat a glob of blood onto the floor of his cell.

The sheriff ignored this and turned back to the deputy.

"*Mr.* Wandry." Deputy Williams stressed the word, and the man in the cell growled. The deputy ignored him and continued, "Mr. Wandry here is Tyler's father."

The sheriff raised an eyebrow and once again looked at the man in the cell. He remembered the handsome Gregory Griddle who wore reflective sunglasses and drove an obnoxiously loud Chevelle and his son with the short-cropped red hair and freckled face. Kent Griddle was hanging out with *this* man's son?

His face scrunched. It didn't make sense.

"Tyler is the boy who—"

The sheriff silenced his deputy with a wave of his hand.

"I know who Tyler is. What happened to his nose?"

The deputy quickly glanced over at the young girl, whose gaze was still locked on the man in the cell.

"He fell," the deputy said, averting his eyes.

"The fuck I fell!" Walter Wandry shouted, once again yanking at the bars. "*This* fucking cunt" — he pointed a bloody finger at the young girl — "elbowed me."

The sheriff took another two steps forward until he was within a foot of the cell.

"I warned you already," he said in a low voice, "use that language again, and I will make sure you end up with more than a bloody nose."

The man in the cell opened his mouth to say something, but catching the seriousness in the sheriff's face, decided better of it. Instead, he turned his head to the side and spat more blood onto the floor.

When he raised his eyes to look at the sheriff again, Paul kept their eyes locked. The man's pupils were massively dilated despite the brightness of the room. He was high as shit.

"Who's the girl?" he asked, keeping his eyes locked on Walter's.

"Came in to see Coggins, said that she has a message written by her uncle saying that she should only speak to him," the deputy replied, his voice even.

The mention of Coggins, just a day after he had gone to fetch him out of the abyss, was such a strange coincidence that his resolve of staring daggers at Walter was broken. He turned to face her and she stared back at him, her pretty green eyes narrowing. This girl, this girl who looked like she weighed less than one hundred pounds, had broken the nose of the junkie in the cell? But when she didn't even falter at his stare, offered nothing—no remorse, no guilt, *nothing*—he knew that she was probably capable of a whole lot more.

"What's your name, kiddo?" the sheriff asked.

"Corina," she said curtly. "Corina Lawrence."

Lawrence.

The word exploded in the sheriff's skull like an atom bomb. Deputy Coggins, the Wharfburn Estate, and now a *Lawrence*. He shook his head and his eyes widened.

There was no way that this was a coincidence.

What the fuck is going on in Askergan County?

His reaction must have been severe, as for the briefest moment, Corina's features softened and he saw a girl behind that mask of anger and dissidence, a young girl who was scared and alone. A flicker of a moment later and this mirage was gone, the hardness returning to her features.

"Did you know my father?" she asked, her eyes narrowing even further.

The sheriff opened his mouth to answer, but the man in the cell behind him interrupted.

"Where's my boy, Sheriff?"

Paul kept his eyes trained on Corina and raised his finger to the man in the cell indicating for him to wait his turn.

Walter snarled.

"Don't raise your finger at me," he continued, the pitch of his voice escalating with every word. "Where the fuck is my boy? I need to find his body!"

His body?

The sheriff turned to face Walter, and saw that the man was grinning, blood dripping from his nose into his mouth and over his teeth, and finally making a bright red streak on his pale chin.

"You heard me: I need to find the body—how else can I get the insurance money?"

The sheriff's eyes narrowed and he bit his lip, fighting back a barrage of insults that were tap dancing on the tip of his tongue.

"Wait your turn," he ordered gruffly, before turning back to Corina.

"I never knew your father, but—"

"Don't you fucking turn your back on me, you black pig!"

Sheriff White spun back around and his hand extended into the cell so quickly that the man clutching the bars had no chance to recoil. He grabbed Walter by the throat; the man was so thin that his long fingers wrapped almost all the way around his neck.

The man coughed once, speckling the sheriff's shirt with a spray of blood. Then the smile returned to his narrow, pale face.

He was enjoying this.

Well, enjoy this, *you fucking junkie.*

Sheriff Paul White's fingers tightened around the man's throat, and he enjoyed the way the creep's smile slowly began to fade. When Walter's breath started to come out of his clenched teeth in bloody bursts, someone shouted from behind him.

"Sheriff!"

Deputy Williams's voice snapped him out of the moment, and the sheriff immediately let go of the man's neck. Walter Wandry stumbled backward into the cell, immediately bringing his hands to his throat and massaging the redness there.

He coughed again and spat more blood on the floor.

When he raised his eyes again, the sheriff saw that choking the junkie had failed to permanently wipe the shit-eating grin off his face.

"You're going to pay for this, Sheriff, you're—"

"Shut up! You earned yourself a night in here, and if you don't shut your mouth, you'll be in there for a week."

The man's eyes darkened and he went quiet, his smirk finally fading.

When he turned around again, the sheriff couldn't bring himself to look at Mrs. Drew, who during this entire altercation hadn't moved an inch. He felt a flushness in his cheeks—embarrassment at the way he had just acted.

What the fuck is wrong with me?

The sheriff cleared his throat in an attempt to regain a modicum of professionalism.

"No, I didn't know your father," the sheriff repeated, again looking at Corina. "But I know about your family."

I know about what happened at the Wharfburn Estate, he felt like saying, but held his tongue. *I know about how your uncle died, and how your dad froze on the ice trying to save your sister.*

The sheriff looked down at the speckled blood on his shirt and almost wiped it away with his bare hands, before thinking better of it; no telling what the piece of shit in the cell was infected with.

No, what was happening in Askergan County was definitely not a coincidence.

What are you doing here, Corina? And what do you want with Deputy Coggins?

15.

COGGINS HAD MADE THIS walk once before, but then it had taken more than twice as long. As it was, the walk from the Wharfburn Estate to the Lawrence family home only took about a half hour, but it was an uncomfortable half hour with the heat continuing to beat down on him relentlessly. The insides of his legs chafed, and he found himself almost constantly picking the fabric of his police pants away from his skin.

When he had woken up this morning, he had had zero intention of going to the Lawrence home, and even now after he had made the dubious decision, he doubted that he would find anything there; after the family had been decimated, it seemed unlikely—impossible, even—that they would have kept the home. But he'd *never* intended to return to the Wharfburn Estate, either, and yet only an hour after waking, he had found himself in the same spot where he had burned the corpse of the thing that Sheriff Dana Drew had become. And for some unknown, *fucked-up* reason, he had put up little resistance when he had been ushered there by his friend that he had alienated from years ago.

Come.

Coggins shuddered.

Askergan County was like a drug, one that he could only stay away from for so long; it induced in him a longing, a need to return, a feeling that was oddly and frighteningly like the magnetic pull he had felt and succumbed to during the blizzard.

No, it seemed unlikely that anyone would be at the Lawrence—or *ex*-Lawrence—home, but then again, he wasn't totally surprised when he turned the corner of the small, narrow road and saw that there was a light on in one of the large windows that marked the front of the house.

It seemed that someone else had felt the pull of Askergan — either that, or they had never left.

He wasn't sure which was worse.

Coggins took a deep breath and tried to wipe some of the sweat from his palms. He couldn't quite place the compulsion to come here, and now that he had arrived, he had no idea what he was going to say or do.

The deputy knocked once and waited.

Maybe it's not even the Lawrences' home anymore—maybe they sold it.

Something deep down inside Coggins hoped that an old man, perhaps with an equally aged schnauzer, would answer the door.

"Sorry, wrong address—my apologies for startling you, sir," he would say, and then promptly leave. Go somewhere else. Anywhere *else*.

But when the shuffling sound eventually made it to the door and it opened a sliver, Coggins's heart sank.

This was the Lawrence home, and it always would be.

"Jared," the deputy said, his voice suddenly hoarse.

The man with the narrow face and dark eyes stared at him without speaking, and for a brief moment, Coggins thought that perhaps the man didn't remember him.

"I'm—" Coggins began, but the man cut him off.

"I know who you are," Jared Lawrence announced, and his voice, like the deputy's, was dry and raspy.

When the man failed to add anything else, Coggins shrugged as if to say, *I'm here, now what?*

Jared bit the inside of his lip, as if contemplating something. Finally, he pulled the door wide and spoke.

"Come in," he managed. "I've been expecting you."

*   *   *

The two men sat in chairs opposite each other across a dining room table. No words were shared for a long time; even when Jared had gone to get some scotch, he had simply poured Coggins a glass without asking—he didn't need to ask. It was in his face, after all, as his six years of insobriety clung to his features like an alcoholic necklace.

And Coggins was grateful; he had needed a drink since… well, since the moment Sheriff Paul White had shown up at the decrepit biker bar and had whisked him away with all of the pomp and circumstance of Prince Charming finally discovering Cinderella.

Coggins took a sip of the copper-colored liquid, enjoying the way it warmed his lips despite the high temperature both inside and outside of the Lawrence home. It felt good. And, perhaps more importantly on this day of strangeness, it felt *familiar*.

Coggins cleared his throat and looked up from his glass.

"You live here alone?" he asked simply, shattering the ice.

Jared nodded, but when he spoke, he averted his eyes, allowing his gaze to drift to the windows at the front of the house. The top window was still boarded up, Coggins noted, only now it was covered in plywood instead of by a piece of soggy cardboard.

"Couldn't give it up," Jared said simply. Then he turned back to Coggins. "Too many memories."

Coggins didn't know how to react to that, as his mind returned to when he and Jared had dragged Alice's limp body through the snow to his house, and how they had found Corina, Marley, and eventually the Lawrence matriarch in various states of consciousness and sanity. Memories, sure, but horrible ones. Ones that inspired nightmares.

"Couldn't leave," Jared repeated, taking a large sip of his scotch. It sounded as if he were trying to convince himself.

When Jared offered nothing else, Coggins let his mind drift, content in letting Jared start up the conversation again if he was interested.

Jared had taken the opposite approach to Coggins following the blizzard: Coggins had fled, burying his thoughts and feelings and memories in drink, while the thin man dressed in the flannel shirt and faded jeans across from him had decided to wallow in those memories, to submerge himself in the horrors. In a way, this was only fitting; after all, Coggins had made most of the decisions at the Wharfburn Estate all those years ago, and it only made sense that he would be the one to actively make a decision to leave. Jared, on the other hand, seemed content — no, *content* was not the right word, maybe *complacent* — to just maintain the status quo.

"I knew you were coming," Jared said suddenly, drawing Coggins out of his own head.

The deputy's eyebrows rose up on his sweat-covered forehead.

Jared nodded briskly.

"I knew you would come back—and I knew you would come back either today or tomorrow or the next day."

Coggins stared blankly at the man with the cleft in his chin and the sad eyes that seemed so very different now than when they had met.

"I knew," he continued, "I knew because I heard it. I knew because we didn't kill it, Brad. Which I guess is probably one of the reasons why I stayed here over the years. Trying to keep watch, to keep guard in case it ever awoke again. Although"—his voice hitched—"although I am not qualified for this job. I... I don't know what to do. Never did."

Coggins felt his throat begin to tighten as he recalled the bone white *cracker* in the plastic bag that Sheriff White had taken back to the station.

We didn't kill it, Brad.

He shuddered.

... in case it awoke.

Coggins shook his head and then opened his mouth to contradict the man, to remind him of how his decision to sacrifice his own brother—Oxford Lawrence—was likely the only reason that both of them were alive today. He *was* the right man, whether he believed it or not.

But Jared didn't let him speak.

"Two nights ago, I awoke in the middle of the night."

Jared took another drink.

"I awoke when I heard my name—my name was being whispered in my head—moaned, even—and I knew that it was back."

The man's eyes reddened, but he fought the tears by finishing his glass of scotch in one large gulp. Jared turned to the small cabinet behind his chair and grabbed the entire bottle and put it on the table between them.

Coggins quickly finished his own drink, and then reached out and grabbed the bottle from Jared's trembling hand. He filled both of their glasses with hefty, three-finger pours.

"I did nothing, of course," Jared said quietly. "But I knew that you would come here and tell me what to do next."

Coggins nodded, although he wasn't really sure why.

All of the preceding events had been like a blur, like a Vaseline-coated dream, and this haze wasn't conducive to thinking of what they would do if it—*Oot'-keban*—was actually back. It was just a bunch of kids, drinking and smoking and maybe even indulging in some hallucinogens, that were scared of getting caught, after all.

But it was also the house and the crab-thing—the *cracker*, as the Griddle boy had called it—that Paul had found in the basement, and the one that he had hit with the homerun swing with the butt of his gun. No way was this all a coincidence.

The fucking crab-things—what the fuck were they?

Jared took another big sip and then stared up at the deputy.

"Tell me—tell me what happened."

16.

"TELL ME WHAT HAPPENED," Corina demanded, her eyes narrowing.

The sheriff's face contorted as if he were wrestling with more internal demons—as he had obviously been when he had grabbed Walter Wandry by the throat.

Don't push too hard, Corina scolded herself.

But *hard* was the only way she knew how to push it.

"I need to know."

The massive man with the gold 'Sheriff' star on his left breast was tucked almost comically behind his small and inauspicious desk. After a brief pause, he looked up at her and sighed.

"What are you doing here, Corina?"

Corina's response was immediate.

"I'm here because of what I saw on the news—I told you that already. I'm here to find out what happened at the Wharfburn Estate—to my *family*. I deserve to know."

She stood with one hand on her hip, her right hip, the hip of her *good* leg, her backpack loosely slung over her shoulder.

The sheriff's face seemed to soften, and he turned to Mrs. Drew, who sat with Deputy Williams at the other desk, looking over some paperwork, likely deciding how they could get rid of Walter—trying to be *political* about it. After all, from what

Corina could gather, Walter's son was the one that had gone missing — the one that had gone to play in the Wharfburn Estate and had not returned.

"Mrs. Drew and Andy, you think you can give us a moment?"

Deputy Williams's eyes flicked up from the papers and he looked at the sheriff suspiciously.

"Boss?"

Mrs. Drew turned next, and she did an even worse job of hiding her emotions. Her grey eyebrows were knitted across her brow, her thin lips pushed together tightly.

Clearly, neither was interested in going back into the hallway where Walter was being held.

Paul gave a subtle chin nod.

"Just one minute. Please."

His deputy made a face as if to say *'what gives?'*, but he slowly rose to his feet. When the man went to grab Mrs. Drew by the elbow and gently guide her out of the room, the woman pulled her arm away. Keeping her eyes trained on the sheriff, she said, "I'm not senile. I can understand a simple *command*."

The sheriff shook his head.

Only after the door was closed and the duo's footsteps receded to the front of the station did the sheriff turn back to Corina.

"Listen, I'm going to be honest with you," he began, interlacing his fingers and placing them on the desk in front of him. "I never knew your dad or his brothers, but I know something *about* them. And — and it's horrible what happened to them, it really is."

The big man chewed the inside of his lip, and Corina knew that he was holding back, that there was something that he wanted to add but didn't. She frowned, trying to figure out what was going on inside his head. As she observed, something flashed over his features, and for a split second, Corina thought that he was scared. And something that scared a man as big and powerful as Sheriff White was something that she probably wanted to stay the hell away from.

But still…she *needed* to know.

"I didn't come here for your sympathy," Corina said coldly. "I came here for information, I came here for Deputy Bradley Coggins."

The sheriff frowned.

"I told you before—he's not here. He's not hiding, he just went to take care of something."

Corina contemplated this. The burly sheriff was telling the truth about this, she was certain. Still, she had come for information, and she was damned if she would leave without it.

"Like I told Mrs. Drew, I'll wait for him to return."

Again the sheriff sighed.

"You can't wait here, Corina. In fact, I don't think you should be here at all. It's—it's—"

"—not safe?" Corina finished for him.

The sheriff shook his head.

"It's not right for you here."

Right *for me?*

Corina shook her head.

"I'll wait."

The sheriff slowly rose to his feet.

He was a massive man, his thick barrel chest barely contained within his police shirt, and his biceps popped out of the tight sleeves like corn from a husk. Corina didn't know if the man had intentionally stood at that moment to intimidate her, but she hoped not—for his sake. She had seen men larger than him fall. And she had felled her fair share.

"You can't wait here," he repeated. "Please, Corina."

Corina, hand still on her hip, stood fast.

"Tell me about the boy, I need to know what happened at the Wharfburn Estate."

I need to know about the children—about the palil.

Her eyes suddenly twitched, and for a split second her grim expression faltered.

It was the word that had affected her: *palil.*

She had heard someone say it before, but she wasn't sure who that person had been. But she knew that it was related to the house, to what had happened to her father.

Why didn't you take me, Dad? Why didn't you take me and Mom with you?

It wasn't fair, of course, as it would have been impossible for Cody, even with Mom's help, to take her and Henri from the house.

But it wasn't fair that she was here, that her father was no longer with them—that wasn't fair either.

"Tell me what happened."

The sheriff looked for a brief moment like he was nearing a breaking point, and upon mention of the boy, his eyes flicked toward Deputy Williams's desk. Corina followed his gaze and spotted a manila envelope on the corner of the fiberboard desk.

The sheriff cleared his throat. It was clear that he was struggling with something, almost as if he wanted to tell her more but just couldn't bring himself to do it.

"I can't tell you," he said finally, his voice for the first time since the discussion began acquiring an authoritative tone. "I cannot reveal the details of an ongoing investigation. I'm sorry, but those are the rules."

Corina shuffled one step to her left toward the desk with the envelope.

"You lost someone in the blizzard, too," she said.

She was taking a chance, of course, because she wasn't even sure that this sheriff hadn't been around when the blizzard had taken place—she hadn't met him before. There was just something in his eyes, a far-off look when he spoke of the snow, that made her think that maybe he had been.

When his face slackened, Corina suppressed the smile; she was right.

She took another step toward the desk.

"We all lost something that night, Corina. But that doesn't mean I can help you here. Listen, I wish I could tell you more, but the truth is, I really don't know anything else." Once again he held up his massive hands palms out. "Really."

Corina, now within arm's reach of the envelope, nodded.

"You sure?"

"Yes," the sheriff affirmed. "Now please, I will let Deputy Cogg—"

A scream from the other room interrupted the sheriff and his head twisted in that direction. It was perfect timing. Corina used this split second to flip her backpack to her hip and reach over to the desk and shovel the envelope into it in one smooth motion. At the same time, she noticed a set of car keys on the desk right beside the envelope, and scooped those in the bag as well.

The bag was on her shoulder again even before the sheriff had turned back to her.

"You better leave," he told her, his voice hushed. "You need to go."

Corina nodded and took a step forward and the sheriff did the same, always standing a protective three feet ahead of her as they quickly made their way out of the office.

Walter Wandry was on his back in the center of the cell, his wide eyes aimed upward.

When they approached, he turned his head on the cold cement floor and stared at Corina and the sheriff. His eyes were a deep red, the vessels in each so swollen that even his eyelids appeared puffy.

"Where's my boy, Sheriff? I need my boy."

The sheriff guided Corina toward the half door that led to the small waiting area.

"Get up," he instructed the junkie in a stern voice. "Get on your feet."

Walter didn't acknowledge the instruction.

"Where's my boy, Sheriff? I need to have his body."

Corina had taken two steps toward the front door when she froze.

Body?

Although she had heard the despicable human in the cell yell this before, it seemed to take on new meaning and it shocked her again.

"I need the body for insurance, you fucking pig!"

Even the sheriff seemed shocked at the man's *callousness* in talking about his son, and it was a moment before he reached to his hip and grabbed the ring of keys that hung there.

"Get up!" he shouted.

Walter ignored him and turned his face back to the ceiling.

"Where is my boy?"

17.

COGGINS FINISHED WHAT WAS left of the scotch in his glass and stared at the empty vessel.

He couldn't believe it, despite having lived most of it; the whole story. The sheriff—his friend, his mentor—and Jared's brother. It was just *so* fucked up. And now this about the crab-fuckers. What did the boy—*Kent*—call them? *Crackers?* Yeah, crackers. Fine, as good a name as any.

Crackers.

"That's it," he said with a sigh. "God, it feels fucked up talk-ing about this."

Jared finished his own scotch.

"Yeah," Jared admitted. "I haven't told a soul."

Coggins raised his eyes to look at the thin man across from him.

"You really think it's back?" he asked, not sure if the ques-tion was for him or for Jared.

Jared looked at his glass, and almost raised it to his lips again before realizing that he had just finished it.

"I think so." He hesitated. "I don't know. I don't even know if it was ever even here. Maybe." He looked away. "I, I saw—"

It was clear to Coggins that although he had bared his soul, this man was still holding something back. Something that had been—*was*—eating him up inside.

"I—"

Something suddenly smacked against the front window with such force that the glass bowed inward.

Coggins immediately jumped to his feet.

"What was that?"

Jared also rose, but he staggered and almost fell back into his chair. Clearly, the alcohol had gotten to him, even though he'd only had half as many glasses as Coggins.

"I don't know," he answered, grasping the back of the chair to remain steady.

Coggins quickly made his way to the window by the front of the house, his right hand hovering over the butt of his gun. Jared followed.

The deputy pressed his head against the glass and looked down, trying to see the grass below. The angle made it impossible, though. He moved his head more to one side, but the new angle didn't help.

"A bird?" Jared proposed with a shrug.

Coggins said nothing, content in just standing there with his face against the glass, trying to see if whatever had struck the glass had fallen to the ground.

"Could be a bird," Jared persevered, but Coggins hushed him.

They stood in silence for a few seconds.

"You hear that?" Coggins finally asked.

Jared shook his head.

"No—"

Coggins hushed him again, and pulled his head a few inches away from the glass.

The cracking sound, like somebody rhythmically cracking their knuckles, became louder.

"There," he whispered.

Jared made a face and shrugged, clearly indicating that he hadn't heard that sound. He took a step forward and leaned his thin face toward the glass.

A sudden loud snap erupted from below the window and Coggins immediately swept his arm out, pushing Jared behind him while at the same time drawing his gun.

A round, dinner plate-sized disc flew into view and landed flush on the window with a *thunk*.

Coggins took a step backward and dropped into a crouch. He used his arm to push Jared even farther behind him, and the man's hot, scotch-laced breath was now on his ear.

Coggins almost fired, but he was reminded of a time when he had shot a random dog, a poor boxer, and he held fast. There was no danger here; at least not yet, not when the glass was intact.

The cracker pressed the underside of its body flush against the glass, its six knobby appendages spreading out in a star pattern. Its underside was a milky white, and in the center was a puckering orifice filled with tiny, sharp teeth.

"What the fuck is that?" Jared whispered, his hands now on Coggins's shoulders.

Coggins didn't answer right away.

As he watched, the cracker's legs flexed at the thickened joints, the points on the end of each trying desperately to grasp the smooth surface. A viscous fluid, like a white jelly, started to form on the edges of the small mouth, which seemed to act as a glue, holding the body in place as the arms slowly curled backward—*double-jointed?*—away from the glass. They cracked as the six joints articulated, each movement accompanied by a distinct sound.

And that, my friend, is why Kent Griddle called them crackers.

Without warning, another one of those singular cracks sounded—this one much louder than the noise produced by the individual joints—and the legs all fired forward at once, their points aimed directly at the glass.

Jared screamed and Coggins used his forearm to shield his face and eyes.

The glass bowed but held.

Coggins pulled his arm away just as the thing's legs rebounded off the glass, and whatever the substance from its mouth was—it *had* to be its mouth—that had held it in place bubbled and the cracker slid down and out of sight. In its wake, it left a nasty white smear on the otherwise clean pane.

Coggins took a deep breath, trying to will his heart rate into slowing. When he went to stand, he felt all of Jared's weight pushing down his back, and found himself locked in a crouch.

"It's okay," he whispered over his shoulder.

When the man's grip remained steadfast, he repeated the words. This time, the man let go and Coggins stood. Then he reached back and pulled Jared to his feet with him.

"What the fuck was that?" the man nearly screeched, his eyes wide.

"One of the crackers," Coggins replied, turning his gaze back to the window. In addition to the milky streak from the thing's mouth, there were six deep indentations in the glass where the claws had struck. "Fucking crackers."

The deputy squinted and scanned the lawn, searching the area for more of the parasites. When he failed to find any, and the noise from the cracker had momentarily ceased, he risked turning back to Jared's frightened face.

"Do you have any guns?" he asked.

Jared's face twisted as he thought about it for a moment.

"I think I have a couple of old shotguns that my dad used to go hunting with."

Coggins nodded.

"But I don't have any permits," Jared added.

Coggins smirked.

"That's all right; don't ask, don't tell. And is there a culvert around here? Behind the house, maybe?"

Jared made a queer face.

"Yeah," he began hesitantly. "All the houses along this strip have them. They were used to get cows from this side of the road to the other side without crossing it, way back when. Why?"

Deputy Coggins nodded, his mind returning to earlier in the day when he and the sheriff had nearly been struck by a cracker in the culvert.

"Because I think I know where these little fuckers are hiding."

Jared's eyes widened once more.

"There are more of them?"

The expression that crossed Jared's features when Coggins nodded was difficult to interpret. It wasn't fear; not quite. If Jared was anything like Coggins, which was becoming more and more apparent the more time Coggins spent with him, then fear was something that had been bastardized by their collective experience in the blizzard. Shock, alarm, surprise, those were all intact, but fear? No, it wasn't fear—it was something else. Something close to fear, a cousin or a step-brother, maybe.

It was vengeance.

"Go get the guns," Coggins instructed, his hand instinctively squeezing the butt of his own handgun.

The man nodded briskly and turned, his previously wide eyes now narrowed to but slits.

"And Jared?" Coggins asked. The thin man with the dark eyes and cleft in his chin turned. "It's back."

Jared nodded.

"It's back, and this time we're gonna kill it for good."

18.

PETE DEVEREAUX PUT THE cigarette to his lips and inhaled deeply. The warm smoke tickled the tiny hairs in his throat before swirling in his lungs.

He sighed.

How long has it been? Three days? Four?

Days melded together without cigarettes, days of shit and hell, of screaming kids and a screaming wife. But now, tucked in an alcove behind the Wellwood Elementary School with his back pressed against the brown bricks and one foot hiked up behind him, he heard nothing. He felt nothing. Except, of course, the surge of nicotine in his lungs and then in his blood.

Pete sighed again, then turned the cigarette in his hand, staring into the hypnotizing red cherry as it ebbed and sparked the thin white paper.

When he could no longer hold his breath, he exhaled a thick cloud of blue smoke that engulfed his head.

He waved the smoke away from his face, and when it cleared he saw a tall woman with long blonde hair spilling in large curls meant to hide ears that were slightly too big, with a lopsided grin on her very red and very plump lips that stood out like a beacon.

"Shit."

He thrust the cigarette to the ground, pulling his foot away from the wall and stomping the smoke from which he had only taken one drag.

One drag.

Pete turned his head to one side and exhaled heavily, trying to force any residual smoke from his lungs.

When he turned back to face the woman, she was approaching fast on her tall black pumps, which, not accidentally, matched her skirt that was probably an inch too short for an elementary school teacher. As she made her way toward him, the woman shifted her shoulders slightly and the wind caught her sheer blouse, flipping it open to reveal the shoulder strap and the top of a nude-colored bra.

Pete Devereaux—or Mr. Dev, as his students called him—couldn't help the smile that formed on his lips. The woman caught this smirk and returned it in spades. A quick glance over her shoulder, and the woman's pace quickened until she was within a foot of him.

"Petie," she whispered, pressing a hand against his hip.

This aggressiveness, so much unlike her, startled Pete, and he instinctively pulled away—or at least he tried to, but she wouldn't let him go. Instead, the woman tightened her grip on his hip and pulled him in closer, driving his thigh between her legs. Even through her black skirt, he could feel her warmth.

"Janet," he said.

It was meant as an admonition, but, feeling that all too familiar warmth, it came out more like a moan. Janet took this as encouragement and bent toward his neck and nibbled on his ear.

The sweet scent of honeysuckle wafted up to him and he felt the front of his slacks tighten.

When Janet snaked her tongue behind his ear, and then traced a line partly down his jaw, he placed his hand on top of hers on his hip and pried it off him, gently pushing her away in the process.

"Janet," he repeated, "what's gotten into you?"

He only said the words because he thought them appropriate. Truth was, he *liked* this new, aggressive Janet.

The woman's plump lips turned into a pout.

"I want you," she whispered and leaned into him again, her tongue darting from between her lips.

Pete smiled.

"I want you too, babe," he started, playing along, "but we can't. Shit, what about the kids? They're supposed to be learning about agriculture. Plants."

The woman turned her head and peered over her shoulder. Pete followed her gaze.

About fifty yards behind them, a dozen children between the ages of five and eight were hunched around a small patch of vegetables in a garden cut out from the grass. It wasn't as if they were alone, left to fiddle with the carrots and lettuce completely unsupervised; no, they weren't *that* irresponsible. Mrs. Biggan was there as well, with her wide hips and frumpy sweater, standing with her hands crossed over her ample bosom. The woman had her back to them, but he knew what face she was making: she was scowling, as she was apt to do. No, there was Mrs. Biggan, but still…

"They *are* learning about planting," Janet whispered as she leaned in again. This time, her hand fell on his crotch, her thin fingers grabbing the tightness there. "And *you* need to learn about planting your seed."

With *seed* she squeezed, and Pete felt a tingling in his balls.

What the fuck has gotten into you, Janet? he thought, and then, *Keep it up and something else will get into you.*

"Mr. Dev?" a small voice asked, and Pete immediately went to push Janet away, but he missed; her hand had already fallen away from his crotch and she had seamlessly put two feet between them. He glanced at her quickly and her tongue darted just a fraction of an inch out from between her full red lips.

Pete shifted his hips, trying to hide the bulge in his pants, and turned to the boy.

"Yes, Dave," he asked, staring at the boy with the thick thatch of messy, dark hair on his head.

Dave looked up at him with equally dark eyes.

"Um, Mr. Dev? Robbie found something in the garden... looks like a crab, or something."

The boy looked away when he said this, as if he thought that he might get in trouble. Dave was one of the more timid of the boys, and he always had a hard time making friends.

Robbie's probably just teasing him.

Pete squatted so that he was at eye level with the boy.

"A crab? What do you mean a crab, Dave?"

Wellwood Elementary was not far from the lake—in fact, not much of Askergan County was far from the lake—but despite having been born in Askergan and having spent all of his twenty-eight years here, Pete had never seen a crab. Crayfish, snails, muscles, catfish, sure, but never a crab.

"I dunno," the shy boy replied, once again looking at the ground. He shrugged. "It looks like a crab. Robbie found it in the lettuce."

Pete glanced up at Janet and was surprised, and more than a little disappointed, that her once lewd expression had transformed into one of concern.

"Show me," she said, reaching for the boy's hand.

Dave nodded and took Janet's hand, and together they made their way back to the garden with Pete in tow.

When they were halfway to the cluster of students, they heard another boy shout.

"I found one too!"

Pete immediately picked up his pace. When another child, a girl this time, also shouted, he broke into a run.

He made it to the first boy, Robbie, before either Janet or Dave. Crouching as he had done before, he put his hand on the boy's shoulder.

Robbie turned to him, his eyes wide in surprise.

"Mr. Devereaux," he exclaimed, barely able get the words out without stuttering, his excitement was so palpable. "I found a crab!"

Pete's gaze followed the boy's outstretched hand, his eyes scanning the patch of lettuce in front of him.

At first he saw nothing, and he crept forward on his haunches a few feet.

"Where, Robbie?"

"There!"

The boy pointed again.

"I don't see—" But then he *did* see.

Tucked behind one of the lettuce heads was a round white shape that kind of looked like a crab shell.

What the fuck?

Pete crept forward some more, then used his right hand to sweep the head of lettuce to one side. He froze.

It looked like a crab—a milky white crab—but it wasn't. For one, it didn't have eyes or claws. Instead, the *thing* had six legs, six knobby appendages, and... and that was pretty much it.

"What the fuck is that?" he whispered, trying to scramble to his feet.

His foot caught in the loose soil, and he fell on his ass, knocking Robbie to the ground when his arm swept out from his side in a failed attempt of maintaining his balance.

Then he heard the six distinct cracks.

"Janet?" he shouted, his voice taking on a shrill quality that he was unfamiliar with.

Before the woman could answer, a seventh crack, this one much louder, much more *distinct*, resonated from the lettuce patch. A split second later, the thing was airborne.

It all happened so quickly that Pete Devereaux never even had a chance to bring a hand up in front of his face before the thing landed directly on his mouth, smothering him. The last thought that ran through his head before his skin was suctioned against the cracker was about his last cigarette.

It had been a good drag, he thought as his eyes rolled back in his head. *Maybe the best.*

PART II – SHEDDING

19.

SHERIFF PAUL WHITE SAT at his desk, his hand hovering over the black phone. It had been a long day, one that had started *fucked up* and had only gotten considerably worse ever since. He knew that he should head back out to the Wharfburn Estate, and intended to do so right after Coggins either returned his calls or made it back to the station himself. He just didn't trust his people alone with the enigmatic Walter Wandry, even if he was locked up.

His next move should have been to pick up the phone and call the neighboring counties to see if they had any missing children as well, but he was hesitant. It wasn't only that he thought it would be a fruitless endeavor, but this whole *thing* had started six years ago with that phone—with the black phone that had once been Sheriff Dana Drew's, but was now his—ringing with a call from the inexorable Mrs. Wharfburn.

Sheriff White's eyes drifted from the black phone to the two desks across from him. One was Deputy Williams's, which was clearly identifiable by the way the papers scattered across the surface—a messy man was he—but it was the other one, the one that was completely empty, devoid of even a notepad or a pen, that held his attention.

Deputy Bradley Coggins's desk.

The words sounded strange after all this time.

Deputy Coggins.

It wasn't the first time that he considered that calling his old friend and partner had been a mistake. He recalled the way the man had started to sweat as soon as they had approached the Wharfburn Estate, and again how he had nearly collapsed in a fit when Paul had thrown the cracker out of the basement, although that might have been warranted.

Yeah, he thought, still staring at the empty desk. *Maybe it* was *a mistake. And where the hell is he?*

'*I need to take care of something,*' the man had said, but what?

Coggins had been gone for over six years, with only a smattering of sightings in and about town, usually around the holidays. Other than that, nada. No phone call, no letter, nothing.

But now he suddenly had something to take *care of*? Now, of all times?

Paul wondered why he had let the man go, why he hadn't pressed a little harder. He supposed that he had been scared of Brad's shaky demeanor, thinking that if he did press, the man might very well crack.

Which brought him full circle, wondering why the *fuck* he had gone and rescued him from Sabra's biker bar just outside of town.

The sheriff instinctively rubbed his right fist where the knuckles were still raw from decking one of the bikers. Then he remembered grabbing Walter Wandry's throat with that same hand when he had called him a pig.

You're losing it, Paul.

There was another shout from just outside the room, one that Paul recognized, as it had been occurring intermittently for at least the last hour.

He heard Deputy Williams's voice next, demanding that the man be quiet, that he shut up and eat his dinner without disturbing them.

And there was that: Walter Wandry.

The sheriff had never met the man before, but a cursory search of his person had produced a wallet with a license indicating that he was from neighboring Pekinish County. Walter was clearly a junkie, a meth head, a heroin addict, but that wasn't the most off-putting part about the rail-thin man with the grey beard, and it had nothing to do with his similarity to the bikers at the bar. No, it was the callousness with which he spoke of his son—of Tyler Wandry—who was still missing. The man didn't care about what happened to the boy, but rather appeared to *want* the boy to be dead, some ridiculousness of needing a body to claim some sort of insurance money.

The sheriff pushed a thumb and forefinger into his eyes.

Damnit. I'm not ready for this.

It had been six years since he had taken over as sheriff, and although by all indications—and Mrs. Drew's biased opinion— he was doing an *adequate* job, until today he hadn't had to deal with anything out of the ordinary—with anything like *this*.

I'm not ready.

And he probably wasn't. For one, he knew he should be back out at the Wharfburn Estate continuing to follow up on finding anything there that might indicate where the boy might have gone. At present, it was just a missing persons case, despite the story that Kent Griddle had told them and the strange eggs and skins that he had found in the Wharfburn basement.

His eyes drifted back to the phone.

He felt like calling Nancy up to vent, maybe ease some of the anxiety that welled within. But he couldn't do that. They had been together informally for the better part of a year, but there was—and likely always would be—a divide between them, a line that could not be crossed. Nancy had made it abundantly clear that while she liked him, her reporting came first.

Enough.

He pulled his fingers from his eyes and looked at the black phone on his desk.

It's time to make some calls.

*   *   *

"Detective Kipling Marshall, Pekinish PD," a tired voice on the other end of the line said.

Sheriff White cleared his throat.

"Mr. Marshall, this is Sheriff White over in Askergan County."

"Call me Kip, please," the man said, his voice coming alive.

"And you can call me Paul," the sheriff responded in kind before quickly continuing, "We are having a bit of a problem up in Askergan and I was wondering if you could help me out with a few things."

There was a short pause.

"Sure," the man answered, his voice changing once again. "Anything to help out. What's up?"

"Well, two days ago a boy…" Paul let the sentence trail off. There was something about the way the man had said *'anything*

to help out' that didn't quite jive with him. His voice had seamlessly transitioned to an *'I'll scratch your back if you scratch mine'*
tone—and that bothered the sheriff.

He decided to play this a little closer to the chest than he had
initially planned.

"Have any boys gone missing from Pekinish lately?"

There was a long pause.

"Boys?" the man answered at long last.

The sheriff nodded.

"Yep, boys."

Kip's answer was immediate.

"No boys. But as you probably know, we had a bunch of
young girls—seven, sometimes eight years old—go missing a
number of years back. Turned the whole county upside down,
but even when the feds came in they left empty-handed. Other
than that, no. And no boys. And not recently."

The sheriff made a face. Something about this man, this *Kip*,
continued to seem off to him. He bit his lip before continuing.

"Thanks, Detective Marshall. Just one more thing, do you
know a Walter Wandry?"

Again, the man answered without hesitation.

"Of course, why do you ask?"

"Well, his son's gone missing and he's causing a real stink
here. Keeping him in the cell until we find out what to do with
him."

"Walter's a piece of work; he's in or out of here once or twice
a week. Fucking junkie—piece of shit womanizer, too. A real
piece of work."

There was a pause before the man continued.

"We can always come pick him up, if you want. I assume he
has at least a few outstanding warrants."

The sheriff shook his head. Even though Pekinish had at least five times the population of Askergan County, and had an actual jail instead of the single holding cell that he commanded over, his intuition—the skill he had somehow absorbed once Sheriff Dana Drew had passed—was indicating strongly that inviting this man to Askergan, especially with the fucked-up things that were going on, was not a good idea.

"We'll bring him to you," he said at last, "but we have to find his son first."

20.

IT WAS NEVER CORINA'S intention to steal the police car, but in the end it made sense; after all, she had no vehicle of her own, and a quick look at Kent Griddle's file showed that the boy didn't even live in Askergan—he lived in a neighboring county at least an hour away.

Still, jumping into that police car and backing out of the parking lot with the lights off felt surreal.

Corina had gone too far this time, she knew it, but she had only done what needed to be done. She had to find out what the fuck was going on in Askergan, and if Deputy Bradley Coggins wasn't around to tell her, then she would find out for herself.

Corina's bright green eyes flicked up in the rearview mirror, half expecting to see the lights of another police car—this one driven by an actual officer of the law—pulling up behind her and signaling for her to pull over. But all she saw was dirt and road.

The thrill of having stolen the car wore off when she made it onto Highway 2 and started heading west, her sights aimed on Pekinish County. As she drove, she flipped the manila file on the passenger seat and glanced over at it periodically.

Kent Griddle: 16 years old.

Her eyes darted to the picture. Kent was a cute boy with short red hair, which was obvious even though the picture paper-clipped to the folder was black and white, with a smattering of freckles on his small nose.

That was all she could glean from the folder—the rest of the time she just kept her eyes on the road.

Corina Lawrence pushed the gas pedal a little harder and the car lurched forward.

If I can't find Deputy Coggins, then maybe you can help me, Kent.

*   *   *

The door opened on the second knock, and although the boy that stared back at her looked a little thinner and worse for wear than the face in the black-and-white photo, Corina had no doubt that Kent Griddle stood before her.

"Kent?"

The boy nodded and Corina closed the folder in her hands. The drive, which she had made in under an hour by speeding most of the way, had given her ample time to come up with a plan for how she would get Kent into the car with her.

She pulled the folder close to her chest and held out her right hand authoritatively. When Kent just looked at it, she smiled.

"Corina Lawrence," she said curtly, "from ACPD. Sheriff White has sent me to pick you up. We have a few more questions to ask about the disappearance of your friend."

A concerned look crossed Kent's face.

"Well my dad's not here right now," he said hesitantly. The boy raised his light-colored eyes and peeked behind her, spying the cop car. Then he looked at what Corina was wearing—faded jeans, a green sweatshirt—and she could see the confusion on his face.

Corina cursed herself for not changing into something a little more professional; even though her bag was nearly empty, she should have at least checked the trunk for a police jacket.

She smiled more broadly, trying to disguise her anxiety.

"That's all right," she continued, "you're not in trouble. The sheriff just had some things he wanted clarified."

The boy's brow furrowed, and Corina moved on to stage two of her apparently ill-thought-out plan.

"They think that they know where he is, Kent."

The boy's eyebrows shot up.

"Tyler? They found Tyler? Is he...?"

Corina purposefully clutched the folder more tightly and held up her other hand.

"I've said too much," she said, blushing. "It's an active investigation, so I can't say anything else. The sheriff, on the other hand..."

Hope crossed the boy's face.

"It's okay that your dad isn't here," she continued, feeling that Kent was nearing his breaking point. "You are sixteen, after all, so you can talk to us alone if you want. The decision is up to you."

Kent's face contorted.

"I—I dunno."

Corina waited for more, but when nothing came, she kicked her plan up into high gear. She tilted her head slightly to one side and smirked.

"I'm not going to lie to you, Kent. I was at the station when you were there, and the sheriff asked me to keep you in the waiting room for a few more minutes while he wrapped up some paperwork."

This was a riskiest part of her plan, as she had no idea how things had gone down with the sheriff. But she tucked her short hair behind her ear and went with it.

"But I was on my damn phone and I didn't get to you in time. Now he's pissed at me."

Kent shook his head.

"But my dad…"

Corina smiled coquettishly and gestured to the police cruiser behind her.

"Truth? I'm not a cop."

Corina shrugged and averted her gaze.

"I'm not even a clerk yet—just an intern. But I really, really want to keep my job. I borrowed Deputy Williams's—do you remember him?"

Kent nodded slowly.

"Well he let me borrow his car so that I could come get you."

She sighed dramatically, laying it on thick.

"I would be very, *very* appreciative if you could come along with me back to the station. I promise I'll have you back here before dinner time."

Corina resisted the urge to bat her eyelashes. She felt sick to her stomach acting this way, but her mastery of Muai Thay and jiu jitsu would not help her here, she knew.

"Well, Kent, what do you say? Are you gonna help a pretty girl keep her job?"

21.

DEPUTY COGGINS AND JARED Lawrence didn't even make it to the culvert; the second they stepped out of the back of the Lawrence house and made it into the woods behind the house, they knew something was wrong. Very wrong.

"What's that noise?" Jared asked in a hushed voice from a few feet behind Coggins.

Jared had a rifle in one hand, with another strapped over his shoulder. But despite the artillery, Coggins was not optimistic of the man's shooting skills, judging by the way he walked crouched over like an early settler hunting Injuns.

"Cracking," Coggins answered simply, holding his own gun—the nine millimeter police issue—out in front of him. "Sounds like the fucking crackers."

Coggins took two more steps onto the dry vegetation at the outskirts of the small wooded area before he saw the first cracker. It was smaller than the one that had struck the window about a half hour ago; still milky white, with the same six knobby legs, but less than half the size. And it was moving toward them at an alarming speed, easily navigating the organic detritus and broken branches blanketing the forest ground.

The deputy held his hand up in a fist, the universal sign for stopping, and Jared obliged. Next, Coggins carefully lowered the gun to eye level. He had no idea if the cracker had seen or somehow *sensed* him and Jared, but based on what he had seen in the Lawrence home and the Kent boy's story, he was taking no chances.

The first shot missed, and Coggins cursed himself for letting his skills fall to the wayside during his six plus years of binge drinking.

Couldn't you have at least gone to a range once in a while?

The second bullet was on target and tore through the hard carapace of the cracker's shell, sending fragments of it flying in all directions. When the smoke cleared, there was nothing left of the creature except for a spray of what looked like runny oatmeal splattered on the mossy grass and fallen leaves.

Jared exhaled loudly, and Coggins could feel the man's subsequent rapid breathing on the back of his neck even at a distance of three feet. He was reminded of being deep in the closet of Mrs. Wharfburn's house, peering wide-eyed at a slit through the door at unspeakable horrors below. He thought of poor Jared's brother, of Oxford, and how even now, even years later, he hadn't worked out if the man's decision to overdose on the drugs meant for the *thing*—for *Oot'-keban*—had been a completely selfless or an utterly selfish act.

The real question is, Coggins thought as he continued to stare at the cracker's mucousy entrails, *what does it matter now?*

"Look," Jared whispered suddenly, extending his finger over Coggins's shoulder.

Evidently the gunshots and the smearing of one of their own had not gone unnoticed. Three more crackers came toward them from deeper in the forest, their white bodies standing out against the dark green-and-brown backdrop. Unlike the first, these three came toward them with more purpose, and Coggins was positive that they were coming for *them*.

Coggins's mind instantly turned to the half dozen eggs that he and Sheriff White had found smashed in the basement.

Where are all of these coming from? Is this it?

As the creatures approached, he raised his gun again and indicated for Jared to pull up beside him and do the same. Then he aimed and barked two shots at the lead cracker.

The first bullet was a direct hit and the thing exploded in a spray of white goo like its predecessor. Jared fired his rifle next, but the shot went horribly wide, taking a chunk out of the tree about twenty feet behind the crackers. Coggins instantly regretted his decision to let Jared use the shotgun—it didn't make sense. Jared should've been using the handgun, and he should've been sporting the rifle.

"Reload," Coggins instructed.

The crackers were coming faster now, weaving across each other's paths, only a couple dozen feet from the two men.

Coggins fired two more shots, but both missed.

"Reload," he said again out of the corner of his mouth.

"I am," Jared spat back, his voice coming out from between pursed lips.

Coggins breathed deep and held his breath.

Then he fired one shot and the back two legs of the cracker closest to them—only about a dozen feet now—exploded, and the thing careened forward. It continued to crawl on its four remaining legs for a moment, leaving a train of the sticky, milky white substance on the dirt behind it, but after another two cracking lurches, it toppled onto its shell and remained motionless.

Coggins immediately turned to the other cracker, but it weaved behind a tree and he lost sight of it.

"Where'd it go?" he shouted. "Jared, where the fuck did it go?"

The man had finally managed to reload the rifle and slowly brought it up to his shoulder again.

"I don't know," the man whispered back.

Coggins remained in the crouched position as his eyes scanned the area where he had last seen it.

But he saw nothing—there was no sign of the white shell.

"Coggins?" Jared whispered, his voice trembling.

Before Coggins could reply, a loud crack that reverberated off the trees exploded from their left.

Coggins whipped the gun around, but Jared was blocking his line of sight and he didn't see the cracker flying through the air. Jared turned a split second later, but the jerky movement was so uncoordinated that the man fell to the ground, somehow pinching off a shot in the process.

A hot white fluid sprayed both Jared and Coggins, but Jared got the worst of it. The stinking liquid splashed his face and he immediately dropped the rifle and tried to clear his eyes and nose.

Coggins leaned over Jared and grabbed the bottom of his t-shirt and wiped most of it away.

"Fuck," Jared cursed, spitting onto the grass beside them. "Fuck!"

He tried desperately to get the tacky substance off his hands, rubbing his palms aggressively on the thighs of his jeans.

Coggins also set about cleaning his own face when he heard the sound.

It was a cracking noise, to be sure, but this time it wasn't the distinct cracking sound that the thing's joints made when they locked into place. Instead, this time he heard a cacophony of cracks that all blended together like the chorus of a steel drum band.

Coggins stopped wiping his face with the sleeve of his ACPD shirt and stared deeper into the forest where he assumed the culvert lay.

His breath caught in his throat.

"Jared, get up," he croaked.

Jared continued to curse with the effort of trying to clear every last ounce of the cracker's blood or fluid or whatever the fuck it was from his face.

"Jared," Coggins whispered again, his eyes locked on the horror that spread out before him.

When the man still didn't answer, Coggins reached down with his free hand and grabbed the man's collar. He missed, and instead grabbed a thatch of the man's hair—which was probably for the better.

Jared cried out and turned to look at him.

"What the fuck, Brad?"

When he saw the look on Coggins's face, he turned and followed the man's gaze.

"Oh my God."

"Get up, Jared," Coggins said, more loudly this time.

Jared scrambled to his feet, grabbing the rifle off the ground beside him.

There were so many crackers twisting and weaving over fallen logs and moss, seamlessly navigating between the trees, that it looked like a foamy sea of white crustaceans coming toward them. Fast.

Clearly, the nest of smashed eggs back in the Wharfburn Estate was only the beginning...

Are they breeding? Where the fuck *are they all coming from?*

But there was no time to think—they were coming right at them.

"Run!" Coggins shouted. He grabbed Jared by the shoulder this time and squeezed the man hard. "Run!"

Together they turned and ran.

The crackers followed.

22.

CORINA LISTENED CAREFULLY TO the boy's story, but when he was finished she said nothing.

"Did you hear me?" Kent Griddle asked, his voice hoarse from all the talking.

Corina nodded slowly. She had heard him all right, but the real question was whether or not she believed him.

Crackers? Really?

"And you told this all to the sheriff?" she asked before Kent got too uncomfortable with the silence.

"I told him," the boy replied.

There was another awkward pause before the boy spoke again.

"Did they really find Tyler? What other questions does the sheriff have for me?"

Corina, lost in thought, continued to drive as she had been for the past forty minutes when the boy had told her about the fishing trip, and then entering the Wharfburn Estate and playing *Ba di bo*.

"Corina? What questions?"

Corina shook her head and turned to face him.

He was cute, even though when he was wide-eyed as he was now, all of his features—his nose, his ears, and especially his eyes—looked a little too big for his small, round face.

"What?" she asked.

Corina shifted her hip and fought the urge to reach down and adjust her prosthetic leg. Even though it was her left leg that had been severed just above the knee, driving was turning out to be a pain. Her rigid prosthetic forced the foot into the floor of the cab, which strained her hip, and she found herself having to continually shift her body in order to try to get comfortable. She had even debated removing the inanimate hunk of plastic and carbon, but thought that Kent might freak out.

He was a skinny boy, and there was zero doubt in her mind that she could take him if push came to shove—even with her leg. But she didn't want that. She liked Kent.

"What questions does the sheriff want to ask me?" he asked, his eyes wide.

Corina shook her head.

"I don't know," she replied.

They drove the next ten minutes in silence, both staring out the windshield lost in thought. The sun was slowly descending from its apex in the sky, taking with it some of the oppressive heat that had blanketed the county over the past week.

In a couple of hours it would be dark, and there was much to be done before that time. The last thing Corina wanted was to be alone in the Wharfburn Estate after dark. After all, that's how this whole shit had started... first with her dad, and then with Kent and his friends. No, the Wharfburn Estate was not a *dark-friendly* environment.

"Hey, how much longer is it going to be, anyways?"

The question threw Corina for a loop and she hesitated.

This was a mistake, as Kent immediately picked up on it and his eyes rapidly turned forward, scanning the gravel road before them for signs of familiarity.

"Not much longer," Corina said quickly, pushing the car a little faster.

Kent started to shake his head.

"No, no, this isn't right—when I came here with my dad, we didn't come this way. This is too—too *urban*." He spat the last word like a curse.

When he turned to look at her again, Corina couldn't meet his eyes.

"It won't be too much longer," she promised. Her tone had unintentionally grown cold.

She liked Kent, but she was still here for a reason.

As they pulled onto a small dirt road, Kent turned his gaze upward to the green street sign emblazoned with the words: Cedar Lane.

"No!"

The boy's hand instinctively went for the door handle, but Corina quickly locked it before he could pull it open. She didn't know if he would jump considering that they were driving forty miles an hour on the small and bumpy dirt road, but she wouldn't risk it. She needed him—she needed him to show her what he had seen.

"Almost there," she said, trying to calm him.

Kent was starting to hyperventilate in the passenger seat as he continued to pull madly on the door handle.

"Let me out!" he screamed. "I won't go back! I told the sheriff I won't go back there!"

When he turned to Corina and his hand reached for the wheel, she drove her right elbow into his ribs just below the boy's armpit. Air gushed from his lungs and he immediately doubled over in pain, his arms wrapping protectively around his core.

"I'm sorry," Corina whispered, pushing the car even faster. "I'm sorry—I just need to know."

*   *   *

Kent had stopped crying and was breathing more normally now. Even when she pulled the car to a stop at the side of the road outside the Estate, the boy managed to maintain some semblance of calm. He was scheming something, Corina gathered, probably trying to figure out how *he* could steal the cop car and get the hell out of there.

This was a nonstarter, however, as she was confident in her ability to keep Kent from misbehaving.

"We're here," she announced, turning toward the boy, and he, in turn, looked at her. When their eyes met, she spoke as deliberately as she could.

"Listen, Kent, I lost my father and my uncle here—and a whole lot more."

She reached down and pulled up the ankle of her jeans, revealing the metal prong that affixed the carbon foot to the plastic lower leg. Kent followed her gaze, and when he saw the prosthesis his eyes bulged.

"What?" he asked simply, his face a mask of confusion.

Yet despite this expression, Corina knew that he was still scheming, probably trying to figure out if he could outrun her considering her handicap.

No chance.

"Listen to me, Kent."

The boy's blue eyes shot up.

"I lost a lot here, and I know that you lost your friend here. I just need to know what happened, what happened to me and my family. To make sure it doesn't happen to anyone else. Do you understand?"

"Tyler?" he whimpered. "You mean they didn't find Tyler?"

"You lied?" he whispered, tears welling in his eyes.

"Do you understand?" Corina asked more sternly.

When Kent refused to answer, her right arm shot out again and the boy instinctively cringed in expectation of another blow. But when she lay her hand gently on top of one of the boy's hands, he looked up with a confused look on his face.

"I need your help, Kent."

It was Corina's turn to fight back tears.

"Please, Kent. I need your help."

Slowly, the boy with the short red hair nodded.

Scheming, Corina thought. *He's still scheming.*

23.

"HEY, SHERIFF, HAVE YOU seen my keys anywhere?"

The sheriff looked up from his desk with tired eyes. He had been at the station for a good twenty-four hours now, and dealing with Walter's outbursts every twenty or so minutes had drained him of what little energy reserves he had left.

"No," he replied plainly, observing his deputy. "Haven't seen them at all."

"And the Kent kid's file? You take that?"

The sheriff shook his head.

"Weird, I left it right here, right on my desk..."

Sheriff recalled the Lawrence girl, so insistent on meeting Deputy Coggins, but then rather quickly and unexpectedly simply agreeing to leave. And moments before that, the Griddle folder had been on Deputy Williams's desk, only moments before Walter had...

The sheriff stood so quickly that his chair toppled.

"Andrew, check to see if your car is in the lot."

Deputy Williams looked at him.

"What? What's wrong?"

"Hurry, go check to see if your car is in the lot! Do it!"

The seriousness of his words prompted the deputy to action. The man shot up and hurried down the hallway. Walter shouted something incoherent as he passed, but these insults went ignored.

Please be there, the sheriff pleaded silently. The last thing he wanted was to have to arrest the girl for stealing a police car. Not a *Lawrence* girl, not after what they had been through.

He heard the phone in the reception area ring and Mrs. Drew answered it.

In a little more than twenty-four hours, all of Askergan County had seemed to have lost its mind, starting with the missing Wandry boy. And eventually he would have to deal with Tyler's shithead father, who couldn't stop yelling about some god damn insurance money.

He bit the inside of his lip, realizing that this insanity had actually started a long time ago; it had started with the storm. The party line at this point—and always had been, ever since he had helped Deputy Coggins craft it—was that a serial killer had attacked and killed Mrs. Wharfburn, and then the sheriff... followed by a couple dozen townsfolk. The man, who remained nameless, faceless, had been killed by Deputy Coggins, and in the process, a fire had started, destroying most of the bodies and evidence.

Convenient? Absolutely. Believable... maybe. Probably not. After all, the worst that Askergan County had to offer before the storm had been an *incident* between a student and a teacher at the local high school—and even that had turned out to be mostly a fabrication. But now six years had passed since the blizzard and the only ones who knew the truth—*all* of the truth, of which even the sheriff wasn't privy—hadn't broken their silence. There was no TMZ exposé on this, and there never would be, no matter how hard Nancy Whitaker pried. And so far the story had stuck—and had become a sort of urban legend.

Stick to a story long enough, no matter how improbable, and a large subset of the masses would eventually accept it as fact. Just look at religion.

But that didn't change the reality that there was something out there. Something bad. Something *old*. Something that had nestled down in Askergan County eons ago and had taken up residence. And like an evicted tenant, it was reluctant to leave, no matter their efforts.

Sheriff White drove his thumb and forefinger into his eyes again and closed them tightly.

Where are you, Brad? Get the fuck back here!

The door chimed as it opened. A moment later, it chimed again, but this time it was followed by Andrew's curses and the sound of running feet.

Mrs. Drew suddenly added her voice to this symphony of sound.

"Sheriff! Grab the line, Sheriff! Something bad has happened out at Wellwood Elementary! Pick up! Pick up!"

"My car's gone, Sheriff! What the fuck—?"

Walter's cackle followed next, the grating sound echoing throughout the small police station.

As a final crescendo, the radio on Sheriff White's hip crackled loudly and he jumped.

"Hello?" he demanded, removing his fingers from his eyes and squeezing the talk button.

"Paul! Whitey, that you?"

Brad. Thank God.

"Brad, what the fuck is going on? You need to get back here, shit is—"

"Paul, get the fuck down to the armory and load up. They're coming, man, they're coming to town and you need to get the fuck ready."

What?

Deputy Williams burst through the half door separating the reception area from the holding cell and their offices. As he sprinted into the office area, his face was white and covered in a sheen.

"My car! Sheriff, my fucking car is missing!"

"Sheriff! Pick up the phone! Wellwood Elementary!" Mrs. Drew hollered again from the front.

So much was happening at once that the sheriff almost lost it.

I'm not ready for this.

It was Brad's hysteria that brought him back.

"Whitey! You need to get ready, get all the guns you have and get ready... they're coming!"

"Who's coming, Brad? Who's coming?"

He was shouting now, standing at his desk and shouting into the phone while Deputy Williams desperately went through the drawers of his desk, pulling out papers and tossing them on to the floor.

"Not who, Sheriff, *what*."

There was a short pause, during which Sheriff Paul White held his breath, his considerable chest expanding to an even more impressive size.

"The *crackers* are coming, Sheriff. The *crackers*."

24.

"**OPEN THE GOD DAMN DOOR!**" Coggins shouted as he continued to yank furiously on the handle.

Jared reached into his pocket and tried to get his keys out while still juggling the two old-fashioned rifles, one slung over his shoulder and the other clutched in his hand.

Deputy Coggins turned and aimed his pistol toward the house, his eyes widening in expectation.

"Hurry the fuck up, Jared!"

Jared finally pulled the keys from his pocket and opened the car door, throwing it so wide that it came whipping back again and smashed against his shoulder. He cried out and Coggins turned to him.

"My door! Open *my* door!"

The old Buick was parked on the gravel driveway off to one side of the house, giving Coggins a clear view of the throng of crackers that flowed out of the thin forest like a roiling white foam.

He had been wrong; there weren't hundreds of them, but *thousands*.

Where the fuck are they all coming from?

When they reached the back porch, some of them seamlessly turned toward the car like a school of fish while others clambered up the stairs and over the back porch, their legs cracking with every step as if someone were driving a paver over bubble wrap. The others would enter the house, Coggins knew, and pass through it before exiting through the front door.

They were coming, and there was no stopping them.

Jared finally reached over and flipped the lock to the passenger door and Coggins threw it wide.

Despite the vehicle's dilapidated appearance—Coggins's fingers were covered with a layer of sap and other tree detritus from touching the roof—it started with a roar on the first try. Just as he was pulling himself inside the car, Coggins caught sight of a shape that looked like a barbecue tucked onto the back corner of the deck. It was covered in a black tarp, and as he watched, the crackers swarmed over it, making white polka dots on the dark fabric. Between their machinating bodies, he thought he could make out the familiar shape of a propane tank tucked beneath.

"Does your barbecue have propane?" he yelled at Jared, hesitating before completely entering the car.

He kept his eyes trained on the crackers that flowed out of the front of the house, spilling onto the lawn and merging with those that poured in from around the side.

"What?" Jared screamed. His hand was on the lever beside the wheel, flexing, wanting to fire the car into reverse and get the fuck out of there, but he couldn't because Coggins's right leg was still firmly planted on the ground. "Barbecue? Get the fuck in here!"

"Do you have a propane tank in your barbecue?" Coggins shouted again, aware that the first of the crackers were within jumping distance now.

"Barbecue?" Jared's voice was shrill, his eyes wide. "Barbecue? Why do you fucking want to know about the barbecue?"

Coggins couldn't wait any longer. He reached inside the car and grabbed the rifle off the seat. In one smooth motion he rotated the rifle around and aimed at the area beneath the barbecue that was covered with a black tarp.

"Just in case you were hungry for some seafood," he muttered and then squeezed the trigger.

The barbecue had a tank, and it was full.

There was a dull, metallic *thunk* as the first round pierced the tank, followed by a hiss of gas releasing beneath the tarp. It was an odd sound, and yet it seemed to harmonize with the chitinous sound of the crackers' movements.

Coggins, surprised that the ancient rifle had actually fired let alone had true aim, reloaded and took aim again.

An explosion erupted almost at the same time as the bark from Coggins's rifle, blowing out the tarp and sending the barbecue flying at least six feet into the air. A billowing yellow-and-red cloud filled the atmosphere, showering Coggins in a wash of hot air and bright light. Squinting against the offending light, he jumped into the car and pulled the door closed.

"Go!" he shouted at an awestruck Jared. He was acutely aware that his own expression matched his friend's; it seemed improbable—impossible even—that his shot would have been so perfectly placed and that the tarp had filled with just the right combination of gas and oxygen to explode. But why shouldn't it work? Why on a day as *fucked* up as today, shouldn't the most unlikely of shots work?

Coggins shook his head.

"Go! Go! Go!"

When Jared didn't react, he reached over and put his hand on top of the man's hand on the gear shift. Then he pulled down, hard.

Jared snapped to and slammed his foot on the gas pedal, spewing up an army of rocks and dirt that skittered across the thrumming shells of the closest crackers.

Jared spun the car around, the rear wheels digging into the loose dirt by the side of the embankment that led down to the water below. Eventually the tires caught and the car shot forward. Coggins whipped his head around as they peeled down the dirt road, affording himself one more look at the carnage that was left in their wake.

The entire back porch had been decimated, leaving in its wake a bubbling stew of white cracker corpses, as if someone had unleashed an uncensored barrage of white paintballs.

Regardless of the hundreds of crackers that had been rendered but a milky smear, there were still more, and they were still coming, crawling effortlessly over the corpses of their kin.

As Jared floored the car—and it responded by issuing a high-pitched whine of protest—a cracker flew up and smacked against Coggins' window.

Peering into that slimy orifice full of the tiny reciprocating teeth, Coggins shuddered.

Askergan, what the fuck is happening to you?

25.

CORINA TOLD KENT TO exit the car first and the boy reluctantly obliged, his head hung low. She followed next, shoving the keys into her pocket after making sure to lock the doors.

The Wharfburn Estate looked pretty much the way Corina had pictured it in her mind all these years, despite the fact that she had never seen it in real life. She was not so naïve to think that her imagination hadn't been impregnated by the blurry image of the house with the blonde news reporter standing in front, but she had obsessed about it for long enough to have formed a distinct visual: ostentatious red brick, overgrown brush leading up to the front, and large Victorian windows blanketing the front. What she hadn't seen on TV, however, was the front door; it simply wasn't there. Instead, the opening was wide, the porch leading up to it and the frame itself marred by streaks of charred wood.

As brave as she was, this house scared her.

"Go," she ordered.

The command was meant for Kent, but it also served to kick her into gear.

When the boy turned his round face to look at her, she was struck by how young he suddenly looked; how young and *scared*. He reminded her of Henri, who had confronted her when Corina had told her and her mother that she was leaving. The girl's eyes had looked just as Kent's did now.

A pang of guilt suddenly shot through Corina at the thought of having left her sister and mother alone—and that she had come here, of all godforsaken places. And had stolen a cop car. And... and... and... her poor decisions kept adding up like gold coins in a purple drawstring bag.

Corina's eyes drifted back to Kent, who appeared to struggle to put one foot in front of the other as he slowly made his way across the lawn.

And kidnapping, she thought glumly. *Don't forget to add that to the list.*

An explosion from somewhere in the distance rumbled through the air, drawing both Corina's and Kent's attention.

The sound had come from Corina's left—about five or ten miles away, she estimated based on the short interval between seeing the orange glow and hearing the sound.

"What the fuck was that?" she asked.

When Corina turned back toward Kent, he bolted.

It would have been impossible for Corina to catch him, what with her prosthetic leg, had he turned and run down the road. But for whatever reason, the boy's first instinct was to head to the car, and when he found his passenger door locked, Corina caught him and slipped a hand under his chin from behind. The boy struggled, pushing off the car with his feet, but when Corina's hand met her bicep and she squeezed, just a little, he stopped fighting almost immediately.

"What the fuck! Who the fuck are you?" he gasped through gritted teeth. Spit flew from his mouth and speckled her forearm.

Corina eased the pressure.

"I need your help," she replied, breathing heavily on the side of his head and ear.

The boy struggled again and she retightened her grip.

"You're insane," he grunted, his hands trying desperately to claw her arm away from his throat.

"No," she said, letting go completely now and spinning Kent around. "Not insane," she said, staring intently into his eyes. "Angry—I'm fucking furious. This place took so much from me, and now it's my time to take it back."

Kent's eyes went wide, and a single tear rolled down his cheek. Clearly, she was doing a poor job of proving that she *wasn't* insane.

"You don't know what's in there," he said, his voice returning to a whisper. "We can't go in there. I won't. We don't even have any weapons."

Corina looked down at herself. What the boy was saying wasn't completely true, of course, as they had one weapon: her.

She had spent the past six years training for something—something that she now realized had been *this*. She was training for *Oot'-keban,* or crackers, or whatever the fuck else waited for them inside the Wharfburn Estate.

Confident that Kent wouldn't try to escape again—at least not in the near future—Corina turned her attention back to the looming Estate. Her eyes scanned the house, looking for something—*anything*—that might give her a hint of what to do next.

That was when she saw it: on the left side of the house, just a foot or two outside the shade that the roof offered, was a small white crab-like creature. Clearly dead, the thing was lying on its back, its six legs pointed like arthritic fingers in the air stiffly gripped by rigor mortis. Corina squinted in the fading sun, trying to figure out exactly what it was.

But she knew what it was: it was one of the *crackers*, one of the parasites that had affixed itself to Tyler's skull... according to Kent, at least.

Corina looked over at the boy, and was startled by the way the boy was hyperventilating and his entire body was trembling, as if caught in an eternal shudder.

"Keep it together," Corina said. "It's dead."

Kent seemed not to hear. The only part of his body that wasn't shaking was his head: it was trained on the dead cracker like a man with tetanus.

Corina felt another pang of guilt, but like before, she forced this sensation aside, burying it into one of the deep recesses of her mind.

"Let's go," Corina whispered. "We don't have to go inside the house."

When Kent still didn't answer, Corina moved closer to him. It had been a long time since she had had any friends, but for some reason, like some bizarre inverse Stockholm syndrome, she felt a bond forming with the redheaded boy. She slipped her hand into his, interlacing their fingers, and was surprised when Kent squeezed her hand. Corina squeezed back and started to move toward the house.

Kent reluctantly followed.

*   *   *

They only saw one other cracker as they made their way around the east side of the house. It was a small thing, even smaller than the dead one that they had passed a minute ago, and it seemed to meander about aimlessly near the back of the property just beyond the swimming pool. Corina was nearly hypnotized by the way the six legs moved up and down in a coordinated manner like organic pistons. It didn't look so much like it was walking on the uneven ground, but more like it was *gliding* across it like a liquid.

Kent, on the other hand, couldn't even look at the thing, and had resorted to burying his head in the back of Corina's t-shirt. She had removed her sweatshirt and left it in the cop car, as the heat and anxiety, and whatever other bubbling mix of emotions that came at her in waves, had caused her to sweat more than usual.

Without warning, the cracker's constant movement ceased, and Corina felt her whole body tense, thinking that they might have somehow alerted the eyeless creature. When the cracker suddenly turned and took off like an arrow into the wooded area, clearly headed west, she relaxed. Somehow, this gave her confidence: they had one weapon, and her body was tuned, ready to go, even if her mind was a muddled mess.

They waited for another moment, frozen in silence, but when it was clear that the thing was not coming back, Corina leaned over her shoulder and shrugged, trying to get the boy off her back.

"It's gone," she told him in a soft voice, "come on."

It took two tries to get Kent to unglue himself from her, and when he did, Corina swiftly made her way across the lawn, squeezing Kent's hand tightly in case he had any intentions of letting go.

Their collective anxiety eased somewhat when they made it completely across the unkempt backyard, following the path of disturbed and broken grass, and stepped into the thinly wooded area.

Still crouching, they made their way toward the back of the property, becoming increasingly aware of a foul smell that wafted toward them like an open sewer pipe.

This is the way, Corina knew. *This is the way to find out what happened to my family — to find out about what happened to* me.

But when Corina made it to another clearing and stepped in front of a grey culvert with Kent in tow, a crippling fear overcame her.

No curious desire, no vengeance-sated *need*, was enough to keep her moving forward.

"Oh my God."

26.

THEY WERE TOO LATE; Coggins's warning to Sheriff White back at the station had come too late.

The crackers had already made it into town.

Their first hint was the small store about a mile from the Lawrence house. The converted shed was set back from a blue slatted house with white trim and matching window shutters. The door to the shed was open wide and two legs hung out of the opening, an 'Open' sign lying on the grass just beyond the person's black shoes.

"Stop the car!" Coggins shouted.

Jared, eyes locked on the road, didn't hear him.

"Stop the car!" Coggins repeated, and this time Jared looked over at him. "Stop the—"

Jared slammed on the breaks so hard that Coggins's head flung forward, coming within inches of smashing into the dash in front of him. As he recoiled, he pulled at his seatbelt, tearing it off of his chest and breathing deep.

He had one foot out the door when he saw it: there was a cracker sitting squarely on what he now realized was a woman's bare chest. This one was not so much white as it was translucent; and it was small, too, not much bigger than a softball.

"Shit," Coggins swore, freezing halfway out the vehicle.

He glanced back down the road, willing away the dust cloud that Jared had made, trying to see if the crackers were following them. When he saw nothing, he turned back to the store and brought his hands to his mouth, cupping it.

"Hey! Ma'am, you okay in there?"

It was a stupid question—an utterly *ridiculous* question—but he couldn't think of anything else to say.

He dropped his hands and grabbed Jared's rifle from the floor of the car. Squinting one eye, he lined the sight with the cracker, grimacing at the sight of its glistening, thrumming shell. He was about to pull the trigger, to send the thing back to the hell that it had come from, when he caught some movement from the woman—a slight twitch beneath her *skin*.

Coggins shifted his field of view. It felt wrong looking at the woman's bare, sagging breasts that hung on either side of her body, like staring at your grandmother in the shower, but he forced himself to stare.

There.

He saw more movement, like fingers pressing through a tight sheet just above her left breast.

What the—?

A hand stuck his leg and his heart leapt into his throat.

"Get in, man! She's dead! Get the fuck in!" Jared shouted.

Coggins swatted Jared's hand away and refocused on the elderly woman again. She *wasn't* dead; he had seen her move.

And then he saw more movement; first her chest again, then her right arm seemed to rise a fraction of an inch.

God damn it, she's alive!

Coggins took a deep breath and turned the rifle back to the cracker, which was now situated just below the hollow of her throat, the faceless shell looking somehow content—smug, even. The rifle barked and the cracker exploded, sending streams of white fluid in all directions. The liquid splattered a row of American flag-bearing teddy bears at the back of the shop, but to Coggins's dismay, the woman didn't sit up. And for a brief moment, the motion in her chest and arm ceased.

"Get the fuck in! They're coming!" Jared shouted, once again pulling at Coggins's pant leg.

Coggins resisted the urge to look behind the car, knowing that if he saw the crackers coming for them, he might lose any semblance of bravery and tell Jared to step on it.

They couldn't leave, not just yet; this woman needed help. A lot of help.

Staring intently at the woman's left arm, he thought he saw movement again.

"Just wait," he grumbled to Jared, still staring down the barrel of the rifle in case another cracker surfaced.

Then there was more movement, but not subtle gestures as before, but a solid pulsating beneath—and somehow *inside*—the woman's wrinkled breasts. A sinking feeling started in Coggins's own chest, as if an invisible man had decided now was the time to stand on him. This inexorable feeling of dread continued to grow as the frenzied activity beneath the woman's skin reached a boiling point and her breasts suddenly tore open, releasing at least a dozen of the milky crackers. The crackers spilled from the bloody ruins of the woman's chest, pausing only to force blood and sinew from the tiny perforations on the top of their shells. It looked like it was raining blood.

Coggins gagged.

Only after the creatures made their way down her body and onto the lawn did Coggins catch a clear a glimpse of the woman's flesh: her chest was torn open, her breasts reduced to ribbons of blood-splotched skin, her nipples hanging around her navel.

Coggins gagged again and felt bile fill his mouth.

But he couldn't bring himself to look away.

As he watched, the cavity of her chest seemed to somehow seal back up again, the blood that ran down the sides of her body and pooled beneath her first reducing to a trickle before stopping altogether. The new skin, disorganized, no longer female, was whiter than the old skin, standing out like different shades of a patchwork quilt. The moment the woman's chest was whole again, the lumpy protrusions, acute angles, started to move beneath the skin of the poor woman's stomach.

There were more crackers buried in her skin.

Coggins vomited on the grass, and this violent act broke the spell. Still spitting puke, he threw the rifle back to the floor and pulled his body fully into the vehicle.

"Go! Drive!" he yelled, flecks of vomit flying from his lips.

Jared didn't need to be asked twice.

When they passed Wellwood Elementary, Jared didn't stop. He simply kept his eyes glued to the road and pushed his shitty Buick to its limits.

Coggins, on the other hand, had his face pressed against the glass, his eyes wide with horror.

27.

"WILLIAMS, GET DOWN TO the armory, now! Bring out as many weapons as you can and put them on the table."

Deputy Williams looked first at the sheriff and then at the black phone that the man had just slammed down hard.

One of his thin black eyebrows rose up in confusion.

"Sheriff? What about my car?"

The sheriff waved his comment away.

"Fuck your car! Go to the armory, now!"

Deputy Williams's face went slack and he quickly turned and fled the room with haste.

Mrs. Drew poked her head into the room next, her expression grim. The woman's always perfectly kept hair, the light grey strands tucked away in a tight bun, was in disarray, with two or three thickets hanging down in front of her face. She didn't bother to push them away.

"Sheriff? Nancy is still on the line... she is nearly hysterical, rambling about Wellwood Elementary." She paused for a moment, biting her lip. "I think you should take it."

Paul nodded and reached for the phone.

"Put her through."

Mrs. Drew left the room and hurried back to her desk.

A moment later, the phone rang and Paul picked it up with the very first sound.

"Hello? Nancy?"

The woman was indeed hysterical.

"Paul? Paul? You need to get out... oh dear God... it's a fucking mess, bodies everywhere—and these fucking crabs... Paul? Paul?"

Paul's heart rate doubled, then tripled.

"Nancy, slow down. Where are you?"

The woman swore and then her breathing quickened. She shouted something to someone else, but Paul couldn't make out the words.

"I don't know," she shouted in between breaths. It occurred to Paul that she might be running.

"Are you running? Nancy, where are you? Think!"

"I—I—for fuck's sake, Jerry, hurry your fat ass up! Sheriff, I just left the school... was heading out there to do some filming of the kids and their new garden... then, Jesus Christ, I saw the worst shit, Paul, fucking horrible shit. The fucking kids... oh God!"

Nancy's voice exploded into a sob.

"Fuck! Their skin was being *sucked* by these fucking crab things!"

Sheriff Paul White's mind immediately went to the story that the Griddle boy had told him about his missing friend. Then his eyes darted to the plastic bag on his desk, the one that contained the dead crab-like thing.

Then he thought of the school—the god damn elementary school.

No.

"Nancy!"

When at first there was no answer, he turned the receiver to his mouth and shouted into the phone.

"Nancy! Listen to me, Nancy, go immediately to Frankie's Diner... go right there, right now! Coggins will swing by and grab you."

He heard what he thought was an affirmation between heavy breaths on the other end of the line.

"And Nancy?"

"Yeah, Paul?"

She was sobbing again.

"Stay inside... please don't let those things near you."

He felt his own tears starting to well.

"Please."

*   *   *

The sheriff hung up the phone again, his hand trembling over the black receiver.

He had just spoken to Coggins, to make sure that he had a car to grab Nancy and Jerry, the cameraman, and his deputy had confirmed what Nancy had told him.

Everyone at the school is dead. And that wasn't all. There were more dead—many, many more.

The whole town was going to shit and he was left trying to poop-and-scoop.

Deputy Williams laid the final gun on the table—a shotgun, Sheriff Drew's old shotgun—among the others.

"That's it," the man said.

The clinking of the metal of gun on gun drew the sheriff out of his own head.

"We need to get ready... they're coming here."

The three of them, the sheriff, Deputy Andrew Williams, and Mrs. Drew, all stood around the table of guns, staring at them as if they expected them to stand up and move on their own.

"We need to get ready," the sheriff repeated.

Get ready? How the fuck *can we prepare for… for this?*

This time, the deputy nodded.

"We have two shotguns, four nine millimeters, four grenades, and two Kevlar vests. Lots of bullets, mostly for the nine mils," he said.

The deputy raised his eyes after speaking and stared at the sheriff with his dark eyes.

"How many are there, Sheriff?"

The sheriff lowered his gaze and shrugged.

A hundred? A thousand? More? Neither Coggins nor Nancy had been clear about that.

"Many," was the answer he opted for.

Sheriff White reached out and grabbed one of the shotguns off the table. With his other hand, he unclipped the protective latch on his holster and pulled out his own gun. Without another word, he tossed it onto the table with the others.

"Five nine mils," he corrected his deputy.

A shout from the other room drew his head from the rather meager table of weapons—a low-level drug dealer had a better stash than this. But this was Askergan County, population one thousand and twelve, not Detroit.

It was Walter screaming again. With all of the phone calls and horrible revelations of what was happening on the outskirts of town, the sheriff had completely forgotten about *him*.

"What do we do about Walter?" Deputy Williams whispered.

The sheriff turned to Mrs. Drew.

"How long has he been locked up?"

The woman's bright green eyes flicked up to the clock and then back to the sheriff.

"About six hours. We can keep him another six without charging him."

Paul nodded. The woman looked so tired in that moment that he felt a pang of sadness. Mrs. Drew had lost her husband and her adopted daughter, and she was slated to lose even more if things kept progressing the way they were.

A school... a fucking elementary school.

Paul shuddered.

When Walter shouted another insult, this one clearly directed at him, the sheriff thought about keeping him in the cell for as long as possible. But twelve hours was the maximum he could keep him without charging him, and even though the man really was a piece of work, he figured it best not to charge him. After all, he had just lost his son.

And rules were rules, no matter how much Coggins made fun of him for keeping them.

The window behind the sheriff suddenly exploded inward, showering the desk he had just vacated with glass. Sheriff White turned with the shotgun leading the way and caught sight of two shapes scampering across and then beneath the desk. He cocked the shotgun.

"Get out of here," he instructed Mrs. Drew and Deputy Williams, who were still behind him. "Get out of here, now."

"I'm not leaving," Deputy Williams replied, and Paul heard him picking up a gun off the table.

The sheriff ducked down and scanned the area below the desk, moving the gun back and forth in a slow arc, searching for any sort of movement. "Go back to the front, Mrs. Drew, and close the door behind you."

The sheriff heard the sound of metal on metal again as another gun was taken from the table, then he heard Mrs. Drew slowly back from the room.

The door closed behind her, and the sheriff and the deputy were alone with the crackers.

It was the deputy who spotted it first, a white crab-like creature huddled in the far corner beneath the sheriff's desk. It seemed to be thrumming in a rhythmic pattern, its shell rising and then falling every few seconds, a movement that was accompanied by the sound of forced air.

Williams, his eyes trained on the thing, gestured with his hand not holding the gun for the sheriff to come to his side.

The sheriff slowly slid over to him and followed his pointed finger. Paul had a good four inches on Deputy Williams, so from his vantage point he could only see six pointed legs pressing into the floor; the *body* was just out of sight. The sheriff motioned for the deputy to keep his gun trained on the thing as he slowly lowered himself first to one knee, then onto his stomach.

Now in full view, he could see its disgusting white shell and the horrible perforations on top pulsating. The sheriff lined the center of the shell up with his shotgun. A second later, he fired.

At first, Paul thought that he had missed the thing as he could no longer see it, or anything, below the desk. He quickly scrambled to his feet and shouted at his deputy.

"Where'd it go? Where'd it go?"

The deputy, lowering his gun, said, "Blamo. You got it."

The sheriff shook his head and leaned down again, trying to catch any sight of the thing.

"You sure?"

The deputy nodded and slowly strode over to the desk. He cautiously bent down and peered beneath it, then came back up, his nose scrunched.

"Splat," was all he said, gulping hard. The sheriff could see that the man was trying to fight back vomit.

The sheriff nodded.

"Good. We need to board —" The words caught in his throat when a funk hit him square in the face. "Oh God," he muttered, bringing his arm up to cover his nose and mouth. "What the fuck is that smell?"

Deputy Williams, his own arm covering his face, didn't reply; he simply gestured to the underside of the desk with his pistol.

"Let's board up the window and get out of here."

Thankful for being dismissed from the now toxic smelling room—an odd mix of chili powder and sewage—the deputy immediately rushed by the sheriff and made his way to the door.

Opening the door alleviated some of the stink, and the deputy took this moment to lean out of the room.

"Mrs. Drew? Come put one of these on," he shouted, meaning the Kevlar vests, "and let's put one on Walter."

Upon hearing his name, the man in the cell perked up.

"I get a gun? I get a gun?" His eyes were wide with excitement, and he started pulling at his long white beard in anticipation.

The sheriff's eyes met his for a moment, but he said nothing. With the stare, the man quieted.

The sheriff's hand drifted to the set of keys—front door, car, cell door, armory door, and handcuff keys—on the large ring on his belt loop and he played with them for a while, enjoying the way the teeth dug into his palm.

We can keep him locked up for another six hours.

Those were the rules.

But based on the shit that was happening in Askergan, could he be sure that he would be around in exactly six hours or fewer to let him go? He thought not.

The sheriff pulled the key to the single cell from his belt and made his way to the cage.

"You're going to listen to me. If you want out, do as I say."

It wasn't a question, or a suggestion; it was a command, an order.

Walter, who was still lying on the floor of his cell, immediately pulled his thin body to his feet. He made his way to the front of the cage, grabbing one on either side of his face with mottled fingers. His eyes were wide, his lips a pale shade of pink that matched his cheeks and forehead.

"Yes, Massa," the man uttered in his best Southern accent.

Walter Wandry's breath was foul, his rotted teeth one hard candy short of falling out of his head.

Even as the sheriff put the key into the lock, he knew that he was making a mistake.

But rules were rules.

*   *   *

Sheriff Paul White had only pulled the door open a quarter of an inch when he heard two sounds happen at almost exactly the same time.

There was a shriek, one that was high-pitched and could have only originated from Mrs. Drew, and a series of successful cracks, culminating with a resounding *snap* that echoed off the narrow hallway.

Instinctively, the sheriff turned and as he did, he dropped to one knee. The key that he had used to unlock the door was still attached by a thin metal string to his belt, and it was stuck in the lock. When he turned, the door swung open.

A blur of brown and white flew past the sheriff, missing the top of his crouched head by mere inches. There was a whoosh of air, and then the cracker flew into the open cell, smacking the back bars with a dull thud.

Walter wasted no time; he quickly spun away from the front of the cage and ran from the cell without any thought of stopping or hesitating. He made his way past the crouched sheriff and into the room that housed the sheriff and deputy's desks.

Collecting himself, the sheriff whipped back around, forcing the cell door closed again. He reached for his gun on his hip, but swore when he realized that he had tossed it onto the table with the others. And after he had shot the cracker, he had left the shotgun on the table as well.

"Mrs. Drew! Downstairs! Now!"

The woman didn't move; she was hypnotized by the creature that was stunned, lying on its side at the back of the cage.

Paul turned to the woman.

"Drew! Move!" He shouted the last word with such vehemence that the woman snapped to action. She quickly bolted, moving quickly for a woman of nearly sixty years wearing a tight black skirt and cream-colored pumps.

When the sheriff turned back to the cage, the cracker had recovered from colliding against the bars. It had propped itself back up on its legs, and now the front part of its shell was tilted toward the sheriff.

Then the legs began to snap into place, each of the thickened joints cracking as it lowered close to the ground.

The sheriff prepared himself, holding his meaty hands out in front of himself.

He would tear the fucking thing's legs off with his bare hands if he had to.

"Bring it, motherfucker."

28.

THE SUN HAD DIPPED low in the sky, but even the long shadows cast into the culvert did nothing to hide the horror within.

Corina Lawrence has somehow propelled her numb body behind a tree, and was now leaning around the side trying to get a clear look at the interior of the culvert. Every once in a while, she glanced over at Kent, who was also crouched behind a tree, but unlike her, his face was buried in his hands. There was a dark stain around the crotch of his jeans—the boy had pissed himself.

Corina didn't blame him.

The naked, cowering boy had revealed himself just after the last of the crackers had fled west. Then the moaning had started.

The boy in the culvert was thin, bordering on skinny, and he was on one knee, his bare back and buttocks facing them. At first, Corina thought that the fading sunlight reflecting off the culvert was casting weird patches of light on the boy's glistening back, giving it a patchwork appearance, but as the light continued to fade and the patches remained, she couldn't be sure.

Another moan from the tunnel, and Corina glimpsed the profile of the boy's mouth go wide. And then she saw it: a quiver of movement beneath his skin, just to the left of his bare spine.

She felt like she was going to be sick.

The movement continued to become more intense, like a writhing horde of maggots consuming a final cube of beef just below the surface. As they pushed harder and harder against his skin, gradually forming a singular, coherent outline, the moan intensified.

A second later, the boy's skin split and a milky white cracker—a *palil*—erupted in a bloody gush. It fluttered for a moment, a strange word to describe a creature that had no wings, and small specks of blood seemed to expel from the top part of the nearly translucent shell. It was breathing; it was taking its first breaths.

Corina's stomach did another barrel roll, and she forced herself to stare at the ground in an attempt to keep from vomiting.

Watching the birth of the *palil* was too much even for her constitution.

A stream of tears suddenly marked her red cheeks.

What the fuck are we doing here?

Closure, revenge, fucking vengeance, none of it mattered now.

Her eyes darted to the boy across from her. Regardless of her own selfish motivations, Kent didn't deserve to be here; he had done nothing to deserve *this*.

After somehow managing to once again keep the puke at bay, Corina looked up again and was taken aback by the fact that the bloody wound on the boy's spine had somehow sealed itself.

She blinked hard, squeezing the last vestiges of tears away.

Did I imagine it? Did I imagine the cracker?

Corina squinted hard, and realized that while the blood was gone, the skin on the spot that she *swore* the cracker had erupted from was different; it was lighter than the rest of his pale skin, a milky white membrane that resembled a patch of vitiligo. A flicker of movement drew her eyes to another shape just below where the previous cracker had emerged. Something was moving beneath his skin again.

And if Corina needed further proof of what she had seen, it was the cracker itself: after spraying all the blood away, the cracker stood poised on the boy's shoulder. A moment later, it scampered over the new protrusions on the boy's back and made its way to the front of the culvert, its pointed appendages tinkling quietly on the metal surface.

The shape in the culvert moaned again, more loudly this time, and Corina dared another glance at Kent. To her surprise, he had pulled his face from his hands and was now peering into the tunnel, his own jaw slack, tears and saliva dripping from his face in such thick rivulets that she could have been convinced that he had just washed his face.

His entire body was shaking.

"Tyler?" Kent whispered.

Corina's heart rate doubled and she gestured wildly at Kent, mouthing the words, *Be quiet, get behind the tree!*

It was no use. The boy stood and took one step into the open.

"Tyler?" he asked again. His expression was oddly blank, as if he were possessed.

The moaning stopped and again Corina, still crouched behind the tree, tried to will Kent back into hiding.

What the fuck are you doing?

When Kent repeated his friend's name a third time—and this time the newly *birthed* cracker at the front of the tunnel tilted backward, as if it had just acknowledged their presence—

Corina had no choice but to stand and make her way to the boy's side. After all, it was her fault he was here; he deserved none of this.

The horrible moan, a low-octave sound that was coming from deep within the crouched form, returned when two new *palil* burst forth in a bloody show.

Kent was now repeating his friend's name over and over again in a wet whisper, sweat, spit, and tears dripping from his chin.

Corina hooked her arm through his, knowing that they had to run, while at the same time aware of how difficult a venture that would be given the uneven forest floor and her prosthetic leg. She doubted that she would be able to navigate it on her own, let alone dragging Kent with her.

The crouched figure in the culvert suddenly twisted, its neck craning toward the opening, toward *them*.

Corina saw his face, and this time her bladder that let go.

Tyler's face was a horrible mess, the skin on the entire left side an opaque, featureless white, too smooth to be that of a boy or a man. It looked like he had received an albino skin graft, one that was much too tight and pulled the corners of his eye and nose out of true. There was a scar that ran down the right side of his face, and it was this scar, oddly, that made him seem human. If it weren't for the scar, Corina wouldn't have been sure.

The boy's eyes were sunken black pits, and his mouth was ragged, his lower lip reduced to bloody strips of dangling flesh. The blood that coated his teeth suggested that he had inflicted this damage on himself.

As her gaze drifted lower, she realized that his entire body was covered in patches of the strange off-white skin, beneath which she saw the stirrings of at least a half dozen more crack-ers. Tyler's body looked like a stained tube sock filled with a family of rats, all desperate to get out at once.

The face suddenly turned and lined up with hers and Kent's.

When the mouth opened, Corina expected another of those horrible moans. With the three crackers having made their way to the opening of the culvert, all leaning forward slightly, puff-ing air through the tops of their shells, she prepared herself to run, knowing that, prosthetic leg or not, she would likely have to drag Kent with her.

A lumpy hand—one that looked nothing at all human, just a solid fist of white calloused flesh—thumped against the inte-rior of the culvert as the *thing*—the *boy*—continued to turn its body.

It wasn't a moan that came out of the ragged hole of a mouth, but words. The sound was garbled, and the words ran together like those of a drunk preacher, but she understood them none-theless.

"Help me," the boy whispered, flecks of spit and blood spraying from the orifice. Another cracker budded from his chest and flopped into his naked lap before scampering to the front of the culvert with the other three creatures.

"Help me, please, God, help me."

29.

SHERIFF PAUL WHITE DIDN'T have to use his hands after all; the cracker was much bigger than the one that he had blasted with the shotgun beneath his desk and it didn't fit through the bars.

With a *thunk*, it fell to the ground again, landing on its side. It tried to scramble to its feet, but it was stunned and careened to one side for a brief moment before finally righting itself.

Sheriff White stared in disgust, unsure of what to do next. The cracker turned and squatted, its joints locking into place as it had done before. Again the sheriff held his large black hands out in front of him, just in case it managed to finagle a way through the bars. But this time it didn't jump. Instead, it simply remained locked in place, motionless.

Deputy Williams came running from the back of the hallway, tearing his way up the stairs two at a time, two small sheets of plywood in his hands. When he saw the sheriff, the boards dropped noisily to the ground and he quickly pulled his gun.

While the sound of the falling plywood drew the sheriff's attention, the cracker didn't move.

"Deputy, stay your ground," the sheriff instructed, holding out an outstretched hand.

"What... what is it?"

The sheriff shook his head.

"Should I shoot it?"

Again the sheriff shook his head, eyes remaining locked on the cracker in the cell.

"It can't get out."

Paul took a small step to his left and the cracker seemed to lean that way. As far as he could tell, the thing had no eyes and no nose... no sensory organs at all, save the orifice on the underside and the strange fluttering perforations on top.

The sheriff took another step closer to Deputy Williams, and then another. With every shuffling movement, the cracker turned a little bit more, the front ridge of the shell that separated the clean white of the underside and the milky top seeming to dip toward him.

I'm watching you, the tilt said.

When he was right next to the deputy, the sheriff spoke, keeping his eyes trained on the creature now locked in Askergan's only holding cell.

"Where is Mrs. Drew?" he asked out of the corner of his mouth.

After the woman's scream, he had heard her run by him, but his focus had been on the cracker and he hadn't seen where.

"In the armory. Where's Walter?"

The sheriff's concentration was broken.

Fuck! Walter!

He turned away from the cracker and headed back the way he had come, back into the office area.

"Keep your gun on it, Williams. And if it moves, shoot it."

The deputy responded by crouching slightly and training his pistol on the cracker.

"Don't fucking move," he whispered.

Sheriff White opened the door cautiously in case there were other crackers inside. After peeking in, he listened.

He heard nothing.

With the palm of his hand, he opened the door just wide enough for his body to fit through, then immediately bolted to the table, picking up a pistol and the shotgun. He jammed the former into his hip holster, and brought the shotgun out in front of him, his eyes scanning the room.

Nothing.

He heard and saw nothing—no crackers.

"Walter?" he asked tentatively.

When there was no answer, he called the man's name again. Still nothing.

The sheriff's eyes drifted down to the table and his heart sank. There was one shotgun, four grenades, and a myriad of shells, but only one handgun. He had one pistol and one shotgun, and he knew both Deputy Williams and Mrs. Drew had one. There had been *five* pistols, however, he was sure of it.

"Williams!" he hollered over his shoulder, keeping his eyes trained on the room before him, still scanning for any movement. "Williams, how many pistols were there?"

"Five!" the deputy cried back.

"Fuck."

The sheriff's eyes slowly drifted upward to the smashed window. He could see what looked like a trail of drops of blood on the sill, the remaining fragments of glass reflecting a deep crimson in the fading sunlight.

The window was small, roughly ten inches high by two feet wide. It was also purposely high above them, with at least a ten-foot drop on the outside, and a few feet shy of that on the inside.

No one could fit out that window.

His eyes drifted downward and he caught sight of what looked like a dusty footprint square in the middle of his desk.

No one could have made that jump.

But Walter Wandry was not an ordinary man... he was a rail-thin junkie who would do anything to get his next hit.

And now he had a gun.

Sheriff White shook his head. There was no way he could have planted a foot on the desk and then slithered his way out the window. Even if he did, there was no way he could have made the drop to the hard pavement outside and then fled without the crackers getting him... could he have?

"Walter Wandry, where the fuck are you?"

There was still no answer.

There was no way the man could have gotten out through the window — except he wasn't here. So where else could he be?

The sheriff grabbed the two Kevlar vests from the table and tossed them into the hallway behind him. Then he picked up the grenades and the remaining shotgun and pistol and slowly backed out of the room.

"Sheriff? Come take a look at this. It's doing... it's doing *something*."

The sheriff backed completely out of the room, and only then did he turn and look at the cracker.

The thing was still hunched, its front rim — if it had a *front* — pointed toward the floor, but it was now pulsating slightly. And when he listened closely, he could hear the air being forced out of the top, a barely audible *whoosh, whoosh, whoosh* sound.

It could be breathing, he thought, but it wasn't continuous; it seemed to have a pattern to it. There were two *whooshes*, two body dips as if to force the air out, followed by a pause and then a longer *whoosh*.

"What the fuck is it doing?" the deputy asked.

The sheriff looked away from the cracker and turned to face Deputy Williams. The man was still in a half-crouched position, both hands clasped on the gun that he held out in front of him.

"Take this," he said, leaning his body toward the man, presenting the weapons. "Take a shotgun."

The deputy turned to face the sheriff.

"And put a vest on."

Deputy Williams nodded and reached for a shotgun.

"What is it do—?"

A crash from the office behind them interrupted Williams's repeated query. Deputy White turned in time to see the other window smash inward, followed by at least a dozen small crackers. At the same time, more began streaming in through the other broken window. The crackers tumbled over one another as they fell to the ground below.

The crackers appeared stunned when they smacked off the desk and floor, but based on what he had seen in the cell, the deputy knew that they only had a few seconds before they recovered.

The sheriff whipped his head around and stared at the cracker in the cell, surprised that despite this carnage, it continued forcing air out of the top of its shell in the same rhythm as before: *whoosh, whoosh,* pause, *whoooooosh.*

And then he realized why.

The cracker wasn't breathing; it was calling to the others.

And the others had arrived.

30.

CORINA LAWRENCE YANKED KENT'S arm so hard that they both nearly toppled. After catching their balance, Kent began backpedaling with Corina, and they slowly moved away from the naked boy in the tunnel and the now half dozen crackers that had arranged themselves in front of the culvert.

"Nooooo!" Tyler moaned, reaching out for them clumsily with his useless, clubbed hand.

Kent hesitated and his posture changed; he leaned forward slightly as if he meant to go to his friend.

No fucking way.

Corina pulled again and this time Kent mobilized. With another yank, she spun him around, and together they ran for the back porch with her half dragging her useless leg. All of those years of practicing a normal gait with the appendage went out the window as she tried desperately to outrun the crackers that she knew were hot on their heels. After a few dozen paces, Kent achieved full control of his faculties and took over. Another few steps and it was him supporting her weight instead of the other way around.

Corina's breathing was loud in her ears, but even over this droning noise she could hear them—she could hear the crackers. They were close.

Corina was nearly dragged up the porch stairs and through the still open doors to the back of the house.

Once they both cleared the doorway, Kent quickly turned and slammed one of the French doors closed, while Corina, still breathing heavily, grabbed the other and did the same.

They locked the doors and turned their attention to the lawn.

The crackers were closer than either of them had thought, and there were more of them now, at least a dozen, maybe more, all seamlessly crawling up the porch steps with their six articulating legs.

Corina instinctively pulled away from the glass doors, reaching out and grabbing Kent by the biceps and urging him to do the same.

The first cracker to make it up the steps locked into place and then flung itself at the glass.

Corina screamed.

The cracker hit the glass with a thud and fell to the ground, where it lay motionless for a second before scrambling woozily back onto its long, multi-knuckled legs.

Two more hit the glass in rapid succession a moment later.

Bam, bam.

It was like a drumroll.

As Corina and Kent stared in horror, another cracker smacked into the glass, only this this time it sent a six-inch-long sliver toward the corner of the pane.

When the next hit, the crack turned into a spider web.

"Run!" Corina shouted, once again spinning Kent around.

They only made it three paces before the glass smashed and caved inward.

Corina could see the open front door—the *doorless* front—right across the kitchen and between the two staircases that ascended upward into darkness. *It* was right there, just past the burnt smear in the foyer.

A crack sounded from behind her and something hit the wall right next to her head.

The open doorway was right *there*, but there was no way they were going to make it.

"In here!" Kent shouted, and for a moment Corina had forgotten that she was not alone—for once, during one of the hard times, one of her dark times, she was not alone.

It didn't matter that the person she was with was just a sixteen-year-old boy that she had met but two hours ago. It didn't matter that she had stolen a cop car and had brought him here under a veil of deception. All that mattered was that she was not alone, and that was good.

Corina skidded to a stop, steeling herself against the desire to turn and look at the throng of crackers that were undoubtedly streaming into the house. Kent was in front of her holding up a small trapdoor in the center of the kitchen. The boy's eyes were wide and he was screaming something unintelligible.

Corina started to run again, but when she tried to stop in front of the hole in the floor, her prosthetic limb buckled and she felt a strange pulling sensation on her thigh. In the blink of an eye, she tumbled headlong into the opening.

Screaming, she managed to grab the edge of the floor with one hand and pressed down as hard as she could.

It worked; pushing down on the ground managed to flip her around as she fell so that when she landed half on the dirt ground roughly six or seven feet below, she did so feet first. The prosthetic limb thankfully took the brunt of the force, and she cried out when the metal bar holding the foot folded backward, bending the plastic shin part into her thigh.

A jarring force fired up her other leg, but this barely registered as something big tumbled through the opening and hit the ground a few inches to her right.

The force of Kent's body hitting the dirt floor was so great that Corina was knocked backward on her ass at least a foot.

The trapdoor slammed closed, crushing several limbs of a cracker hovering above the hole with a sickening crack.

And then they were immersed in darkness.

*   *   *

The cracking above, a sound that was thankfully muted by the floor, went on for several minutes before fading away. The scampering eventually receded, too, as the crackers presumably fled through the broken door at the back of the Wharfburn Estate.

Despite the fact that the creatures were gone, Corina's heart was still beating a mile a minute. It took another few minutes to realize that it wasn't *just* her heart rate that was rocking her body. At some point after he had fallen, she had unknowingly grabbed Kent and was now holding him close, and the boy curled up against her heaving chest.

What the fuck are we doing here?

It wasn't quite pitch black in the basement, as there was a thin rectangle of light seeping in through the cracks that separated the trapdoor from the floor. But as evening bled into night, Corina knew that this too would eventually fade.

Neither of them said or did anything for the first little while, content in sitting in each other's arms, attempting the impossible task of trying not to think of the horrors that they had just witnessed.

But Corina, for one, couldn't build a wall fast enough to keep them out of her mind.

The scar. It was the scar on the boy's cheek, the one thing — the *only* thing — that made his mangled face and horribly distended body *real*, made it look *human*.

And she couldn't help but think that something like this had happened to her uncle — to Oxford.

Had he been turned into one of those... those breeders, like Tyler?

She shuddered hard, and when she turned her eyes downward, she was surprised to see that Kent was staring up at her.

His face was glistening from tears, and the light from above cast strange streaks on his face, as if he were staring out from bars of a prison cell. And maybe he was; maybe he was a prisoner. After all, Corina *had* kidnapped the boy.

It was just so foreign, thinking that she stole a cop car and kidnapped Kent only to bring him here. It was wrong. But did it matter now?

What mattered now was surviving.

When Kent spoke next, it was as if the boy had read her mind.

"Are we going to die down here?" he whispered.

His eyes were huge, round orbs that took up his entire face.

Corina shook her head violently.

"No," she said. Yet, despite her denial, she started to sob. "No, we are not going to die."

Kent opened his mouth to say something else, but the next sound that Corina heard wasn't the boy's voice. Instead it was something else. It was a crack.

This crack was unlike the sounds above, which were muted by the ceramic tiles and subfloor. This was a loud crack. A crack that came from *inside* the basement.

31.

SHERIFF PAUL WHITE PULLED the shotgun trigger and the cracker inside the cell exploded in a geyser of thick white fluid.

"It won't be communicating anymore," he muttered.

Deputy Williams didn't hesitate turning his handgun on the crackers that were still spilling in through the office windows. There were so many of them now that there no longer seemed to be spaces between them; they covered the floor and desks like a writhing white duvet. The deputy fired off six or seven shots, and the sheriff turned in time to see several of the much smaller creatures explode.

"Get the ammo!" Sheriff White shouted, stepping into the room himself and strafing to his left. He squeezed off another blast of the shotgun and a cracker that was readying itself to launch instantly became into a smear of white milk.

The deputy fired again and then took two large bounds forward, scooping up two of the boxes of nine millimeter bullets.

Most of the crackers that had already fallen from the two smashed windows had begun to regain their bearings and were poised to jump. The sheriff heard a loud crack from his right and turned in time to see a small, baseball-sized cracker flying directly at him. Having expended the five shells in his Remington 870, the sheriff swiveled his body while turning the shotgun

in his hands at the same time. As he had done before in the culvert with Deputy Coggins, the sheriff smashed the cracker with
a full swing of the butt of the gun, sending fragments of hardened bone and shell flying in all directions.

*Coggins was right; maybe I should have been a baseball player.
Maybe that kind of pressure would be easier to deal with.*

Another cracker flew at him, and he just barely managed to
turn sideways to avoid it. The cracker landed hard against the
back wall behind him, just to the right of the open door, and lay
motionless, legs skyward.

"Grab the shells, too," the sheriff shouted, backing toward
the door.

Deputy Williams scooped as many of the shells as he could
manage while still holding his gun out in front of him before
quickly retreating with the sheriff. Another two crackers flew
at them before they could flee the room. The first barely missed
the sheriff, while the other smacked the deputy square in the
chest. Thankfully, at some point during the melee, or perhaps
before it started, the deputy had managed to put the Kevlar vest
on, and the cracker bounced off the hard material harmlessly,
leaving a milky smear over the ACPD initials and crest.

"Go!" the sheriff shouted, watching as the now flock or herd
or pride or whatever the fuck you call a horde of crackers began
to line up in front of and on top of his desk. There were so many
of them now, with more flowing in through the windows every
second, that they looked like a miniature army.

The call the thing in the cell had made had evidently been
heard—and obliged.

Paul pushed the deputy out the door behind him and then
backed out of the room, quickly pulling the door closed. A second later, they heard three successive thumps strike the other

side of the door with such force that the brass doorknob rattled in the sheriff's large hand.

"Fuck!" Deputy Williams shouted. He put the ammo on the ground in front of him and then wiped at the sticky smear on his vest. When he pulled his hand away, thick tendrils of the milky white substance clung to his fingers. "Sick!"

The sheriff ignored his comments.

"Take the other vest and give it to Mrs. Drew, then hole yourself up in the armory."

His eyes drifted to the large glass windows that flanked the front of the police station. These were made of thicker glass than the small windows in the office room, but he didn't know how long they would hold if the crackers turned their attention to them next.

The doorknob rattled in his hand again as several more of the crackers smashed against the door.

No, the windows won't hold forever.

"Go!" he shouted to his deputy, a man he had known for just over six years.

The man's narrow face twisted, and when he didn't move immediately, the sheriff realized that the man was very much like Coggins—not his twin, surely, but similar enough. The man cared about him and he cared about Askergan. He was one of the good boys.

"What are you going to do?" the deputy asked as he bent down and picked up the Kevlar vest.

"Got a couple of calls to make," the sheriff said. "I'll join you in a minute. Now go!"

The man nodded, and then he scooped up all of the ammo and guns and piled the stash on top of the Kevlar vest still draped over his arms.

The man was *like* Coggins, but he wasn't Coggins. Coggins wouldn't have left him then.

A cracker suddenly struck the front window of the police station with such force that it bowed inward, followed by a wobbling back and forth, causing a strange acoustical pressure in the sheriff's head. The window was large, at least six by eight feet. When another cracker struck the glass, he thought he saw the beginnings of a crack near the center of the massive pane.

Two calls; I need to make two phone calls.

The glass wouldn't hold for much longer.

32.

"FUCK ME!" COGGINS SHOUTED as the car skidded off Highway 2 and careened onto Main Street.

The gas station marking the intersection was on fire, the walls of the small shop twisting and warping as the yellow-orange flames licked up the sides. But this wasn't what had drawn the obscenity from Coggins.

It was the crackers; they were everywhere.

Somewhere in the sea of white, Coggins spied an iconic plaid shirt—something one particular man wore every single day, even on a hot day like today. Coggins hadn't seen the man in over four years, but a simple glimpse of the red tartan pattern and he knew the body lying face down on the tarmac by pump three was that of the proprietor, Andre Merckle.

Coggins swallowed hard.

"Drive! Keep going!" he instructed Jared, just in case the man had any reservations about stopping.

He did not.

The sun blinked below the horizon and the street lamps flicked on as they made the corner, casting an eerie blue glow on the street before them.

Coggins's mouth dropped open.

The street was teeming with crackers, hundreds and hundreds of them, all moving in one direction, smooth and effortlessly, like an organic blanket.

Jared snarled and flicked on his headlights. The closest dozen or so crackers stopped moving and dipped either toward the lights or the rumble of the engine, and Jared floored it.

The tires spun madly as they tried to keep their traction on the crushed shards of cartilage, bone, shell, or whatever the fuck the ungodly creatures were made of.

Coggins wound down his window and leaned out, scrunching his nose at the stink that hit his face like a blanket. Eyes watering, he reached back inside the car and grabbed the rifle.

Coggins's first shot took out three crackers; the bullet passed right through the first two before deflecting off something hard and rebounding to take out a third.

"Yee-haw, motherfucker!" he shouted into the warm night air.

He squeezed off another shot and another two crackers were reduced to milky smears.

Coggins ducked back into the car to reload, and just as he pushed another round into the chamber, his cell phone rang. The sound was so foreign that he almost dropped the rifle. Instead, he placed the gun across his lap and grabbed the phone.

'Whitey' flashed on the display.

"Coggins! Look out!"

Coggins turned back to the open window just in time to see a cracker flying through the air. Jared yanked the wheel to the left and the cracker missed the open window. Instead, it smashed into the rear window, blowing it inward in a shower of glass.

"Fuck!"

The cracker landed on the backseat, but was stunned by the impact, lying curled on its side, three of its six legs flailing awkwardly in the air.

Coggins leaned between the seats and flipped the rifle around, driving the butt end into the underside of the shell.

"Get it out!" Jared shrieked, trying to keep the car on the road as he continued to run over dozens of the crackers, even while the vehicle continued to pick up speed.

"Uh-oh."

The rifle butt had driven some of the tiny teeth backward in the orifice, but it also seemed to bring the thing back to its senses. It flipped over onto its legs, then began lowering into place, the joints cracking into place.

"What do you mean *uh-oh*?" Jared shouted. He swerved to the right and the cracker's shell in the backseat tilted in the opposite direction in an effort to remain planted.

It worked.

"No uh-oh, Brad, no fucking uh-oh!"

Coggins acted fast, flipping the rifle around.

"Cover your ears," he muttered.

"What?"

A shot rang out in the car.

*   *   *

Smoke.

Milk.

Ringing.

Coggins plugged his nose and tried to force air through his ears, but it was no use; all he heard was ringing in his ears.

He waved a hand in front of his face, clearing the smoke from the rifle blast.

The cracker was gone, destroyed. The bullet, which had been fired at a distance of only about a foot, had completely disintegrated the cracker and had ripped through the backseat and buried it somewhere in the trunk.

Coggins blinked again, trying to catch his bearings, to recover his senses.

He flipped forward in his seat and turned to stare out the windshield. The part of Main Street that they were presently on was not as covered in crackers, with only a couple dozen of the creatures spreading out before them.

Coggins stretched his jaw, once again trying to get his hearing back. When this accomplished nothing, he put a finger to his ear and felt something wet. When he looked at his finger, the pad was covered in red.

Fuck, blew out my eardrums.

He realized that above the low rumble of the engine and the perpetual ringing in his ears, there was another sound: Jared was screaming something at him.

The deputy turned to look at the driver.

The man's eyes were wide, as was his mouth, the latter stretched so far that the cleft on his chin completely disappeared. He was yelling so loudly that a vein in his forehead bulged and spit flew from his lips.

But Coggins couldn't hear him.

Coggins leaned in close to the man's mouth, close enough that he could smell the man's whiskey breath, but it was no use; he could hear the sound that Jared was making, but it was like one obnoxious low-frequency drone, and he was unable to make out the words.

He stared at the man's lips instead.

Where the duck is the HOCKEY?

Coggins squinted, holding up his hand and turning it in the air, trying to get Jared to repeat it.

Why is the fuck MOCKING?

It dawned on Coggins that he could still speak, and he shouted, "Slower, what the fuck are you saying? I can't hear!"

His own words came out sounding like Portuguese, all nasal vowels that didn't make sense.

Jared swallowed and looked back to the road. He swerved to smash another few crackers, then righted the vehicle in the center of the road.

Thankfully, the road was completely abandoned, which was not completely unusual for a Tuesday evening in Askergan County. Coggins hoped that most people had fled the town or were locked safely in their homes... the alternative being an option he didn't want to entertain.

Andre Merckle—poor Andre and his fucking plaid shirts.

Jared turned back to him then.

Where the fuck is Frankie's Café? he mouthed.

Coggins was confused at first, but when Jared indicated the cell phone, he understood.

Nancy! Jared mouthed. *We need to pick up Nancy at Frankie's Café!*

It made sense now—the sheriff had called them to pick up Nancy.

Coggins immediately turned his gaze out the windshield and began scanning the side of the road for Frankie's Café.

"There!" he shouted, pointing out his open window. "There! There! There!"

Jared yanked the wheel to the right and aimed the headlights directly at a small, dimly lit café at the side of the road.

Please be there, Coggins thought. *Don't make us wait.*

The interior of the café was dark, and there were no signs of movement.

Jared almost smashed into the café's sign—an iconic green-and-white crest adorned with the word *Frankie's*—swerving at just the last second to avoid it. He pulled right onto the sidewalk, lining up Coggins's door with the entrance.

As Coggins continued to scan the interior of the café, Jared turned his attention to Main Street.

There were far fewer crackers now than when he had first turned onto Main Street, partly because he had turned some of them into a milk smoothie, but also because most of them were on the grass now, all heading for one specific place.

And now that place became clear.

The crackers were heading for the police station.

Jared's heart sank. The lawn of the ACPD station, which was roughly a quarter mile in the distance, appeared to be much darker than the surrounding area. In fact, had it not been for the well-lit ACPD sign, he wouldn't have been able to recognize it at all. As it was, the sign blinked every so often, not because of an electrical issue, but because the crackers were swarming all over it.

A hand suddenly reached across his seat and hammered on the horn. The loud *beep* cut through the silence, and several of the crackers still on the road stopped in mid-step. The horn rang again, and then a third time before Jared swatted Coggins's hand away.

Jared's own ears were ringing, especially his right, but the left was better as he had managed to bring a hand to cover it a split second before Coggins had fired the rifle. Still, it was difficult for him to echolocate the shouting that he heard now.

He turned to Coggins and saw that he was half out of the car, pulling open the rear door on his side. At first, he thought that it was Coggins who was shouting, but the sound was too high-pitched to be the deputy's voice.

A flicker of movement inside the café, a flash of yellow from just below the window, drew his eye. A second later, a blond woman in a tight yellow dress bolted from the darkness, making amazing speed as she traversed the twenty or so feet from the bar to the door, despite wearing heels and crouching at the same time.

The woman leapt into the backseat of the vehicle, causing it to sway with the impact.

Jared turned his eyes back to the road and saw that the few crackers that had stopped with the horn honks had started moving again. Except now they were coming toward them — and fast.

He slammed the car back into drive, but a shout stopped him before he jammed his foot on the gas.

"Wait!" the woman in the backseat screamed. "Wait! One more!"

Jared looked back at the café. A fat man with a camera that looked like it was straight out of the eighties blundered his way across the floor of the café at less than half the speed of the woman.

Hurry!

The first of the crackers was crossing the sidewalk now, and it would only be a few more seconds before it would be within striking distance.

"Coggins!" Jared shouted. "Coggins!"

A heavy thud from the backseat and the car dropped a few inches. Jared, eyes still fixed on the crackers that were lowering themselves into striking position, heard a door slam closed, then another.

"Go! Go, go, go!" Coggins shouted.

His words were unnecessary; Jared had already slammed on the gas and the car lurched forward, crushing the crackers just before they leapt into the air.

33.

"PUT IT ON!" SHERIFF White instructed Mrs. Drew.

The woman was looking at him with a strange expression on her face, one that twisted her lips downward, pulling her face into a deep frown.

"I won't," she replied, sadness in her green eyes.

Sheriff White stepped toward the woman and held the Kevlar vest out to her.

Mrs. Drew was not intimidated by his advance or his size.

"I'm not a cop," she said firmly.

"Mrs. Drew—" Deputy Williams began, taking a break from loading the two shotguns and reloading his pistol.

Sheriff Paul White held up a hand to silence him.

"I know you are not a cop, Stacey—no one said that you were—but I need—"

The woman finally broke the sheriff's gaze.

"Dana was the cop. He was the one who was supposed to protect us. And now he's gone, and so is Alice. And I'm here. Alone."

A tear ran down her cheek and she quickly wiped it away with her thumb.

The sheriff stood and stared at the woman for a moment, his jaw slack. This was the first time since he had met her at least a decade prior that he had seen this side of her. It wasn't that she was a cold woman, *per se*, but she was calm, cool, collected, and direct. Always direct. But this… this seemed so out of place that for the briefest moment, Paul considered that perhaps one of the crackers had gotten to her already, caused some sort of extreme mood change.

Sheriff White glanced to his deputy, and saw his own shocked expression reflected in his face.

The sheriff cleared his throat and regained his composure.

"You are not alone, Stacey," the sheriff said softly. "And Dana was a good cop—a great sheriff. But now I need you to help me, the new sheriff. *I* need your help. *Askergan* needs your help."

He presented the vest to her again and she looked up at him. There was no fight left in her eyes. The woman nodded.

"I need you to put this on," Paul continued. "And I also need you take one of these." He held out a pistol. She looked at the gun. Even though this was the second time that she had taken the gun, the first being back in the now infested office room, he felt it pertinent to ask her if she had ever used it before. "Have you—?"

Mrs. Drew sniffed harshly and took the vest. Her thin hand shot out and grabbed the gun by the butt. In that instant, the sheriff knew the answer, but she replied anyway.

"Dana showed me; I can shoot."

"Well you probably won't have to use it, but—"

"I can shoot," she repeated.

The sheriff nodded and helped affix the vest, strapping the Velcro around her back and sticking it to the front. Then she surprised him by pulling back the chamber on the pistol and checking to see if there was a round in there. There was.

Deputy Williams pumped the shotgun.

"What now, Sheriff?" he asked, his face serious.

Sheriff White stared at him unsure of how to respond.

What now indeed.

*   *   *

A horn sounded upstairs, and at first the trio in the dank basement that served as both the ACPD armory and evidence room ignored it. But when it honked again, three times, long and loud, the sheriff stopped midsentence and looked up at the ceiling.

Nancy.

The thought rocked him.

Nancy and Coggins are here!

During his battle with the crackers upstairs, he had forgotten that Coggins was going to retrieve her.

"Stay here," he instructed to Mrs. Drew, pointing a finger directly at her. Then to Deputy Williams, he said, "You take one of the shotguns, I'll take the other. Coggins is back."

The deputy nodded and tossed one of the Remington shotguns to Paul. The sheriff caught the weapon with one hand and then put his pistol back into its holster with his other.

"Keep that ready, Mrs. Drew, just in case," Paul said, indicating the pistol on Mrs. Drew's lap with his chin.

Aside from the breakdown a few minutes ago, the woman was ice cold. She had nerves of steel, it seemed, which didn't surprise Paul. After all, she was Dana Drew's wife.

The breakdown had been a blip, that was all. The woman was as confident and composed as ever. The outburst and tears had been a blip brought on by extreme stress. Mrs. Drew would be fine; she always was.

The sheriff shook his head, trying to clear it.

"Come on," he instructed Deputy Williams.

Together, they headed toward the sound of the horn.

*   *   *

The glass at the front of the station was still holding, but barely. The outer pane had been smashed, with only a handful of jagged triangles clinging to the frame. The inner pane had its own collection of spider web cracks that splayed out from multiple locations. Some of these cracks were deep ravines.

It wouldn't hold for much longer.

The sheriff and his deputy strafed cautiously along the wall opposite the still closed and locked office door, which was curiously intact. Paul listened closely as he inched his large body forward, but he couldn't hear any sound within.

Where the fuck did they go?

The cell door was still open, the white smear in the corner affirmation that what had happened earlier—what was still happening—wasn't some sort of collective delusion.

The horn honked again, and the sheriff's attention was drawn again to the front windows.

"Get behind me," he instructed to the deputy.

The cell's footprint took up most of the hallway, making it difficult for the sheriff to turn and square up his shoulders so that he could keep the shotgun out in front of him.

Sweat dripped down his forehead and traced a line down his cheek, but he fought the urge to brush it away. Instead, his eyes scanned the reception area, moving back and forth in a sweeping motion, ready to fire off a blast if *anything* moved. When he saw nothing, he raised his eyes and stared through the cracked pane of glass.

There was a car out front, one headlight slicing through the darkness like a spotlight, illuminating a sliver of lawn. The other headlight was smashed, the bulb dark.

A shot rang out, and the sheriff caught a glimpse of a form leaning out of the passenger window, spraying bullets from what looked like an antique hunting rifle.

What the fuck?

So many questions rushed through his mind that he felt his teeth chatter.

Who the fuck is that? And what is he shooting at?

The sheriff hurried to the window, indicating to Deputy Williams to remain tucked in behind him.

It was Coggins—thank *God*, it was Coggins.

He scanned the car. When he caught sight of a woman in a yellow dress—albeit a much darker, grimier version of the one he had seen earlier in the day—he felt a weight come off of his considerable chest.

Nancy.

Nancy was in the car, which had been driven onto the lawn and pulled over the sidewalk just a few feet from the door. But as he continued to squint, trying to understand the dark interior of the vehicle using only the light from the station, he realized that she wasn't the only other person in the car; there was a man in the driver's seat, a man that, despite the twisted sneer on his thin face, looked familiar. And that wasn't all; there was *another* man in the backseat, a man so fat that his girth looked to be forcing Nancy against the door, despite the fact that there were only two of them in the backseat. The man had a large, antique-looking camcorder still attached to his shoulder.

The sheriff lowered his gun and ran for the door. He unlocked the deadbolt and then rested his hand on the push bar.

Before swinging it wide, he rapped his knuckles off the glass as stiffly as he dared, trying not to smash the pane.

Nancy and the driver immediately looked over at him, their expressions matching masks of horror mixed with relief.

Then he held up three fingers.

"One... two... three!" He lowered a digit with every word, and on three, he thrust the door to the police station open.

Nancy opened the car door and leapt across the three or four feet separating the car and the station, and landed directly into the sheriff's arms. He backpedaled, catching her with one hand.

Deputy Williams reacted immediately, pushing past the sheriff, leading the way with his shotgun. He squeezed off one blast, leaning the gun out the door so as not to deafen the sheriff and Nancy. The sheriff, now a few feet from the entrance, caught sight of a spray of white liquid through the glass.

Deputy Williams stepped aside and the cameraman came next, rolling awkwardly from the vehicle before slamming against the sidewalk. The man, his dark hair hanging in grimy strings over his face, scrambled on all fours until he was well within the station. As soon as he had passed, the deputy took position again in front of the still open door, waving his shotgun across the lawn.

The driver came next, throwing his door open and grabbing another antique rifle from the center armrest and pulling it with him as he crossed the divide.

Coggins was last, but even when Deputy Williams shouted—*screamed*—at him to come inside, the man didn't even turn. Instead, he squeezed off a few more shots with his rifle at crackers that were just out of the sheriff's limited viewing angle. When the rifle was empty, Coggins switched to his handgun, firing off two, three, and four shots even as Deputy Williams continually yelled at him to come inside.

Is he on some kind of suicide mission?

Sheriff White released Nancy and then made his way to the door, pushing Deputy Williams out of the way.

"Coggins!" he bellowed in his deep voice. "Coggins, get the fuck in here!"

Coggins turned, a confused look on his face. But when he saw Paul, he smiled — the man actually smiled.

Suicide. The man was insane and wanted to go out in a blaze of glory.

Coggins turned back to the lawn and fired off one more shot, then pulled himself out through the window, and scrambled onto the roof of the car, rifle in one hand, pistol in the other.

It dawned on him that the man wasn't suicidal, at least not now, and that he was going to jump.

The sheriff's eyes went wide.

"Coggins?"

Deputy Andrew Coggins leapt from the roof of the car into Sheriff Paul White's open arms, knocking him backward and onto the ground. With the sheriff's foot out of the way, the glass door to the police station swung closed.

The air was knocked out of the sheriff's chest, and he grunted. When he opened his eyes, Coggins's red beard was right in his face.

"Miss me, big fella?" Coggins asked, a sly grin on his face.

Sheriff White shook his head, trying to clear the stars.

"Get the fuck off me," Paul finally managed after catching his breath.

He shoved the much smaller man to his right, and Coggins rolled off and pulled himself to his feet.

As the sheriff did the same, he saw blood coming out of both of Coggins's ears.

No wonder he didn't come when Williams was calling him.

The sheriff went to Nancy first, wrapping his big arms around her and pulling her in tight. Then he kissed her forehead lightly.

She was trembling.

A resounding snap suddenly filled the ACPD reception area, and both deputies and the sheriff turned in time to see a large crack form on the inner pane, spreading into a snowflake pattern extending from the center where the cracker had struck it.

"Get up," Deputy Williams said to the cameraman, who was still on his back, feet up in the air like an overturned turtle. His awkward camera was still attached to his shoulder, and the sheriff now realized it was actually affixed with some sort of modified sling.

Confident that Nancy was unhurt, the sheriff turned to the driver of the vehicle next, a thin man clutching the barrel of a rifle that was so old that he was concerned even the man's thin fingers might crush it.

"You," he instructed, "get behind me—we need to get downstairs before the window shatters."

The man nodded and helped the cameraman to his feet before heading back down the corridor toward the end of the hallway.

Coggins was next. Although he still couldn't hear what the hell was going on, he had seen the crack and knew that it was only moments before the glass broke and they were infested with crackers.

*   *   *

Coggins watched Sheriff White lean forward, his face twisting into a frown.

"Wait, *what?* Jared—your name is Jared Lawrence?"

The man with the short brown hair and the cleft in his chin nodded.

"Jared Lawrence," he confirmed.

Coggins immediately realized why he looked familiar, but let the sheriff answer anyway.

"Corina…"

The words came out more of a mumble, but Jared picked up on it immediately and his expression suddenly changed.

He stood and took an aggressive step toward the sheriff.

"What about Corina?" he demanded. "How do you know her?"

There was pain mixed in with the anger clear in his voice and narrowed eyes.

Neither Coggins nor the Sheriff responded; instead, Mrs. Drew answered for him.

"She was here," she said simply, keeping her eyes fixated on the pistol that she still held in her lap.

There were six of them sitting on uncomfortable folding chairs surrounding the table covered in their collective arsenal: Sheriff White, Coggins, the cameraman, Nancy, Mrs. Drew, and Jared. Deputy Williams was at the top of the stairs, his ear pressed against the thick metal door, shotgun in hand.

Jared, now standing, turned his venomous gaze from the sheriff to Mrs. Drew.

"What do you mean, '*she was here*'?"

Mrs. Drew shrugged.

"She came in here about six hours ago, looking for Coggins."

Coggins was struggling to read lips, his eyes bouncing back and forth from face to face. He was having a hard time keeping up with the conversation, but one thing was clear: Jared was not happy. And he recognized something else, too—his name. Mrs. Drew had just said, '*Coggins*'.

Uh-oh.

Jared turned to him.

"Brad? What the fuck?"

The sheriff interrupted before things got heated.

"Sit down."

When Jared ignored the order and took another step toward Deputy Coggins, the sheriff repeated the request, this time with more force.

"She was here… but then she left. She stole" — the sheriff indicated Deputy Williams at the top of the stairs — "Deputy Williams's car and left about two and a half hours ago."

Jared's face transitioned from anger to shock.

"She *what*?"

The sheriff nodded.

"But, it doesn't matter now. What matters is getting the fuck out of here and dealing with those — those *things*."

"Doesn't matter? Doesn't *matter*? My fucking niece is out there with those things and it doesn't *matter*?"

Coggins was getting better at reading lips, and he thought he had a better grasp of what was going on. He recalled a time long ago, a time that he had forced into the deep recesses of his brain, when he had told Jared that they would have to leave his brother Oxford. The man was having none of it then, and was going to have none of it now.

"We'll get her," Coggins said, and all eyes suddenly turned on him.

Jared made a face.

"What? We'll get her," he repeated with a shrug.

He wasn't sure if he had meant to say the words, or if he had intended only to think them; as before, he had forgotten that although he couldn't hear for shit, his own speech was just fine.

It was Jared who answered, crossing his arms across his chest.

"How?"

"I think you guys should see this," the cameraman suddenly piped in.

Unlike the rest of the people around the table, the man didn't seem that interested in the ongoing discussion. Instead, his eyes were focused on the archaic video camera that he had only just recently detached from his shoulder.

"How, Brad? How the fuck are we going to get out of here— get by those things—and find her?"

"Guys?"

The cameraman again.

"We can find her," the sheriff interjected. "All of the cruisers have a tracker in them—we can find her. Getting by those things, however—"

A loud crash cut off his sentence, a bombastic thud followed by the unmistakable sound of breaking glass.

The crackers had broken the front window.

The sound that followed, the sound of hundreds, maybe even thousands of tiny, pointed legs scampering above them sounded as if someone had spilled an entire collection of marbles across a ceramic floor.

And the sound grated on them; it grated like a jagged fingernail on an exposed tooth root.

Nancy, who hadn't said anything since making her way to the basement, suddenly rose to her feet and began backing away from the table, trying to put as much distance as she could between herself and the stairway leading to the upstairs.

"Nance, it's okay," the sheriff said, trying to calm her. The woman's breathing was coming in short bursts, and he was concerned that she would soon start to hyperventilate.

"Nan—"

There was a thud at the door, and Williams instinctively moved down a step. The thud was followed by another, and then another. Soon, the thuds became continuous, like an unwanted drum solo.

Even the sheriff had been holding his breath, but he released it when it was clear that no matter how many times the crackers banged against the thick metal door, it would hold.

This wasn't glass, this was two inches of aluminum.

It *would* hold.

"Guys!" the cameraman shouted, and this time the sheriff finally acknowledged him.

"What?" he demanded.

"I think you should see this."

The fat man didn't wait for a response this time. He turned the viewfinder of the camera around and aimed it at the sheriff. It took both him and Coggins a few minutes before they realized what, exactly, they were watching.

It was Wellwood Elementary, and it was horrible.

34.

"GET IT OFF ME!" Kent screamed, swatting madly at the leg of his jeans.

Corina whipped out her phone and quickly flicked it on, the glow from the small screen shining an off-white light on Kent's pants.

She caught a glimpse of something moving into the shadows, but it had been too fast for her eyes to focus on it.

"It's gone," she said, her voice tight.

Maybe it wasn't one of them. Maybe it wasn't a cracker.

But they had both heard the sound; the unmistakable sound of a cracker pushing itself off the dirt floor of the basement.

Kent took a deep breath and rolled out of her arms, looking up and down his body for any sign of a cracker or anything else.

"Keep the light on it!" he demanded.

His hands worked frantically from the top of his worn sneakers up to his knee.

"Where did it go?" he asked. Like Corina, the boy's voice was high and tight.

"Where did—?"

Kent screamed and clutched at the inside of his left ankle with both hands.

Corina pushed him off of her and he fell onto his ass. Reaching forward, she shoved his hands away and grabbed the leg of his jeans and roughly hiked it up to his knee.

She could see nothing in the shaking light of her phone, nothing except his thin, pale leg and…

"Fuck!"

A milky white cracker, no bigger than a large moth, was attached to his ankle, just above the bone.

"Get it *off me!*" Kent yelled.

Corina stared in horror at the creature that had wrapped itself around Kent's ankle like an organic house arrest ankle monitor.

As she watched, it suddenly clamped down hard and Kent screamed again.

"Take it off!"

Corina snapped out of it and reached down with one hand and grabbed the thing. Her intention had been to grab ahold of it and pull, but her hand immediately recoiled. It was surprisingly cold and slick to the touch, and she had felt air rushing through her fingers.

What the fuck?

"Please," Kent pleaded. He turned his round face up to her, and she realized that his cheeks and chin were slick with tears.

Corina looked away from him and scanned the room. There, within reach, was a foot-long splinter of wood. She snatched it up and turned back to Kent.

When Kent realized what she intended to do, his eyes bulged from their sockets.

"No!" he screamed.

But he was a split second too late; the wood was already in motion.

Corina brought the piece of wood down on the shell, careful not to break Kent's ankle in the process.

A *thunk* echoed off the moist brick walls, and for a brief moment, Corina thought that she had killed the thing. Its limbs, which were wrapped almost completely around Kent's thin ankle, seemed to relax.

But it was not dead, not even close.

As she watched in horror, the cracker's legs retracted inward, and then started to push *under* Kent's skin, dissecting it.

Corina's stomach lurched as blood began to soak the top of Kent's white sock.

Corina raised the piece of wood again, but it was too late. The cracker had burrowed itself under his skin, somehow flipping around so that the tiny mouth surrounded the tear in his skin.

"Oh my God," she whispered.

Kent swooned, and his head banged off the dirt ground before Corina could get her hands beneath it.

"No," he moaned, and his eyes rolled back.

*   *   *

The pain was mostly gone now; either that, or Kent had become accustomed to it.

He was lying flat on his back, his head resting in Corina's lap, his pale face staring up at her. His left leg was straight, the blood filled sock and shoe as far away from them as possible.

Even though Corina knew she was supposed to comfort him, she found herself unable to look away from the hard outline of the cracker buried beneath the tight skin on his ankle.

It should have been me.

The irony of the thought was not lost on her as, had it been her left ankle that the thing had latched on to, they would both be fine—it wouldn't have been able to dissect the carbon fiber prosthetic foot.

As she stared at those tiny, reciprocating teeth, her mind kept drifting back to Tyler in the culvert behind the house, his skin tightening and then budding as more crackers were birthed from his flesh.

Why did I pull my hand back? Why didn't I rip it off?

Nearly six years of training. Muai Thay, jiu jitsu, boxing. Six years. Six years and she couldn't even pull off a fucking over-grown beetle from Kent's leg. Kent... Kent, who she had kid-napped and brought here.

Corina turned her face skyward, staring into, and beyond, the rotting wooden beams of the floor above.

"Fuck!" she screamed.

There was a smattering of movement above as the crackers stirred in response to her voice, but she didn't care.

This was fucked.

When she finally mustered the courage to turn back to Kent, he was still staring up at her.

He was terrified.

"Don't let me end up like Tyler," he whispered, his eyes welling with tears again. "Please."

Corina managed a meek nod even as her own tears started to fall.

"I can dig it out," she whispered, once again reaching for the pointed stick that she had struck the cracker with.

Kent shook his head.

"It's too late," he whispered, his voice barely audible. "I can feel it... I can feel it *inside* me."

Corina started to sob.

"It's not too late," she stuttered.

Kent turned away. It took Corina a moment to realize that he was showing her the side of his neck.

Corina could not believe her eyes. She put one hand on the side of his head, and used the other to pull down the collar of his t-shirt.

It looked like his neck was vibrating, but it was not a steady, regular pulsing of his blood through his carotid. Instead, it seemed to be twitching.

"No," she moaned.

The twitching became more obvious, and before long she caught a glimpse of a faint outline of an oval shape—of something hard, of something familiar.

"No," she said again, letting go of his head and pulling his shirt collar back up.

Why? Why am I back here?

When she finally managed the courage to wipe her tears away, Kent was back in her lap staring up at her. Only this time he had an embarrassed look on his face.

Corina sniffed, confused by the expression.

"Corina?" the boy whispered, his light orange-colored eyebrows rising up his forehead.

Corina sniffed again and nodded.

"Yeah?"

"I've never kissed a girl," he said, his pale cheeks reddening.

Despite their situation, Corina couldn't help but smile.

She used the sleeve of her t-shirt to wipe away the mucus from her nose and mouth. Then she helped Kent rise from a prone position to being half seated.

"Please," he pleaded, staring into her green eyes, "please don't let me end up like Tyler—I don't want to end up like *him*."

A tear ran down Corina's cheek, but this time she didn't wipe it away. Instead, she closed her eyes and leaned into Kent, ignoring their collective smell of sweat.

Her lips met his in a kiss that was surprisingly tender. His lips were soft, pleasant, and gentle.

Before the kiss was over, she slipped one of her hands from his face down to the base of his throat.

Corina pulled her face away and stared into his eyes.

"I'm so, so sorry," she whispered, then turned him so that he was sitting in her lap, his back against her chest. He didn't resist.

She continued to snake her right arm around his throat, trying to be tender, to be gentle, like the way that he had kissed her. When her hand made its way all the way under his chin and reached the bicep of her other arm, she squeezed.

Kent never said another word.

After a full two minutes, the boy's heels stopped clicking on the dirt basement floor of Mrs. Wharfburn's Estate, and Corina released the choke.

Again she turned her eyes skyward, tears streaming down her cheeks in thick rivulets.

"Why?" she screamed until her throat was hoarse. "Why?"

PART III - INFESTATION

35.

"TURN IT OFF," SHERIFF White whispered, averting his eyes. "Please, just turn it off."

The cameraman closed the viewfinder and they waited in silence. Coggins felt like he was going to vomit. Nancy and Mrs. Drew had averted their eyes after the first crab had budded from the bare chest of a boy who could have been no older than six or seven.

In the midst of all of this, Coggins and Jared shared an exchange that indicated that while what they were seeing was new, it was similar to something they had witnessed before. A *knowing* exchange.

Silence ensued for some time.

It was Deputy Williams who finally broke it.

"I don't hear them anymore," Deputy Williams said from the second rung of the staircase, his voice flat. He had remained on the steps when the cameraman had shown the footage that Nancy and he had taken. It would have been impossible for him to make out the details, but it was clear by how pale his face was and how he kept swallowing as if something were stuck in his throat that he had seen enough.

Coggins tilted his head and listened, his hearing having returned somewhat after clearing the blood from his ears. It was true; not only had the crackers stopped throwing themselves at the steel door, but he couldn't hear their claws scratching across the floor upstairs, either.

"What does it mean?" Deputy Williams asked, swallowing hard.

"The fuck if I know," the sheriff answered. He turned to Coggins. "We had one of the fuckers caught in the cell upstairs... and after a while, it..." His eyes darted to Williams's. "It *called* to the others."

Williams nodded, and Coggins thought about that for a moment. His mind flashed repeatedly to Andre Merckle, the gas station owner, lying face down on the tarmac. And he thought of the woman in the small souvenir shop not far from where he had met up with Jared. Had they been breathing? It was difficult to tell, what with the crackers budding off of them. But he thought that maybe they were. Was the thing in the cell somehow communicating with the crackers in the bodies? Telling them to produce more *palil*—to send them here?

Coggins cleared his throat and looked at the odd group of people around the table: the elderly woman; Nancy, who had since crept over to the sheriff and was buried in his chest; Jared, his thin features looking chiseled by the fluorescent lighting; and the fat cameraman still staring into his dark viewfinder as if he expected something to suddenly appear on the screen, something that would teleport them all out of there; out of this place, out of this situation.

An odd mix of individuals, all brought together and now sharing a singular purpose: survival.

"We need to draw them away from town," Coggins said at long last. "We need to go to the source."

Another hush fell over the group.

The *source*. Even to Coggins, who had uttered the words, they sounded strange, but oddly appropriate.

Sheriff White leaned down and kissed Nancy's smooth, damp forehead. She looked up at him with her bright green eyes and squeezed him tightly.

"I think you're right," the sheriff finally said.

His mind flicked to when he and Coggins had travelled out the back of the Wharfburn Estate, and how he had smashed one of the crackers that had lunged at them with the butt of his gun.

"And I think I know" —he looked at Coggins, then at Jared — "I think *we* know where the source is."

*   *   *

"And what do I do?" the cameraman asked, his voice high and tight. The man was holding the camera over one shoulder, and as he adjusted the strap, the fat below his chin started to flap.

The sheriff stared at him.

"Do what you do best," he replied. "Tape it."

The man's wide face went blank for a moment. Then he brought a hand up to one of his chins and scratched at the greasy stubble. He nodded, and an expression of calm passed over him.

Williams removed his Kevlar vest and handed it to Nancy. The woman's short blonde hair was clinging to her jawline in thin, wet strips, and there was a streak of dirt directly in the center of her forehead. She had since ditched the high-heeled shoes that she had been wearing, and now that she had, she was at least a foot shorter than Sheriff White. When she turned her face up to him again and leaned in for a kiss, Paul had to crouch down considerably. He closed his eyes as he kissed her, loving the warmth that spread from his lips and billowed throughout his entire body.

Sheriff White pulled away and helped her put on the Kevlar vest. Then he reached into his holster and removed the pistol.

He handed it over without reservation—unlike Mrs. Drew, he was positive that Nancy knew how to use it. In fact, she was probably the best shot of all of them.

But she wouldn't be firing today, not if he had a say in it.

The sheriff's dark eyes drifted over to Mrs. Drew next, and whatever calm had spread over him suddenly vanquished. The woman had been more or less silent when they had formulated their plan, which wasn't at all like her. Now, her brow was perpetually furrowed, thick creases forming on the usually smooth, albeit aged skin.

Thinking about Dana? About Alice?

It was impossible to know.

'I'm all alone,' she had said. The sheriff glanced around again. Clearly, the woman had meant *right now*, but also something else. A loneliness that ran deep.

Paul White frowned, but before he could give this much thought, Williams spoke up.

"I'll lead," he offered, but the sheriff immediately shook his head. He reached for the shotgun on the table in front of him and tossed it to Coggins.

The deputy caught the gun and made a sour face as he pumped it.

"Feels familiar," he muttered, a comment that made little sense to the sheriff.

"No," Sheriff White instructed, "you fall in behind me and Coggins. Jared, you pull up the rear."

Deputy Williams opened his mouth to say something, but the sheriff cut him off.

"Andrew, behind Coggins."

Williams's eyes darkened. When they got through this, the sheriff knew, he was going to have to set some ground rules — break some of the tension between his two deputies.

If. If we get through this.

To clear his head, he turned to Nancy and leaned down and kissed her on the lips again. Then he kissed her for a third time. They didn't exchange any words; none were necessary.

He turned to Mrs. Drew next.

"Just go," she said flatly before he had a chance to say anything.

Sheriff White nodded.

"You come last," he instructed the cameraman.

The man nodded voraciously, the skin below his chin making an audible slapping sound.

After scooping up the four grenades and distributing them — tossing two to Coggins, one to Williams, and keeping one for himself — the sheriff made his way to the bottom of the stairs and waited for them to line up, single file, in the order that he had instructed.

Then, gritting his teeth, he took the first step, feeling his heart leap into his throat and adrenaline surge into his fingertips.

This was it.

*   *   *

"What the fuck."

It wasn't a question but a statement, and even though Coggins had said the words, it was a sentiment shared by all.

The upstairs was empty, devoid of any crackers. In fact, if it weren't for the white smear in the corner of the cell, the sheriff might have convinced himself that none of this had been real — that the infestation had never happened.

He led the way, staying high, while Coggins came next keeping low, trying to collectively cover as much of the area in front of them as they could. Then came Williams and Jared, both of whom looked scared, their faces long and pale. The cameraman lagged much farther behind, the old-fashioned camcorder strapped to his right shoulder, the red recording light like a sniper's laser.

The interior of the police station was empty, but as they slowly made their way to the broken front window, they soon found out why.

"Oh my God."

This time, no one was sure who had spoken.

The men spread out in the reception area, staring at the scene that unfolded before them, their jaws slack.

They were staring at hundreds — no, *thousands* of crackers, all lined up just outside the station. The entire expanse of lawn in front of the station, and the parking lot beyond that — in fact, for as far as Paul could see by the dim street lights, there were crackers. Even the Buick that Jared had driven up to the door was covered in them, the entire hood a sea of those long, jointed legs and the milky white shells.

That wasn't the worst part, however; the worst part was the sound. They weren't cracking, as the men had become accustomed to, which, in this case, might have been better. Instead, the men were accosted by the sound of rushing air, as each of the thousands of the creatures forced air through the tiny perforations on their shells at the same time. Rocking, pulsating…
communicating.

It was like a nightmare; the boogeyman had crawled out from under the bed and was breathing its sour breath on their necks.

Deputy Coggins leaned into the sheriff from his right and whispered, "What are they waiting for?"

The sheriff, his shotgun aimed at the crackers on the roof of the car, kept his eyes on them when he answered.

"I don't know."

"How the fuck are we going to get to the car?" Coggins asked next.

The sheriff's answer was the same.

"I don't know."

They had expected to see a couple dozen, maybe even a hundred of the crackers on the way to the car, but none of them could have expected this; not thousands of them, not all lined up, fanned out, waiting, watching, *thrumming*.

No one moved. No one, save the crackers, breathed.

What did they do now?

A noise, the sound of the metal basement door flying open, broke the silence, and the sheriff immediately turned to see Nancy and Mrs. Drew bust through the doorway, the pistols held out in front of them as they made their way to the front of the room.

"No!" the sheriff yelled, turning his body completely. He waved his arm at the two women like a madman. "No! Go back downstairs!"

That was it. Whatever calm had been holding the crackers in place broke, and the air was filled with the sound of cracking joints as they started to lower into place, readying themselves to jump.

Coggins fired the first shot, and the spray of pellets took out at least a half dozen of the tightly packed crackers just outside the smashed window.

Williams' and Jared's pistols barked next, and more cracker bodies, the front wave, were sent flying backwards, their bodies reduced to the now all-too-familiar milky white smears.

The sheriff turned back to the car and ripped off a shotgun blast, the pellets embedding themselves into the roof of the car, taking a handful of the crackers with them.

"No!" he continued to shout even as he fired.

He turned back in time to see Nancy and Mrs. Drew pull up the rear, firing their own pistols.

They had taken out at least fifty of the damned things before the first flew at them.

The men rolled out of the way and most of the crackers overshot their targets, flying over their heads and into the station behind them.

Williams and Jared turned, firing at the crackers that were behind them now, while the others kept firing into the throngs of crackers that kept coming at them.

Any thoughts of making it to the car, despite the fact that it was practically within arm's reach of the front door, left the sheriff's mind. They were going to go out in a blaze of glory, but they *were* going to fucking go out.

A large cracker just missed the sheriff, but when it hit something soft and he heard an accompanying *whoosh*, he turned in fear. The thing had struck the cameraman in the chest and had knocked him to the ground. Evidently it had failed to find purchase, as it landed a few feet to the man's left. The cracker scrambled to right itself on its tall legs, then immediately scampered back toward the fat cameraman with amazing speed.

As the sheriff watched, the cameraman spun his body in a deft move he did not appear capable of doing and delivered a swift kick to the thing's underside, sending it back into the air.

Nancy turned and shot the thing before it hit the ground, showering them all in a white paste.

"Die, you motherfuckers!" Jared shouted, and took several steps toward the throngs of crackers that amazingly just missed him as they flew by.

Coggins also began to move forward, and it was clear by the way he was heading to the window and not to the door that he too had given up hope of heading to the source.

The plan had changed; it had become what the sheriff had feared when he had first seen Coggins leaning out of the car window—it was now a suicide mission, one designed to take out as many of the fuckers as possible.

Fucking Kamikaze.

As the sheriff fired off another blast of his shotgun, one of his hands fell to the grenade on his hip.

The plan was now to take out as many as he could, even if it meant taking himself—*them*—out in the process; no way did he want to become an incubator like the kids at Wellwood Elementary.

Sheriff White bit his lip hard and charged at the window.

"Die!" he heard himself shout along with Coggins.

He became acutely aware of the fact that there was someone beside him now—a flash of yellow in his periphery.

Nancy.

Well, if he was going to go out, at least he had her by his side.

36.

THEY HEARD THE RUMBLE long before they saw its source. It was like a heavy drone trying to break through the high-pitched cracking that filled the night air.

"There!" Deputy Williams shouted, pointing a hand down the dimly lit Main Street.

A cracker hit him in the chest, and then another, but he swatted them off of the Kevlar, then turned his pistols—one in each hand now—and blew them away before they could even scramble back onto their legs.

Deputy Coggins turned his head following where Williams had pointed. There, ripping down the highway going at least a hundred miles an hour, was the outline of a dark blue muscle car. A Chevelle, if he wasn't mistaken—a loud Chevelle, one that sounded like it was a fucking jumbo jet and not a car.

Coggins fired another shotgun blast and then quickly reloaded his weapon, stepping behind Jared, who continued to fire as Coggins filled the shotgun with five new shells.

When he looked up again, the car had jumped the median and was now on their side of the road, coming straight for them.

Coggins fired off another shot.

Right at them.

"Get the fuck out of the way!" he shouted, grabbing Jared and pushing him to his right.

Sheriff White, standing side by side with Nancy, dove out of the way, forcing the woman down to the floor.

The driver hammered on the e-brake at the last second, sending the Chevelle into a skid that smeared a good hundred or so crackers across the lawn. The engine hissed and popped, and the sound was followed by a thick cloud of smoke that leaked out from cracks in the hood. The acrid smell of burnt rubber added to the foul scent of the annihilated crackers.

Williams fired again and again, taking out more crackers while they flew all around them. It was hard for Coggins to keep track of all of them, and he had resigned himself to aiming his gun behind them, trying to make sure to pick them off before they crept up on them and latched onto their skin. Twice, he had hit one just a few feet from either the sheriff's ankle, or one of the cameraman's fat hands.

He reloaded his pistol—he'd already tossed the shotgun off to one side as soon as he had run out of shells—and realized that he only had one magazine left. This was going to end soon, he knew, but for some reason this fact didn't bother him as much as it should have. In some strange way, it was almost a relief. Being back here, beside his best friend Paul White and his new friend Jared Lawrence, was somehow cathartic, as if he were earning back some cred that had been lost when he'd left—when he had fled, abandoning those who cared for him and the town that he loved.

A sound like running water and a blast of heat at his back drew his attention back to the front of the station.

For a second, Coggins forgot to keep shooting.

What the fuck? What in God's name?

A man—or a woman, he had no way of knowing—had stepped out of the passenger side of the car brandishing what looked like a... *hose?*

Coggins blinked hard, then looked over at the sheriff and Deputy Williams. Both of their faces were incredulous, and for a brief second they too forgot to keep firing. But this mattered little as the crackers were also distracted, turning and tilting the front ridges of their shells toward the car and the man who was dressed in what looked like a whole array of white garbage bags. The bags were wrapped around his entire body, clinging tightly to his skin by duct tape. The figure was holding what looked like a garden hose and a garden nozzle, and every time he squeezed the trigger, an arc of flame at least eight feet long erupted, immediately setting dozens of crackers alight.

This was no garden hose to spray your kids on a lazy Sunday afternoon. This was a homemade fucking *flamethrower.*

Coggins, still in shock at this strange, demented WHO worker with the improvised flamethrower, fired off another shot and sent fragments of flaming crab spraying through the air.

The driver's window rolled down and a handsome man with medium-length brown hair peered out at them.

"Evening, boys," he said with an odd smirk. Before they could respond, he pulled a massive handgun—a gun that was so large that it might more appropriately have been called a hand *cannon*—from somewhere inside the cab and immediately started opening fire on the crackers.

For the second time in less than a minute, Coggins's eyes nearly bugged out of his skull.

This has to be a dream. It just has to.

The man with the flamethrower pulled down his reflective aviator sunglasses and peered over at them, his face covered in a sheen of sweat.

"Boys," he said through gritted teeth and with a slight nod.

A second later, Sheriff White appeared at Coggins's side.

"Greg Griddle," the sheriff stated.

And at that moment, Coggins realized that the man in the driver seat of the smoking Chevelle was the man from earlier in the day—it was Kent Griddle's father.

"Where's my boy?" the man with the hand cannon demanded.

Both Coggins and the sheriff exchanged confused looks.

Deputy Williams squeezed off another few rounds and made his way to the front of the window, putting one foot outside the glass.

There appeared to be fewer crackers now—at least this was Coggins's perception, based on the fact that he had to duck less often. It appeared as if some had fled from the improvised flamethrower, or were just confused by it.

The huge pistol from the man in the driver's seat fired again.

"Got your call, Sheriff—more than happy to lend a hand."

Greg turned his attention to the closest cracker and turned it into cottage cheese with one squeeze of the trigger.

"Where is Kent? Where's my boy? Neighbor said a cruiser came and got him this afternoon."

All three lawmen raised an eyebrow.

A cruiser? The stolen *cruiser?*

A scream from somewhere behind them drew their attention away from the flamethrower and the man in the driver seat of the Chevelle with his hand cannon.

It was Nancy; she had stopped shooting and was attending to Mrs. Drew, who, at some point during the melee, had fallen to the ground and was now lying with her eyes wide, her mouth open. The cords in the woman's neck stood out like re-bar.

"No!" Sheriff White roared, and ran to her fallen body.

Coggins slowly backed away from the window, shouting for Williams and Jared to keep shooting.

By the time they had made it to Mrs. Drew, it was too late. Coggins felt a lump form in his throat when he caught sight of the unmistakable outline of three crackers—one on her right arm, one on her left, and one on the nape of her neck immediately beyond where the Kevlar ended.

"No!" the sheriff said again, but this time his voice was languid instead of furious.

The creatures had already burrowed beneath Mrs. Drew's skin, causing deep stretchmarks in her armpits and beneath her chin that had already started to fill with blood.

Coggins was strangely hypnotized by the acute shapes beneath the woman's skin, and without thinking, his right hand stretched out with the intention of touching the cracker embedded beneath her throat. Thankfully, Sheriff White swatted his hand away before he made contact with the hard shell.

The sheriff went for the back of her neck and propped her head up, looking into her eyes.

Coggins heard the all-too-familiar cracking sound and looked up in time to see a cracker flying through the air, aimed directly at the back of the sheriff's exposed neck. The deputy rolled to his right, grabbed the empty shotgun from the floor, and then swung the butt in a wide arc.

It wasn't a direct hit like the sheriff's had been in the culvert behind the Wharfburn Estate, but it was solid enough to send the thing spinning back in the direction that it had come.

Maybe I should have been a baseball player, too.

When he turned back to Mrs. Drew, she was trying to pull herself to her feet despite the sheriff's protests.

"Let me up," she cried. A grimace suddenly attacked her features, and Coggins caught stirring beneath her skin, like a ripple over calm water. Based on what they had seen on the videotape, he knew that it wouldn't be long before more crackers started budding.

"No," Coggins heard himself moan. Even with his muted hearing, that one word was loud and clear.

First Alice, then Sheriff Drew, and now... *this*.

Tears streamed down his face, but he did nothing. He was paralyzed in fear, frozen in guilt, immobilized in grief.

"Let me up," Mrs. Drew repeated, and this time the sheriff obliged.

The woman stood and staggered, needing the sheriff to steady her.

"I'll distract them," she slurred. "You go fucking kill the bastards. Kill all of them."

Mrs. Drew's green eyes were wide. There was sadness in them, but there was also anger.

The sheriff, now seeming to understand what she was trying to do, went to grab her, but she was deceptively quick despite her affliction. The woman sprinted across the reception area, sliding between both Jared and Deputy Williams, who continued to fire their weapons at the crackers that seemed to have recovered from their shock at the man in the garbage bags wielding the flamethrower.

"I'm coming, Dana! I'm fucking coming!" the woman screamed as she ran onto the lawn.

As soon as her first foot hit the lawn, the closest crackers dipped toward her. The woman made it maybe twenty paces before the first of the crackers launched themselves at her. Like a giant spider swinging on an invisible web, its legs spread wide, it struck her in the back of the neck and stuck. A second later, another cracker hit her, this time on the back of her arm. And in the blink of an eye, Mrs. Drew was covered in them, a veritable walking, then stumbling, mass of crackers, all desperate to find a small piece of her bare skin to burrow beneath.

"No!" the sheriff bellowed just as Greg Griddle's hand cannon erupted, sending a bullet directly through the back of Mrs. Drew's skull.

The woman's arms flew out to the sides as the front of her face was blown out in front of her in a spray of blood and brains. Then she collapsed to the ground and remained motionless.

Coggins, still weeping, turned away from the wife of his departed idol. The thick black smoke still billowing from the hood of the Chevelle caught his eye.

"Jared, get in your car!" Coggins screamed as he made his way over to the front door. Despite the fact that Mrs. Drew had since fled this world, the crackers appeared distracted, trying to figure out what to make of Mrs. Drew's corpse while at the same time trying to avoid the ever present sprays of flame.

They had a few seconds, Coggins surmised, if that, to make it to the car.

"No!" the sheriff screamed again, squeezing off another few rounds.

"Jared!" Coggins repeated. "Get the fuck to the car. And Greg! You get in there, too! We'll find your son!"

Jared stopped shooting and ran to his car, hopping through the smashed window. The man in the white garbage bags turned the flame toward the front of the car as Jared pulled open the driver-side door, offering them cover. A wave of heat hit Coggins like a wall as he too bolted through the window and toward the car.

"Stay here, Reggie," Greg shouted to his friend with the flamethrower.

Greg Griddle flew jumped into the passenger seat. A moment before Coggins closed the door behind him, he turned back to face his friend, Sheriff Paul White.

Nancy had pulled herself to her feet and was now standing beside the big man, reloading her gun, clearly intent on offering more covering fire.

They needed to hurry as there had been more, hundreds more, crackers than could be accounted for by the white smears or the flaming shell fragments on the lawn. They would be back, Coggins knew, and they had to draw them away—they had to draw them back to the source, to the Wharfburn Estate.

For a brief second, Coggins's gaze met the sheriff's dark eyes. There were tears streaming down his face, and Coggins felt a hitch in his throat.

Even though his hearing was still poor, and the flamethrower roared just outside his open window, he heard the words that the sheriff spoke loud and clear.

"Go get this motherfucker."

This. Not *these.*

Go get this *motherfucker.*

Go get *Oot'-keban.*

37.

THE BASEMENT HAD TURNED dark and cold.

Corina Lawrence shivered. She had no idea how long she had been down there, but it must have been at least a few hours. And once again, she was alone.

She could no longer see Kent, but could feel his head cradled in her lap. He had long since passed, but she couldn't seem to let him go. There was no room for solace in Corina's life, but if she could feel a smidgen of respite, the impetus would have been that she had granted the boy his final two wishes: she had been his first and only kiss, and the movement had stopped beneath Kent's skin. The crackers appeared to have died shortly after the boy himself had passed, as if whatever lifeblood they were suckling from him was no longer useful or valid. And thus she had succeeded in granting his second wish: the boy would not become like his friend Tyler.

Corina had used the glow of her phone to illuminate small patches of the basement around her after her throat became too raw to continue screaming.

There were furs—*skins*—soaked in some sort of fluid just behind where she sat. There were also what looked like broken shells or eggs or *something* buried beneath these furs, but she lacked both the means and the gumption to investigate further.

One glance at her prosthetic leg, and Corina knew it didn't matter what was in the basement with her, so she stopped looking. The only exit was somewhere about seven or eight feet above her head. Under normal circumstances, she might have been able to make the jump and pull herself out. But not now, not with her twisted and broken carbon fiber foot.

She was going to die in the basement.

Corina shifted Kent's lifeless head in her lap and ran her fingers through his short hair.

She could feel the familiar tingle in her lower lids as tears tried to form, but none came. She was all cried out. For whatever time interval had passed since she had snaked her forearm beneath Kent's chin, she had cried for everyone — for Kent, for Oxford, for Henri, for Mom, for Grandma, even for Grandpa... but most of all she had cried for her dad, for Cody. God, how she missed him.

And yet it was all his fault.

If Cody had been here, if Cody had taken *her* and not Henri, none of this would have happened.

It wasn't true, of course, but that didn't matter. Rationality had been whisked away when she had stolen the police car, while the fabric of reality had been punctured and torn when she'd kidnapped Kent.

A flurry of movement from above drew Corina out of her mental spiral, and her ears perked. After their initial frenzy in response to her screams, the crackers had stopped making any noise from above. Somewhere in a dark recess of her mind, she had come to grips with the fact that the crackers had likely resigned themselves to just waiting for her to come out, conserving their energy to burrow under her flesh to make new crackers as they had with Tyler and as they had tried to do with Kent.

Fuck you. I'm down here for good.

There was no stronger desire in the animal world than the need to reproduce, and these things were living—and dying—proof of that. She could not know if the things above were subject to natural selection, to evolution, but it didn't matter; the necessity to procreate was an innately secular construct.

The crackers needed to live, and to live they needed *skin*—they needed *flesh* to infest and incubate.

But now, somewhere in the darkness above her head, the crackers stirred, revealing their presence with the archetypal cracking of their tough, cartilaginous joints.

Corina waited and listened.

Soon she picked up the sound of something else, something far off, but something that was becoming increasingly familiar.

The crackers' stirring increased in intensity, and before long they were all scampering back toward the French doors that they had smashed through earlier in the day.

What's happening?

Then the other sound increased in volume and she realized what it was: the sound of an engine, of a car.

Corina's eyes went wide.

A car! Someone is coming!

Corina swallowed hard, trying to lubricate her raw vocal cords.

"Help!" she screamed. Her voice was dry, hoarse, but she didn't care. "Help! I'm down here!"

38.

THE WHARFBURN ESTATE WAS eerily quiet after Jared shut the engine off. Deputy Coggins scanned the front of the house, his eyes moving back and forth rapidly, his finger on the trigger of his pistol. Gregory gripped the massive handgun—which Coggins now saw was a Desert Eagle .50—in two sweaty palms.

Not only was the place quiet, but it appeared deserted as well; not so much as a bird chirping or a squirrel foraging for a nut.

Nada.

Where are you fuckers?

"There," Gregory said, pointing a trembling finger off to the right of the Estate.

The man had been on edge ever since they had tracked the stolen cruiser to the Wharfburn Estate, but now that he had seen the vehicle, his anxiety had become palpable. Deputy Williams's car was pulled awkwardly onto the grass, tucked partway beneath one of the large oak trees, as if either the person driving it had either been a shitty parker or had attempted to hide the vehicle.

Corina, Coggins thought. *Not a* person *driving it*—Corina *driving it.*

Coggins looked at Gregory Griddle and saw something in his eyes. The deputy didn't have much family—only his demented mother was still alive—so he didn't much comprehend the bond that Jared had for first his brother, then his niece, and he *definitely* didn't understand what Greg was going through with his missing son. But what he *did* understand was that look that occasionally passed over these men—a look that indicated one thing: that they would stop at nothing to get back the person they loved.

Coggins felt a strange weight on his chest. Part of him felt envious that he had yet to forge such relationships—*am I even capable?*—while the other part desperately wanted him to help these men succeed. Eventually, the latter won out.

"Look!" Jared shouted, breaking Coggins's train of thought.

Coggins turned in time to see a white streak of that fluid in the doorway, organic movement that could only mean one thing: crackers.

He opened the door and stepped out, pumping the shotgun. *This ends here.*

"I'm heading 'round back," he informed the others, fingering one of the two hand grenades that were attached to his hip.

Jared Lawrence answered.

"I'm going inside with Greg—going to find Corina."

"And Kent," Greg added.

Both Greg and Jared finished loading their own guns and all three of them exited the vehicle.

Coggins grunted and prepared himself to face the demon that had haunted him for all these years.

This ends here.

39.

SHERIFF WHITE HAD ONE bullet left. One single, solitary nine millimeter Parabellum brass-cased bullet. It was all that stood between him and Nancy and the crackers.

After Jared, Coggins, and Greg had left in the car, he too had made his way outside, coming up beside the man with the makeshift flamethrower—this *Reggie*, as Gregory Griddle had referred to him—and together they had managed to keep the crackers at bay. Nancy was still shooting, too, but she lingered inside the station, hovering over the cameraman who, unsurprisingly, had managed to twist a fat ankle and was confined to half lying, half sitting on the floor by the cell. In a way, they were all shooting—only the cameraman was using film instead of rounds.

It dawned on him that both Nancy and her cameraman would be better off *inside* the cell, particularly so that the larger crackers couldn't get at her.

Sheriff White fingered his final round and glanced over at her. Nancy was sweating, and her yellow dress, so vibrant earlier in the day, was now smeared with an equal number of black grease marks and white stains. She had since tossed her white pumps and was barefoot, and her hair, the blond bob that was usually so meticulously arranged for the camera, was stringy and damp with exertion. Still, despite her considerably grungy appearance, when she squeezed off a round from the pistol, he couldn't help but feel aroused. There was just something about women—*his* woman—and guns.

A blast of heat hit the right side of his face, forcing him to move away from Reggie and his flamethrower. The sensation faded quickly, and he turned to see the arc of flame extending out from the modified garden hose sputter and then cut out.

"Shit," Reggie swore. He reached back into the passenger seat of the car and picked up the propane tank with one hand. Although it was obvious even with the ridiculous white garbage bags covering his body that the man was in good shape, the tank lifted easily—*too* easily.

When Reggie raised his eyes and met the sheriff's, his expression was grim. Sheriff White had a matching expression, one that was clear from his reflection in Reggie's aviator glasses.

"Empty," he replied simply, then promptly removed his glasses and tossed them on the lawn.

The sheriff swallowed hard and thumbed his final bullet into the chamber. Then he turned his eyes on the infestation.

One of the larger crackers was crouched just behind the ACPD sign, its shell lowered and tilted to the east. Taking a deep breath, the sheriff lined the center of the shell with the sight, but hesitated before blowing it away.

It seemed to be moving—rocking, even. Two puffs of air, then one, then a pause, then a long puff.

The sheriff's finger tightened on the trigger, but he continued to refrain from shooting.

Just like the one in the cell before it, this cracker was communicating again.

"Hey," Reggie shouted from beside him. "Hey, look! They're leaving!"

The sheriff moved his finger from the trigger to the trigger guard and pulled his eyes from the cracker.

Reggie was right; the remaining crackers on the lawn, and dozens more that had slunk into the shadows and behind the building when the man had pulled out his flamethrower, suddenly emerged. Only now they seemed less concerned with attacking them, and instead were set on getting *across* the lawn and back onto the road. To head east. To head to the Wharfburn Estate—to Deputy Bradley Coggins.

Nancy shouted something, but the sheriff was distracted and didn't make out the words. He turned toward her and saw that she was smiling, her full lips parting to reveal a row of perfectly white teeth—TV teeth, he liked to call them.

Regardless of what she had said, Sheriff Paul White couldn't find it in him to smile back—not after what had happened.

As the crackers started to flood across the lawn, seemingly oblivious to the police station and its inhabitants now, Paul caught sight of a form on the grass not twenty paces from where Gregory Griddle had parked his Chevelle.

It was Mrs. Drew. The woman's arms were splayed out from her sides, the back of her head a bloody mess.

The sheriff didn't blame Gregory for shooting her; in fact, if the man hadn't done it, the sheriff himself would have probably pulled the trigger. But now, staring at her limp body, the ACPD letters on the back of the Kevlar vest just barely visible in the dark, her exposed arms lumpy and ungainly, he started to cry again.

This is fucked.

He could bear it no longer and looked down, tears streaming down his face. When he looked up again, Reggie was staring at him, a pained expression on his face. The sheriff didn't need the man's glasses to know that his own face fostered the same hopeless expression.

"I'm sorry," was all the man said.

The sheriff glanced at Mrs. Drew's body again, and his mind wandered to what Coggins had told him about the flaming gas station and Andre Merckle's body at the edge of town, on the corner of Highway 2 and Main Street.

His large hand instinctively went to the grenade that still hung from his belt, and one of his fingers worked its way inside the ring.

There was one more thing to do.

He eyed the Chevelle, and was glad to see that the black smoke had finally stopped leaking through the seams of the hood.

Sheriff Paul White sniffed hard and wiped his nose with the back of his hand.

"Think this thing will run?" he asked quietly.

More crackers scampered across the lawn, some of them coming within a few feet of the two men without hesitating. Not fully trusting their intentions, the sheriff kept his gun with his last bullet trained on the ones that came closest to them. There were more crackers than they had ever thought—even when they had first made it upstairs from the basement—and Paul was glad that he had sent Coggins away. Detroit PD wouldn't have had enough bullets to pick off every last one of them, let alone Askergan County's sheriff, two deputies, and a handbag full of mixed candies.

Besides, whatever the fuck Coggins was doing out by the Estate seemed to be working. For now. He just hoped that his friend didn't meet the same fate as Mrs. Drew... or Dana Drew, for that matter.

Sheriff White swallowed hard and turned back to Reggie.

"Let's go, then," he said, his voice tight. "One more thing to do."

The man nodded, and began tearing away the white garbage bags from his body, revealing muscular, tanned arms beneath.

"Let's fucking do this."

40.

GREGORY GRIDDLE SQUEEZED THE trigger and the massive pistol bucked in his hand, the sound so loud that it momentarily deafened him. A cracker fleeing through the kitchen, trying to make its way through the smashed French doors at the back of the Estate, exploded, sending milky tendrils in all directions.

"Kent!" he shouted as he continued to make his way through the burnt foyer. He swung the flashlight in a wide arc across the room. "Kent!"

Jared fired off a few shots of his own, but his gun seemed woefully inadequate compared to Greg's, and his poor aim didn't help, either.

There were only about a dozen of the creatures inside the house, but they all seemed disinterested in Greg and Jared, and instead were intent on trying to get out of the house. For once, the damn things were running from them, and not the other way around.

"Corina!" Jared yelled, adding his voice to Greg's. "Corina! Kent!"

There was little hope in this place of death, Greg knew. The Estate stunk like rotting flesh, and there was a stillness about it that belied any life—except, of course, for the scampering white demons.

But he wouldn't give up. Not for his son. His *champ*. His fucking *boy*.

"Kent!"

He squeezed off another round, cognizant of the fact that he only had two bullets left and only one more magazine in his fishing vest.

This bullet ripped through the nearest cracker and embedded itself in the stove behind it.

The Wharfburn Estate was so dry that even the smallest ember from the bullet from Greg's gun started a fire. A small flame ignited behind the stove, but this hungry fire spread with amazing speed. Before Greg could even aim his pistol at the next cracker, the wooden cabinets had started to burn. It would be but minutes until the floor ignited, but none of these facts meant anything to Greg. All he wanted was his son.

"Kent!"

Then he heard something: a faint, hoarse voice, the slightly baritone nature of which undercut the bright clicking of the cracker claws on tile and the sizzle and crackle of the burning kitchen.

"Corina!" Jared shouted, but Greg hushed him, bringing a finger to his ear to indicate that the man should listen.

There.

"You hear that?"

Jared nodded. He began scanning the kitchen, trying to echolocate where it was coming from.

Greg perked his ears and concentrated hard. It was becoming more difficult to hear now that the flames had seized and consumed the oak cabinets.

There. It sounds like... sounds like... 'help me'!

"I'm coming, champ!" he screamed at the top of his lungs. "Hang in there, I'm coming!"

Oblivious to the crackers that were moving fluidly around and between his feet, still desperately trying to exit the now burning house, Greg turned his attention to the cupboards closest to him. He flung the first one open, one that had yet to be kissed by flame, shouting his son's name as he did.

Nothing—nothing but cleaning supplies.

He flung open the next cupboard, aware that the heat from the burning wood behind and above him was growing in intensity.

Still nothing.

"Kent!" he screamed. "Where the fuck are you?"

"Help me!" The words were still muffled and difficult to make out.

Gregory looked skyward for a second, trying to clear his mind, to block out the other sounds and pinpoint the shouting.

It was stifled, muted, nearly inaudible... it had to be coming from the cupboards. Unless...

Gregory whipped around and grabbed the fridge handle in his left hand.

It made sense, hiding in the fridge. After all, the crackers wouldn't be able to get him in here.

He took a deep breath and yanked opened the door, prepared to embrace his son as he fell out.

Nothing.

"Fuck!" he shouted, slamming the door closed.

A blast of heat hit the right side of his face, and he immediately turned to the fire. The cupboards that he had just flung open were ablaze, the entire kitchen becoming an inferno.

The heat was so intense that Gregory was forced to raise his hand in front of his face. What a moment ago he had dismissed as an inconsequential fire was soon going to force them all from the Estate—with or without Kent or Corina.

No, Kent can't be in the cupboards. He would have come out by now… he has to be somewhere where he can't *get out.*

But where?

"Kent, where are you?" he shouted, the tears on his cheeks mixing with the beads of sweat.

"Greg!" Jared shouted. "Look!"

So consumed with finding his son, Greg had completely forgotten about Jared. At the sound of his voice, he turned immediately to face him.

Jared was crouched on the floor, his long face twisted in a grime-smeared frown. His thin fingers were looped through a small brass ring embedded in the floor.

"Open it!" Gregory shouted, running to Jared.

He crouched beside the man as Jared pulled the trapdoor open and peered inside, his heart thudding in his chest.

41.

COGGINS USED THE DARKNESS to slink around the side of the house unnoticed by the crackers.

He had his pistol in one hand and a flashlight in the other — but the light was turned off. Despite the sun having long since dipped below the horizon, it was still hot out, and the air had an eerie stillness to it that was disquieting.

When he turned the corner, he heard shots from inside the house, but he ignored them and pressed onward. It wasn't that he didn't care about Corina Lawrence or the Griddle boy — he did, especially after watching what had happened at Wellwood Elementary — but that was not his task; not now, anyway.

His task was to end this.

He fingered a grenade on his belt.

It was his task to finish this one way or another.

Deputy Bradley Coggins crept around the swimming pool, staying close to the house. As soon as he crossed from the concrete area that surrounded the pool to the grass, he immediately caught sight of the crackers, even in the darkness. Even with their six tall legs, the white creatures struggled to navigate the overgrown brush. The crackers paid him no mind, and Coggins extended them the same courtesy.

As he reached the first trees of the forest behind the house, he caught sight of even more of the white bodies, despite the fact that the light coming from the house—he was acutely aware that there was a fire of some sort—was barely bright enough to illuminate just a few feet in front of him. And as he made his way as quietly as possible through the tree line, his visibility faded to near zero.

But he heard them. He heard their disgusting joints clicking and clacking, a cacophony of popping that grew into a furious crescendo as he made his way deeper and deeper into the darkness. For whatever reason, his fear of the crackers, so acute, so *tangible* just an hour or so prior at the station, was gone. Perhaps it was the fact that they showed no interest in him—this was undoubtedly a contributing factor—but it was something else, too. There was something bigger here, something more important, something that took precedence over even these parasitic crustaceans.

Coggins's breathing was slow and even, his body relaxing as he mentally began to prepare himself for... something. For *Oot'-keban*, maybe.

A shudder ran through him as he recalled the beast that had possessed Sheriff Dana Drew all those years ago, making him do those horrible things... skinning people, *eating* people.

Coggins shuddered again, not from fear this time, but from revulsion.

Another two steps and he slowed; there was something different now—something had changed.

It took him a few seconds to realize that it was the sound. Or, more specifically, it was the *lack* of sound. There was no wind, no rustling the leaves above, no shots from the house about a hundred feet behind him, and, most disturbing of all, no cracking.

Coggins took a deep breath and raised the flashlight.

Then he clicked on the light.

His chest seized, his heart stopped.

42.

CORINA LAWRENCE STARED UP at the face that leaned into the basement.

It can't be.

"No," she moaned, her mind trying to retract into itself.

It's not real, it's not real, it can't be real.

It was Cody, her *father*, leaning into the basement, leaning in to take her to another, better place.

She swooned, almost falling onto her back, but then the man above started speaking and her mind snapped back into focus.

It wasn't her father, it was her uncle; it was Jared. He was saying something, his narrow jaw moving up and down, forming what should have been words, but she heard no sound.

Slowly, as if the air in the basement had been replaced by some sort of dense ether, she gently moved Kent's head from her lap and placed it on the dirt floor beside her. Then she rose to her feet, or at least tried to, but failed due to her twisted prosthetic limb.

It dawned on her that the kitchen from which Jared leaned down had a strange yellow glow, illuminating his face like a campfire.

Did they somehow get the power on?

His lips continued to move as he leaned farther into the hole, stretching his pale arm into the basement, reaching, longing for her.

Corina pressed herself up onto her one good leg and waited for a moment to catch her balance. She found that although the twisted foot of her prosthetic leg would be useless for walking, it could be used to prop her up. With a grimace and a grunt, she shuffled forward, moving within a few feet of the opening. Her movements were slow, languid, as if she were moving under-water. Her mind was sending the messages to her limbs, but she couldn't *feel* her body. It was there, of course, but, like her mind, it was numb.

Another shuffle, another drag of her leg, and she was directly below the opening in the floor.

"Jared," she said, but like the words coming from her uncle's mouth, she didn't hear these, either.

It seemed impossible that he was here. Part of her thought that she had died.

But then their fingers touched, and Corina snapped back into her body. Time sped up, like an internet connection skipping frames to bring a video back up to real time.

"Jared!" she shouted. The words were loud—too loud, in fact, as the sound echoed off the basement walls.

She heard something else, too.

Jared hadn't managed to get the power back on—the light was coming from a fire.

The heat hit her first. This heat was different from the dank, warm air of the basement. This was an acute sensation, one that sent her invigorated body into a state of readiness—a warning, her extremities tingling, indicating that she needed to get ready to move.

Fight or flight or freeze.

Freezing was not an option.

Corina stretched as far as she could, and while her fingers again brushed against Jared's, they couldn't seem to lock them together.

She released the hold and took a deep breath. The next time she reached, she put all of her weight on her good leg.

This time, she grabbed her uncle's hand and squeezed.

Jared snaked his other hand into the hole and grabbed her wrist. He grunted and his face strained with the effort, but with her unable to jump, he only managed to raise her a few inches off the ground.

As Corina watched, her body once again becoming a star-burst of energy as the heat from the fire above grew more intense, Jared turned to someone just out of view and shouted, "Help me!"

A split second later, another face appeared above her. Although she was certain she had never seen this man before, he looked familiar to her.

He had pleasant features: a small nose, eyes that bordered on beady, and perfect hair, although it was damp with sweat around his temples.

It was Kent's father, of that she was sure.

Corina exercised all of her willpower to avoid shrinking back into the corner of the basement to wait for the fire to take her.

"Take my hand," the man said to her as Jared let go.

Corina stared at that hand for a moment, knowing that this was her way out, her way of surviving, but not entirely sure that this was what she wanted.

After all, she had prepared to die and had reconciled with the fact. Coming back from that dark place was not a menial task.

She turned her gaze to Kent's lifeless body on the floor of the basement, only a foot from the animal skins and ruptured eggs. It was dark down there even with the fire spreading up above, but she managed to make out his face nonetheless.

It looked like he was smiling in death.

Corina blew him a silent kiss, tears again streaming down her cheeks. Then she reached for Gregory Griddle's hand.

She was done quitting.

43.

THE ENTIRE EXPANSE OF lawn before him was surrounded by crackers.

There were thousands of them, all lining the mossy ground, their bodies pushed together so tightly that their shells overlapped. It was a sea of ubiquitous, organic white, and all of their shells were dipped downward toward him in expectation—or perhaps *anticipation*.

The side of the hill surrounding the culvert was also covered with the things, their multi-jointed legs allowing them to cling easily to the steep embankment. They also surrounded the mouth of the culvert and lined the inner surface.

But that wasn't what had taken Coggins's breath away. That had been a result of the boy.

"Help me," the boy whispered. The sound was horrible, as if his one end of his vocal chords had been wrapped around a wrench and someone was turning it like a crank.

Coggins's hand started to shake so violently that he dropped the handgun. The gun clanked off the shells of the crackers that had silently surrounded his feet. They did nothing to avoid it.

Only the boy's face was noticeably human—and even that was undergoing some sort of metamorphosis that would render it unrecognizable in time. In place of the boy's arms were flat flaps of white skin, huge rectangles of flesh that were stretched to the inside of the culvert, affixed to the corrugated metal interior by the milky white substance that the crackers seemed to exude from their orifice. The boy's legs were much the same; there were no discernable bones, only sheets of skin that were glued to the bottom of the culvert. The poor boy's body looked like a patchy white sheet, and it had been stretched so far that it almost filled the entire culvert. There was something akin to ribs in the center of the boy's taut skin, but Coggins wasn't sure; they were but spokes poking through the patchy, thin sheet.

But then there was the face; a boy's face, a boy with buzzed black hair, a narrow nose, heavy bags beneath his small eyes, and thin lips that were stretched at the sides. A pink scar traced a line down the right side of his face, starting from the outer corner of the eye to the corner of his mouth. When the boy spoke, as he did now, in a horrible, trembling voice, it grated on Coggins the way the sound inside the Wharfburn Estate six years ago had caused pressure to build in his head.

"Help me, Bradley Coggins. Help me."

The voice was clear now—the voice was human. The thing that uttered those words, however, was not.

44.

CORINA FELT HERSELF FADING as the man, the one that her uncle called Greg, the father of the boy that she had killed in the basement, wrapped his arms around her back and beneath her knees. The heat of the blaze was intense now, a deep, dry heat, but she shut her eyes before she caught sight of the flames that had turned the entire Wharfburn house into an inferno. Acrid smoke filled her nose and throat, and she coughed, but even this seemed distant, detached.

Corina hadn't slept in a long time, and all of the raw emotion of the day had left her more than drained; it had left her empty.

The burnt smell subsided and the air cooled, but only a little, and she assumed that Greg had carried her out of the house now.

"Here, you take her," the man said, and she felt her body being transferred from Greg's strong grip to one that was more tenuous.

"You can't go back in there," she heard Jared say.

"My son, I need to find my son!"

Corina was so tired, but her eyes rolled forward at the mention of the man's son.

"He's gone," she whispered, her voice hoarse.

There was a brief moment of silence, and all that could be heard was the splintering and popping of the Wharfburn Estate as the abandoned house was completely engulfed in flames.

"What?" Greg shouted, grabbing her shoulders and shaking her briefly.

Corina's eyes snapped open, and there was a deep sadness hidden in those green pools.

"I'm so sorry," she whispered, "Kent is gone. He—"

Despite feeling empty, more tears came, streaking her pale cheeks.

"—he's gone."

The man's face contorted and he opened his mouth in a wail.

"No!" he screamed. "No!"

Corina let her eyes close again, and she felt Jared instinctively lean over her a little more, his body shrouding hers protectively.

"It can't be," she heard Greg Griddle say, but his voice seemed far away. "Not my boy! Not my champ!"

Her body slumped as Jared suddenly reached forward with the hand that was tucked under the back of her knees.

"No," her uncle cried. "Greg! You can't go in there!"

"Champ! I'm coming for you, champ!"

The man's voice was even more distant now, but Corina didn't know if it was because he had moved back toward the house, or because everything sounded muted now as the darkness that surrounded her mind settled in.

Sleep. I need to sleep.

"No! Greg! You can't go in there! You can't…"

But the words faded into oblivion as Corina slipped into a deep sleep; a long, dark, unfeeling slumber that lasted for days.

45.

CRACKERS WERE BUDDING FROM the boy's flattened skin almost every few seconds now, first blebbing before their mostly translucent bodies fell to the culvert floor.

As he watched the newly born *palil* fall, Deputy Bradley Coggins's mind drifted back to when Oxford had sported the skin suit and had stumbled down the stairs to wait for *Oot'-keban*. Then the man had injected himself with the lethal cocktail intended for the beast. His mind skipped around like a scratched CD, and the next image was of the spaceship in the bathroom, the one with the yellow lights all the way around, and the biker hooker between his legs, blowing him.

Oot'-keban had been there, too. He was sure of it.

"I was a good man," a voice suddenly said, and he snapped out of his reverie. It was the boy talking, of course, but it also *wasn't*. Its eyes were different, rounder somehow, brown, and older.

"I was a good man, I just made some mistakes… I didn't deserve to be eaten alive."

It was Oxford's voice.

The boy's head suddenly twisted to one side and the mouth spread wide, a horrible burping sound coming from deep within the sheet-like torso. When it turned back to face him once more, it was no longer Oxford.

"Why did you kill me?"

A chill ran through Coggins despite the fire that blazed at his back.

"Why, Coggins? You were one of the *good boys*... one of us."

Coggins felt his bladder let go.

It was Sheriff Dana Drew. It was his voice, his *eyes*. It was him... in someone else's flesh.

The head twitched again, more rapidly this time, and the mouth opened wide, the same horrible burping sound coming forth moments before it snapped closed. Then it turned and looked directly at Coggins.

"You abandoned me, Brad. I needed you—I *still* need you, Brad. I thought you loved me—I thought you would protect me."

No. It can't be.

But of course it *was*, as much as the thing that had once been a boy, a drug addict, a sheriff.

It was Alice.

"I needed you..."

Coggins was lost in the face, in the vision, the beast, the *Oot'-keban*, and he felt his feet moving forward without his consent.

Come

    Come

        Come   *Come*

Coggins's eyes rolled back in his head, and he felt the crackers now, all of their pointed limbs pressing on his feet and ankles. They didn't frighten him anymore; they were no longer aggressive, they were... *comforting*.

Alice... I'm coming, Alice.

FLESH 273

An explosion suddenly rocked through the forest, sending a shockwave through the crackers. The trees shook, dislodging leaves and branches, and the ground quivered beneath Coggins's feet. The crackers started to move about again, anxious at this new sensation, their joints articulating in multiple directions at once.

Coggins felt his eyes roll forward, and with this some of his senses began to return.

What am I doing here?

The hand not holding the flashlight fell to his side, brushing against something round and hard.

Where is Alice?

As his vision began to focus, it once again landed on the thing before him. Only this time it had the face of a boy, the face of Tyler Wandry, complete with the pink scar that marked the right side of his face.

Join me, Bradley. Join me, help grow my palil. *Breed my* palil, *my crackers.*

Coggins wasn't sure if the sound was in his head or outside, as the lips of the boy before him, stretched as they were, hadn't moved.

Join me, Brad. Join me.

The words repeated in his head over and over again, even as his hand tightened on a grenade at his side.

Join me. Join me. Join me.

He pulled the grenade from his belt and hooked his finger through the loop. He would go down like Oxford, sacrificing himself for all of them if he had to.

But it ended here. *Oot'-keban* would end here.

Join me. Join me.

Come

Come   Come
    Come Come Come

Coggins pulled the pin on the grenade.

"Fuck you," he spat, tossing the grenade into the culvert. "Fuck you."

In his head, he heard an oddly familiar sound; a deep, rumbling laughter that rattled his molars and made his vision spin.

46.

WHEN SHERIFF PAUL WHITE pulled up to the flaming Wharf-burn Estate, he expected the worst.

He was not entirely disappointed.

There were two cars on the lawn: Jared's car, which Coggins had left in with both Jared and Greg, and the police cruiser that Corina had stolen.

But he saw nothing else.

"Where are they?" Nancy asked from the passenger seat, her voice meek.

The sheriff didn't reply, but his chest tightened as he put the car into park.

"Wait here," he instructed, and the woman with the short, dirty, sweaty blonde hair nodded.

The air outside smelled of burning wood, but it was a welcome relief from the smell of gasoline that Paul had become accustomed to over the last hour.

Sheriff White breathed deeply as he quickly made his way across the lawn. His heart rate quickened when he reached the cruiser first, recognizing that it was completely empty. His gaze inadvertently glanced at the burning house, but it was too far gone to know if there was anyone inside; and if there had been, there would be nothing he would be able to do for them.

Paul's breathing regained some semblance of normalcy when he recognized the outline of figures in Jared's car, but as he grew nearer, any relief that he felt faded. There just weren't enough of them. There was someone in the driver seat, completely still, and another, hunched form in the backseat. But that was it.

Five, there should be five of them.

Somewhere in the distance, he could hear the siren of Askergan's only fire engine wailing on the wind. Instinctively, he turned his gaze toward town, and although the trees prevented him from seeing any of the skyline, the sky itself was an eerie yellow. Like the Wharfburn Estate, Askergan was burning; and the sheriff was okay with that.

The big man used two knuckles to gently rap on the glass of the passenger window. He now recognized three figures in the car, one in the driver's seat, and *two* in the back, one huddled up and cradled in the other's arms.

It was Deputy Bradley Coggins who rolled down the window. His face was streaked with blood and grime, and his beard appeared glistening. There were dark, almost black circles around his eyes.

And something in his eyes was missing; the wit, the sarcasm, the *humor*—gone.

"Coggins," the sheriff said softly, feeling a weight fall off his chest. "Thank God you made it. You won't believe—"

Coggins slumped back in his seat and he turned away from the sheriff.

"It's over," he said flatly. He was staring straight ahead, his eyes locked on the burning Estate through the windshield.

"—the damn crab-things," the sheriff continued, despite his confusion. "The damn *crackers* or whatever you want to call them, they all stopped *moving*. The fucking things just flipped over and *died*."

Coggins's reaction was not what the sheriff had expected. Truthfully, he wasn't sure what he'd expected — relief, surprise, satisfaction — but he definitely did not expect this: apathy.

"Coggins?"

The man didn't respond. Instead, he opened the car door and exited the vehicle. As Coggins slowly walked around the car to greet him, the sheriff peered into the backseat.

The second figure was Jared Lawrence. The man's head was pushed back against the headrest and his eyes were closed. Tears streamed down his cheeks. In his arms he held the nineteen-year-old Corina, her face relaxed, her breathing rhythmic. The girl's left leg was twisted beneath her at an odd angle, but before the sheriff could lean in and get a better look, Coggins arrived beside him.

The man smelled foul, but the sheriff didn't smell all that good either; gasoline had splattered his clothes when he had removed all of the pumps at the station, just prior to setting them on fire.

"It's over," Coggins repeated in the same flat tone.

The two of them were standing side by side now, staring at the Wharfburn Estate, which continued to burn like a massive bonfire. The entire house was engulfed in huge yellow and orange flames that had already blown out every window and had turned the red bricks black.

They were going to have to leave the lawn soon; as it was, the heat from the house was almost overbearing.

The sheriff shielded his eyes against the blaze. Then he shook his head.

"Almost," he said, laying a gentle hand on his friend's back.

He left Coggins and headed to his own car, surprised to see that Nancy had fallen asleep in the front seat.

As quietly as he could, Sheriff White reached in and popped the trunk, then grabbed the red gas can from inside.

Coggins was standing exactly as he had been before, staring at the burning Wharfburn Estate.

"Come with me," he said, gently tugging on Coggins's arm to get him moving.

They walked together across the lawn, turning their faces slightly to the side to avoid the full brunt of the heat.

The sheriff's eyes scanned the sticks on the lawn.

"There," he said when his eyes fell on a particular branch in the center of the lawn about halfway between where he had parked the car and the burning porch.

The sheriff grabbed the branch and tried briefly to move it back and forth. Recognizing the strange way that it seemed to stick and stay in both directions, he nodded.

"This is it."

Coggins looked at him with a queer expression on his face, which was actually a relief to the sheriff—the man wasn't completely gone after all. Coggins turned his gaze to the base of the stick and started to squat, but Paul stopped him by grabbing his arm.

"Don't," he said. Then he proceeded to empty the gasoline on the stick and at the base, making sure that the dark, empty space on the ground around the branch was thoroughly saturated.

"I came here before, you know," the sheriff said, pulling a book of matches from his pocket. "I was here right after you left to go on leave. And I came to this very branch. At the time, I wasn't sure why I came to this stick instead of any of the others, but now I know."

Coggins looked at him, but instead of confusion as Paul expected, something akin to understanding crossed his features.

"I was drawn to it."

The sheriff lit the match and the stick immediately burst into flames. The tendrils licked down the dried shaft and then hit the earth, causing another burst of fire.

Both men stepped back.

For several seconds, nothing else happened. Then there was a puff, like a slowly deflating balloon, and then some sort of mist came out of the ground, sending a shower of sparks into the sky.

Coggins went to move forward, to take another look, to investigate, but again the sheriff stopped him, this time by grabbing his arm with a firm grip.

Eventually, the fire on the grass burned itself out. The house, on the other hand, continued to burn in front of them.

"Now it's over," the sheriff said.

Coggins nodded.

The two men said nothing for several minutes. Even when the upper level of the Estate collapsed onto the first floor, they said and did nothing.

At long last, when the Estate had been reduced to a pile of burning rubble, the sheriff spoke.

"What are you going to do now?"

Coggins, eyes still trained straight ahead, said, "I don't know."

His gaze drifted to the yellow sky—a tangible reminder of the fire that burned in town.

"Askergan needs you, Brad."

Another pause.

"What Askergan?"

The sheriff shrugged, his own eyes turning to the burning sky.

"Askergan will be rebuilt; Askergan needs good people like you—like us. Askergan needs the good boys."

Coggins nodded, but it was clear that he had no intentions of reliving his days as a deputy any time soon.

"You have Deputy Williams, and he's like my twin."

"As long as you don't go back to Sabra's biker bar," Sheriff Paul White quipped. He was surprised at how quickly he had come up with the insult, and also that he had been in a state of mind to make it.

Coggins made a face—*almost* a smirk. *Almost.*

"Oh, you don't have to worry about that… drove by it on the way here. Let's put it this way"—he turned back to the burning house—"the dirty bastards all have crabs."

Epilogue

THE ROOM WAS WARM and smelled of flowers. A quick glance at the bedside table revealed the source of the smell: there were two vases, one with fresh flowers, the other with ones that were mostly dead, the yellow daffodil leaves drooping, their ends starting to dry out.

Mrs. Drew, Coggins thought as he stared at the flowers. *Now that she's gone, someone has to bring new flowers.*

Coggins reached out and searched for her hand, finding it tucked neatly beneath the crisp white linen. He untucked the sheet—the woman on the bed before him had always hated that in hotel rooms; being tucked beneath the sheet made her feel like she was being entombed.

'I feel like I'm a mummy,' she had said. *'I'm too young to be a mummy.'*

Coggins squeezed her hand gently, his heart breaking when he felt how pliable her skin was, and at how this action elicited zero response from her.

He cleared his throat and just started speaking with no forethought. It was best this way, he surmised, given that she hated scripted speeches almost as much as she hated tight sheets.

"Alice," he began, staring at her pale face, "I miss you. I miss talking to you, I miss holding you, I miss kissing you."

The tears were coming freely now, but Coggins didn't care. Even if they hadn't been alone, if they had been in a crowded bus stop or in line at one of the amusement park rides that she loved, he wouldn't have cared. His emotions were just too raw, too all-encompassing.

"And I'm sorry... I'm *so* sorry. I don't know why I haven't visited. I guess—I was just too fucked up, I guess. I don't know. But I'm here now, and while it may not be worth all that much, it's all I can do—all I can give."

He wiped the tears from his cheeks with the back of his hand, but was almost immediately overcome with emotion again. Coggins buried his face in the crook of his elbow, while his other hand still squeezed Alice's tightly.

"Is it gone?"

Coggins's sobs caught in his throat and his eyes snapped up. But his vision was watery and he couldn't make out her face.

"Is it gone? Did you get it all, Brad?"

Coggins wiped the tears away, but when his vision finally cleared, her face was as it had been before: relaxed and still.

"Yes, Alice, it's gone. It's gone forever."

A few minutes later, Coggins left the room, his tear-stained cheeks glistening under the long-term care facility's fluorescent lights. He was so lost in thought that he almost stumbled into a nurse on the way out.

Coggins cleared his throat.

"Excuse me," he asked.

"Yes?" the woman asked in a soft voice.

"Alice, Alice Dehaust?"

The woman nodded.

"Yes, I know Alice."

"Well," he sniffed again. "Well, she doesn't like the sheets tucked in around the corners."

The woman nodded, her face pleasant.

"Okay," she replied. "I won't make her bed too tight."

"Thank you," Bradley Coggins replied, wiping more tears from his face. "Thank you."

End

Author's Note

The most common question I get asked is, "Where do your ideas come from?"

The answer to that is easy.

I hate blizzards, so I wrote Skin.

I hate basements, so I wrote Crackers.

I hate creepy crawly critters, so I wrote Flesh.

I hate... well, you are going to have to read Book 4, PARASITE, to find out what else I hate.

The first three novels in this series are different in many respects, but they also share the pervasive themes of family, survival, and helplessness. I had boatloads of fun writing them, and I hope that they kept you entertained for a good hour or two. If you enjoyed them, then I'm preeeeetty sure that you will enjoy Book 4 in the Insatiable Series as well. *AND* if you enjoyed them, I really hope that you can spare a minute of your time to post a review wherever you bought this book. Reviews are the number one factor determining whether or not I can put out more books.

One minute for you to put up a review, a lifetime for me to continue to write better and better books.

Together we can rule the world... or in the very least spend a few hours being entertained by the written word.

Take care,
Patrick Logan
Montreal, 2016

Sign-up to my *no spam* newsletter at www.PTLBOOKS.com to receive *FREE* e-books!

And don't forget to…

Grab your copy of Book 4 in the *Insatiable Series*, **PARASITE**, out now!

Made in the USA
San Bernardino, CA
10 September 2017